THE PERIL OF THE PACIFIC
By J. Allan Dunn

Off-Trail Publications
Elkhorn, California

Front cover art by John A. Coughlin from
People's, July 1916

THE PERIL OF THE PACIFIC
By J. Allan Dunn
Copyright © 2011, Off-Trail Publications
ISBN: 978-1-935031-16-1

OFF-TRAIL PUBLICATIONS
Elkhorn, California

Printed in the United States of America
First printing: September 2011

CONTENTS

— — *THE PERIL OF THE PACIFIC* — —
Serialized in PEOPLE'S magazine

— — § — —

J. ALLAN DUNN
1872-1941

What Dunn Knew
By John Locke

A MAXIM TRADITIONALLY OFFERED BEGINNING FICTION WRITERS is to "write what you know." Don't make the problem harder by inventing the world. The reader needs to sense reality in the fiction, and the real world of the author's experience provides the surest path. Genre fiction, however, often aims to enthrall the reader by dramatizing larger-than-life events.

When J. Allan Dunn broke into the pulps in 1914, he had to wrestle with this conflict. He was a quick hit, and thus his work was in demand by the genre-fiction mills. He was also an unemployed man in his early forties, in drastic need of a steady income. Circumstances quickly forced him to convert from a dabbler in the craft of writing to a hard-working productive professional. Instinctively, he must have known he couldn't be too predictable, couldn't sell the same essential story over and over; to prolong his success he would have to mix it up as much as possible.

Dunn's greatest resource, beyond his inherent ability, was that, by 1914, he was extremely well-traveled, especially in the western United States. He had a great many sights and settings stored in his memory. It's not surprising, then, to see him draw upon his varied background in his early tales. He also tried his hand at different genres; adventures, at first, for *Adventure*; then sports stories for *Top-Notch*; a crime short for *Top-Notch*; even a romance for *The Parisienne*.

And, of course, westerns; his first attempt appeared in the May 1915 *Adventure*. Dunn's reputation, based on a twenty-seven-year career in the pulps, would be as an adventure-story author, but in fact his most productive genre was the western, accounting for well over half of his output. His adventure stories add up to about a quarter, and his last major genre, detective and mystery, ranked third.

Dunn became one of the big-name authors of the pulps, familiar to the majority of regular readers. His stories weren't in every pulp magazine, although it may have seemed that way. By the time he died in 1941, he'd made well over 1,200 pulp-magazine appearances. During his pulp-writing career, his adventurous past became an ever more distant memory and his fiction took on the characteristics of a reliable, time-tested product. The specific settings of his past appeared less frequently, replaced by the generic west, the big city, the anonymous small town. The challenge of being original must have become an increasing burden, until finally he realized it didn't matter, and then it was just a matter of going through the motions; indeed, of selling the same essential stories over and over.

The Peril of the Pacific, serialized in *People's* from July through November 1916, was the longest story yet of Dunn's budding career, at 62,000 words; and the best example of him tapping his past.

Dunn's central setting is San Francisco. He moved to the city in October 1904; it remained his primary residence until his writing career caught fire. After that, he always lived within hailing distance of the Manhattan publishing empire. For most of his time in San Francisco, Dunn worked in the Publicity Department of the Southern Pacific Company, which explains the references to SP in *Peril*. The Department's job was to promote tourism on the company's railroad. They published *Sunset* magazine, which was sold heavily in the east, to tout the virtues of the west. Dunn worked for a time as an editor for *Sunset*; he also wrote the occasional article, e.g. "Motoring Over the Overland Route" (February 1907). His research often called for travel on the company's trains.

Southern Pacific established a resort on the Monterey Peninsula, about 120 miles south of San Francisco. Called Del Monte, it consisted of the luxury Hotel Del Monte; the surrounding grounds; the Del Monte golf course, the premier west coast course of the day; and the famed Seventeen Mile Drive, which winds along the Pebble Beach coast. SP's Coast Line Railroad extended to the peninsula and included a stop at the hotel. Dunn made a number of visits to the resort, traveling by train. His references to Del Monte in *Peril* undoubtedly refer to the hotel and grounds.

California's Central Coast encompasses the Monterey Peninsula at the southern tip of Monterey Bay, and Santa Cruz at the northern tip. Dunn was very familiar with the Central Coast, and all the railroad stops between San Francisco and Monterey; they all feature prominently as settings in *Peril*, e.g. the Santa Clara Valley in the Bay Area; and Gilroy, Watsonville, and the Pajaro Valley on the Central Coast.

The full extent of Dunn's travels aren't known, but we can assume from his detailed descriptions of other places in *Peril*, that he had visited them. These include the Pinnacles, a set of rocky formations on the east side of the Salinas Valley; it's now a National Monument and a popular hiking and rock climbing spot. An outdoorsman, Dunn probably hiked the area himself. He must have taken the rail down the valley. Here, he gives the view from an "aëroplane":

> Their course lay along the Salinas Valley, between two spurs of
> the Coast Range. Fields and hamlets were a blur beneath them in

their rapid flight, spurning the air with the speeding propellers. Twice a train, vomiting blotches of smoke, passed, one north and the other south, where the railroad followed the river.

The Salinas Valley was eventually to gain a more lasting literary identity, as Steinbeck country.

In Part Five of *Peril*, Dunn evocatively describes the Farallons, a line of rocky islands twenty-seven miles west of San Francisco. Later, he describes Santa Catalina and the other Channel Islands that lie off the coast of Santa Barbara and Los Angeles. Dunn was an experienced yachtsman and it's quite possible he visited these places on private excursions. He learned his seamanship during five years spent in Honolulu, prior to moving to San Francisco; which also explains his knowledgeable references to Hawaii.

One of the fascinating aspects of *Peril* is in the differences from modern California that it reveals. It's amusing to read Dunn describe Los Angeles as twelve miles inland, now that the unbroken sprawl has long since spread to every flat area of coastline.

Dunn sets key scenes in Pajaro, midway between Monterey and Santa Cruz. His hero, Grahame, says: "There's a big colony of Japanese in the Pajaro Valley, making fortunes out of apple lands." It was indeed the premier apple-growing region at the time; commercial apple orchards remain but the center of the industry has moved to Washington state.

Some differences simply consist of name changes. The Del Monte grounds and golf course are now part of Monterey; while Seventeen Mile Drive has been reduced to a twelve-mile loop inside Pebble Beach, while still retaining the original name, which sometimes leaves tourists wondering what happened to the other five miles. Goat Island, in San Francisco Bay, is now called Yerba Buena Island, and is the conduit for the two spans of the San Francisco-Oakland Bay Bridge. Little Nippon, the center of Japanese life in San Francisco, is now called Japantown, and is several blocks from where Dunn locates it.

Some of the more striking observations pertain to the isolation of the far west: " 'The Pacific coast is a separate country by sheer geography,' said the spokesman for the committee, 'shut off from the continent by the Sierra Nevada and Cascade Mountains.' " This was the west prior to commonplace air travel, and a vast network of paved roads. To easterners, it would have felt like a distant, even fabled, land. Dunn exploits the isolation in formulating the story. The west can be easily reduced to chaos by sabotaging a few key elements of infrastructure, water supply lines, train routes, bridges, leaving the eastern United States establishment powerless to respond in a timely manner.

• • •

Dunn plants clues to other aspects of his past in *Peril*. For example, in San Francisco he was known as a "clubman," someone whose social life circulates around club activity. He belonged to the Bohemian Club, and other organizations, and would remain a clubman throughout his life. The protagonists of his stories often belong to clubs. Dunn must have thought of the club as a central unit of society. A number of fictional clubs figure into *Peril*: the San Francisco Aëro Club, the San Francisco Motor Boat Club, the Army and Navy Club; the Japanese belong to the Chrysanthemum Club. Dunn's protagonist is a thorough clubman. His experiences, no doubt, mirror Dunn's:

> In San Francisco, Grahame lived at the University Club. Its atmosphere was congenial, and there were a number of its members who were kindred spirits. Some of them belonged to his fraternity, some had been of his own year at the University of California. They had a table set apart for them at dinner, and generally forgathered daily. They were a clean-cut, efficient-looking crowd, none of them drones . . . When they talked together, it was of the vital topics of the day, and the conversation was apt to be tinged with expert opinion. Among them were transportation, light, and power men, chemists, lawyers, architects, engineers, doctors. Grahame was not the only wealthy one; there were others who managed their own affairs of considerable magnitude, big ranches, lumber, and shipping interests.

Dunn lived in San Francisco during the Great Earthquake, although he and his wife came through unscathed. The destruction of San Francisco described in *Peril*, written in 1916 but set four years into the future, was explicitly modeled after the earthquake: "The sun shone on a ruined city. Once more San Francisco was devastated by a catastrophe almost as swift and disastrous as the earthquake and fire of 1906." He describes famous structures that were destroyed, including the building which housed one of the city's leading newspapers: "Before the full horror of it all could be fully sensed, the second shell struck the Call Building midway in its height, and sent its upper stones hurtling, with their occupants, into Market Street as a child might strike a toy tower of wooden blocks." This is the scene depicted on the cover of the July 1916 *People's*, which published Part One, a view looking down Market Street to the Ferry Building. The Call Building, with its distinctive dome toppling over, is central to the scene. The painting is based on famous photographs of post-Earthquake San Francisco.

One of the buildings destroyed in the quake was the luxury Palace Hotel on Market Street, downtown, one of the world's largest hotels. It was rebuilt, and reopened in 1909; its reincarnation remains in business. Dunn set a key scene of *Peril* in the Palace's magnificent "palm room," commonly known now as the Garden Court. In February 1912, Dunn helped organize the Mardi Gras Ball held in the Court, one of the grand parties held at the rebuilt hotel. It's noteworthy that he doesn't describe the destruction of the Palace in *Peril*, although it was situated in the heart of his assaulted area; as if, for sentimental reasons, he couldn't bear the thought.

Since *Peril* is set in its author's future, and features speculative technology, it thus can be considered, tangentially, a work of science fiction. Dunn, on rare occasions, employed elements of fantasy, and on even more rare occasions, scientific elements. He submitted a ghost story to *The Thrill Book* in 1919, but it went published. In fact, despite his twelve-hundred-plus appearances in pulp magazines, he is only to be found in a magazine of the fantastic on five occasions: *Thrilling Mystery* (October 1935), *Unknown* (June 1939), and *Unknown* (January-March 1940, three-part serial). The vast majority of his material is set in the real world, at least as the pulps defined it.

Dunn's key speculative element in *Peril* is the helicopter. Our hero, Grahame, describes it in Part Two:

> "It has long been foreseen that the dirigible has reached its limitations, and that the aëroplane is in the same predicament. The one is merely an improved balloon, the other a glorified kite. The air machine of the future is the helicopter, the machine projected by Jules Verne as he prophesied the submarine, independent of air currents, rigid, powerful, capable of rising and descending directly to or from the ground and of hovering in a fixed spot against a mile-a-minute gale, or moving at a speed of a hundred miles an hour in either direction."

This would have been quite exciting to the reader of 1916. At that time, helicopters were still in the experimental stage; realistic working helicopters would not exist until the '30s. Dunn may have read about the experimentation in a magazine like Gernsback's *Electrical Experimenter*, and projected their potential usefulness in war.

Grahame's new aircraft, the *Aërolite*, is a seaplane and a triplane. Both features were still in development in 1916; Dunn presents a functional aircraft. His projections are wrong on two counts: the triplane would eventually prove to be an impractical design; and the fixed-wing aircraft would not be made obsolete by the helicopter. He seems to assume that the helicopter and the fixed-wing plane would share similar top-end speeds, and thus, owing to its maneuverability, the helicopter would prove to be the better design. In showcasing the capabilities of aircraft in warfare, from fighting to reconnaissance, he's reflecting the popular interest generated by World War I aviation, and entering into the speculation that many people would have been making at the time.

Submarines had been famous since Jules Verne had immortalized the *Nautilus* in *20,000 Leagues Under the Sea* (1870). By 1916, they were in use by the world's large navies, and Dunn avoids projecting futuristic capabilities onto them.

Set four years forward, *Peril* provides speculation on the course of history. In Dunn's version of the future, America resists entry into the Great War:

> Washington was in a turmoil. Not since the anxious days when the United States Congress, represented by President Wilson, strained every resource to preserve a neutrality that should comport with the honor and dignity of the nation had there been such a ferment in the capital city, a ferment that leavened the entire country with unrest.

He further speculates that England (and Canada) would be bailed out by Japan, and thus obligated to side with Japan against the United States:

> And the rumors grew to assertions that England and Canada— under the terms of a treaty amended in the last stages of the European war for special aid rendered by Japan at a desperate moment in Great Britain's Asiatic affairs—would respond to Japan's summons for men, munitions, and money, the three essential M's of warfare. And Canada had a veteran army of over a quarter of a million men, ready to pour across the border.

Dunn nearly contradicts himself in Part Three, where the constitution of the helicopter fleet is described: "The aviators for the twelve machines, men chosen from survivors of the European War, were assembled about the flyers." We naturally assume these aviators to be American, but soon discover that the head instructor, La Rue, is "a man medaled for bravery and efficiency in the French corps." Dunn isn't explicit but, presumably, all the aviators are European mercenaries.

Peril is the type of Asian invasion story that would appear periodically in the pulps well into the '30s. Dunn spells out, in many passages, the preoccupation with racial distinction that was so common in pulp fiction. Grahame says, of the Japanese invaders, "we'll teach them a lesson that will last for all time, that the white man is master." The half-Japanese Ogden Kirby is referred to as "that hybrid devil." The war is described as "white man against brown, as it had been through all the ages." The enemy hold equivalent views; the Japanese Count Kato complains about the prohibition against Japanese settlers becoming American citizens:

> "You give citizenship to black men. Is the Malay—if you will, the Malayan—Mongoloid, less than the negroid race? Is yellow a deeper stain than black? There are many Chinese in California whose children, of both sexes, vote and hold property rights."

Dunn was reflecting commonly-held prejudices that circulated around decades of immigration and debate. In the mid-19th Century, Chinese workers had been brought to America to provide cheap labor in the gold fields, or on the railroads. In 1882, the U.S. Congress passed the Chinese Exclusion Act, which barred immigration from China. Employers responded by importing labor from Japan, and other Asian nations. Ninety percent of the Japanese settled in California, a heated debate during Dunn's years in San Francisco. Japanese immigration was restricted by the Gentlemen's Agreement of 1907, made between the U.S. and Japan. The continuing immigration of Asians was a matter of national concern when Dunn wrote *Peril*. The novel serves the debate by presenting a putatively plausible scenario in which America's Japanese non-citizens unite into a fifth column to undermine domestic security in advance of the Japanese invasion from the sea. *Peril* answers the question as to where the loyalty of the Japanese immigrants lies; following the standard xenophobic suspicions, they *all* obey their ancestral homeland. After the Gentlemen's Agreement, Japan successfully lobbied to be excluded from additional immigration legislation, such as the Asiatic Barred Zone Act, passed by Congress on February 4, 1917, not long after *Peril* had concluded in *People's*. In Dunn's imaginary future the argument still rages in 1920: "I tell you, major, every time that alien immigration bill comes up in Congress, I can see the Japanese fleet getting up steam in their boilers."

It's easy now to look upon the xenophobic fears of 1916 as both quaint and ugly reminders of a prejudiced past, but it wasn't strictly a product of fevered imaginations. World War II was characterized, after all, by grandiose assertions of ethnic identity by both the Germans and Japanese. Dunn is prophetic in imagining the form the backlash against Japanese-Americans would take. Grahame, speaking about the insurrectionist Japanese in California, says: "We may be able to intern them—providing they are unarmed." Of course, Japanese-Americans were to be interned during WWII. Adding an irony, Dunn uses Tanforan as key location in *Peril*. Tanforan Racetrack, just south of San Francisco, was constructed in 1899; it was also used as an airfield during the early years of aviation, which gave Dunn the inspiration to make it his helicopter base, presumed safe from Japanese attack. During WWII, Tanforan became an assembly center where Japanese-Americans were held before being relocated to the interment camps.

• • •

The Peril of the Pacific is an interesting piece, but would not likely be considered among Dunn's most riveting stories. It's quite heavy on exposition, and analysis of the geographical, political, and military aspects of a possible war—and rather short on character interest. *Peril* plods where most of Dunn's best work carries the reader along effortlessly. The novel does hold a special distinction, though. In utilizing Dunn's background to a far greater extent than any of his other stories, it tells us where he'd been.

July ~1916   15 Cents

PEOPLE'S

THE PERIL OF THE PACIFIC

BY

J. Allan Dunn

Author of "Boru", Etc.

Cover artwork by John A. Coughlin

The Peril of the Pacific
by J. Allan Dunn

Part One: The Shadow

I
THE TRIAL TRIP OF THE "*AËROLITE*"

THE BAND PLAYED A QUICKSTEP, company by company the battalions marched from the parade ground to their barracks, and the reviewing party strolled toward the headquarters of General Lancaster, chief of the Pacific division of the United States army, located at the Presidio, the military reservation at San Francisco, California.

The review had been an informal affair, a little more elaborate than the regular daily parade and drill, in honor of the visit to America of Viscount Lieutenant General Yasushiko Iwashami. The two officers chatted in English as they walked ahead of the rest of the little party, consisting of two of the Japanese general's personal aids, the Japanese consul and his secretary, an equal number of General Lancaster's staff, and a civilian addressed as Ogden Kirby, a resident of San Francisco, evidently a close acquaintance of the consul, and known to General Iwashami. To General Lancaster he had been introduced as a man interested in the general promotion of affairs between Japan and the United States, a go-between on commercial matters, not entirely unconnected, perhaps, with governmental purchases for the former nation.

Brown-haired, blue-eyed, clean-shaven, with an aggressive chin and a subtle suggestion of military bearing, despite his avowedly pacific occupation, his short figure was the only one of the Caucasians that did not top the men of Nippon. The soldiers were tall and rangy, the Japanese below the average stature, with convex noses, skins yellow rather than brown, and of slender, almost delicate, physique.

General Iwashami was an exception to his countrymen, save in height. The contrast between him and General Lancaster, as they walked ahead, was a marked one, emphasized by their trailing shadows. The American was a type of the United States officer, lean everywhere, gray eyes beneath white eyebrows, gray hair, mustache and imperial, vigorous, emphatic in walk and gesture. Beside him, the Japanese looked almost froglike, though his squat figure shared also the other's emphasis of force and command, mingled with confidence. His scanty hair was gray, his face brown, his nose large, his lips thick, and the eyebrows thin. Inclined to corpulence, his thick neck was closely joined to square shoulders. Above prominent cheek bones, his narrow eyes were beady, inscrutable, and keen. He was of the mixed Mongoloid Malayan type, as opposed to the Korean cast of his companions. Lancaster was eminently Anglo Saxon, unhyphenated in descent. As they talked on military affairs in the technical terms of experts, it seemed the meeting of two strong men from Orient and Occident on the border line where East and West must meet—the shores of the Pacific Ocean.

Three women awaited them on the steps of headquarters. Irene Lancaster, daughter of the general, blond, lithe, and good to look upon, with her father's gray eyes in franker, less assertive, reproduction, and in her bearing a hint of athletic propensities; her aunt, Mrs. Houston, a widow, whose mourning had been long discarded and forgotten, talkative, and with an air of cordiality to the opposite sex that in a younger woman might have been termed flirtatious, her somewhat faded, but carefully retouched, charms revealing their artificiality beside the fresh complexion of her niece; and the wife of the Japanese consul, quiet, almost shy, dressed in a tailored suit of modern cut, that fitted, yet somehow held the hint of masquerade.

"Are you coming up to the house, father?" asked the girl, after introductions had been effected. "For refreshments."

General Lancaster looked at the watch on his wrist.

"I am expecting to hear from Grahame," he said. "I told him the parade ground would be cleared by four o'clock."

A soldier came up quickly to the general, saluted, and handed him an envelope.

"From the wireless station, general," he reported.

General Lancaster read the message aloud:

> "Five miles outside Golden Gate, five thousand feet above it. May
> I descend?
>
> GRAHAME.

"Tell him 'yes.' See to it, Webster, will you, please?" said the general to an aid who hurried away as his commanding officer turned to his visitors.

"Bruce Grahame," he explained, "is a friend of ours who is trying out a new air machine to-day, the *Aërolite*, a triplane. He is more than a dabbler in aëronautics, though one could not call him a professional. He is, in a way, an amateur auxiliary of the army. He is going to help us try out certain things at our annual maneuvers at Atascadero later this week. To-day he lands on our parade ground."

"Equipped with wireless, I see," said General Iwashami. "Hydro—or aëroplane?"

"A seaplane, I believe, with equal facilities for lighting on land and water. My daughter really knows more about it than I do. I have merely talked it over briefly with Grahame."

The Japanese turned his searching eyes upon the girl. Ogden Kirby moved closer to her.

"You are interested in aëronautics?" he asked.

Irene Lancaster surveyed him evenly from her somewhat superior height. Apparently she was not particularly impressed by the man.

"Not to qualify as an expert," she answered politely. "But Mr. Grahame is an old friend of ours."

"Here comes the advance guard," said the general. "Every machine that can raise a plane is up to-day." He gave command, and an orderly brought several pairs of field glasses, which the party proceeded to focus to suit their eyes.

The sky was brilliantly blue, with but a random trade cloud or two to accent the azure. In the northwest, black specks revealed themselves in the powerful prisms as a host of aëroplanes, flying rapidly toward the reservation, dipping and hurdling in the lofty vagaries of the air, biplanes most of them, a few carrying a passenger beside or behind the pilot.

Above and behind them, like a hawk scattering a flock of pigeons, soared a machine that rushed onward without apparent deviation from the air lane it had chosen, rapidly overtaking the rest. Its three tiers of planes were in shadow, but the sun's reflection flashed from its metal struts and supports, and turned its untarnished guys to lines of light. In place of the ordinary boat-shaped vehicle, pilot and passengers were inclosed in a car of aluminum with oval windows, the forward openings of which accented its resemblance to some mammoth insect.

"He would have to dull that metal work for war purposes," said Iwashami, his glass swinging in the arc of the swiftly approaching triplane.

"He intends to. He hasn't decided on the best color as yet," said Irene Lancaster.

Her father smiled at her. The Japanese lowered his field glasses and gazed at her shrewdly.

"I suppose in Japan a woman is seen and not heard," she thought, with a mental *moué* of rebellion.

The minor air machines were wheeling to right and left, remounting in swift spirals or swinging aside to give right of way to the triplane that alone had permission to land on the parade ground. Suddenly the *Aërolite* swooped with stiff-set planes, plunging earthward as if bent on destruction, gliding of its own momentum, with its powerful engines silent. Some unseen hand within the cabin plucked at a halyard, a ball of bunting ascended a metal rod, and broke out into a flag that whipped fiercely in the breeze, the emblazoned banner of the Stars and Stripes.

A burst of spontaneous cheering arose from the soldiers assembled about the parade ground, and from the group at headquarters. The quick-witted bandmaster, his musicians still undismissed, batoned them into the "Star-Spangled Banner" as the great machine tilted its planes and turned the bolt of its descent into a curve, as, on wheels and skids lowered under its water pontoons, the *Aërolite* lit upon the center of the parade ground, and, like a great bird running with outspread wings, came to rest opposite General Lancaster and his party.

A door opened in the side of the cabin, and three men stepped out, one commencing to walk about the machine in the role of mechanician, the others, both dressed in olive shirts, breeches, and puttees, approaching headquarters.

Both saluted, the shorter of the two with a military precision that bespoke the soldier he proved to be on introduction. The other, Bruce Grahame, was a young giant, two inches over six feet, with broad shoulders, from which his body tapered, V-fashion, to a pliant waist, close-clipped hair above a tanned face, smeared with streaks of grease that his companion shared, but redeemed by a frank smile from even teeth between clean-cut lips, and a pair of eyes that looked straight at and seemingly part way through you, in the direct purpose of their gaze.

Congratulations were bestowed upon Grahame, and the party moved closer to the machine, which, even at rest, its twin screws motionless, seemed strangely vital, almost capable of soaring aloft from its own volition.

"The latest thing in aëroplanes, I take it," said General Iwashami, appraising it with intelligence.

"Not quite the latest," replied Grahame, "but about as far as any one has gone with vertical propellers, I think. We are experimenting along other lines."

"Ah, helicopters!" said the Japanese sagely.

"Were you satisfied, Bruce?" asked General Lancaster.

"We climbed the first twenty-five hundred feet in eight minutes, and a full five thousand in fifteen," answered Grahame. "The stabilizers worked like a charm. Of course, we have room for another man, but we were carrying fifteen hundred pounds, exclusive of the weight of the machine. A third of that was fuel and oil, a third live weight, and the rest tools and instruments. The engine was a little over-vigorous, and we got spattered, but we might fairly call it a success, I think. Potter has the actual figures."

He nodded to the lieutenant who had accompanied him.

"Was this an official trial?" asked Ogden Kirby.

Grahame raised his eyebrows.

"I mean, are you expecting to sell to the government?"

Grahame looked at the speaker indifferently.

"I am an amateur," he said. "If I can help to discover or perfect methods of aviation that will increase the efficiency of the army or the navy, I shall certainly offer the benefit of any such developments to the United States government as a matter of patriotism."

Ogden Kirby exchanged a few words with the Japanese general in the latter's own language, and, undeterred by the lack of cordiality shown toward him by Grahame, again addressed him:

"General Iwashami would, I believe, be delighted to make a flight, if you would extend him an invitation."

Uncertain as to how well the general spoke English, Grahame hesitated for a moment. The Japanese officer smiled and bowed.

"I should be glad," he said, "to be the guest of so distinguished an amateur."

"I am sorry," answered Grahame, "but I am afraid I shall be obliged to decline the offer."

The words were spoken without emphasis, but to all present they conveyed the idea of a direct refusal, rather than inability to comply with the request. There was a little silence, pregnant with veiled antagonism.

"Oh!" said General Iwashami trenchantly. "The plane, then, is out of order?"

"It is unable to accommodate your excellency," replied Grahame firmly.

"Some other time, perhaps," suggested General Lancaster smoothly. "Grahame will be at Atascadero three days from now, at the annual army maneuvers. So, I trust, will you, general."

"I am afraid not," answered the Japanese. "My time is limited and very much occupied. Even now I am forced to leave you."

He turned and exchanged a rapid staccato of Japanese with the consul, and, with all his party, made a ceremonious farewell that was yet markedly impromptu. The suggestions of General Lancaster that they partake of refreshments fell upon politely deaf ears, and the Nipponese entered the automobile that had brought them, and drove away, imperturbable and seemingly complacent, but leaving behind them the sense of antagonism already promoted between Grahame and General Iwashami.

"You've offended him, my boy," said General Lancaster, returning from his farewell courtesies. "Was the machine really out of commission?"

"It was not," said Grahame, his frank face hardening.

"Then why—" commenced the general.

"Because, sir, I do not believe that in the present condition of friction between Japan and the United States—and California in particular—it is advisable to place a trained expert of what may possibly become a hostile country in a position to examine our defenses."

"Pooh, pooh, sir," said General Lancaster. "I am the best judge of that."

Grahame bowed.

"You may remember, sir," he went on respectfully, "that, as commodore of the San Francisco Aëro Club, I protested against the entry of either Japanese or Chinese aviators in the flight competitions held five years ago, during the Panama-Pacific Exposition. I was overruled by the committee, but it did not alter the fact that an alien aviator, with the aid of a camera, could register the position of every battery that the artillery arm had taken pains to secrete. The Presidio is filled with signs and set with sentries to prevent the ordinary citizen acquiring knowledge that every airman, if he cares to take the trouble, can ascertain in an hour's flight."

General Lancaster tugged at his mustache. There were side looks not unexpressive of approbation among the officers, and the general's face reddened as he noticed them.

"I regret that General Iwashami should have been treated with discourtesy," he said abruptly.

Ogden Kirby, who had lingered by the automobile to talk with the Japanese, interposed:

"General Iwashami is desirous of obtaining a number of aëroplanes of the latest model for the Japanese government," he said. "He wishes to make a personal trial that might lead to purchase."

"Doubtless," said Grahame. "If I ever enter the aviation market, however, it will be to sell machines for defense, not offense."

He turned on his heel and approached the girl.

"You understand, do you not, Irene?" he asked, in a low tone.

"I think you have unnecessarily placed father in an unpleasant situation," she answered, flushing. "That Japanese bugaboo of yours is becoming an obsession, Bruce."

"I am sorry if I displeased you or your father," he answered. "But the *Aërolite*, like its master, is purely patriotic in purpose. I am sorry you were not up with us to-day. You've always wanted to make a flight. Will you let me take you down to Atascadero on Friday?"

"No," she said crisply.

Bruce Grahame bowed to her decision. The girl turned to Ogden Kirby.

"You've lived in Japan, Mr. Kirby?" she said. "I want to ask you some questions. I think, as a race, they are delightful. Aunty and I are planning for a trip to Chrysanthemum Country very soon."

They plunged into an animated conversation, as, led by General Lancaster and his sister, the group strolled toward the general's personal quarters. Grahame, his eyes following the figures of Irene Lancaster and Kirby, failed to join them. A grizzled major, seamed and tanned of face, took him by the elbow.

"You gave the K.O. shrapnel, Bruce," he said. "Confidentially, there's a heap in what you said. I've always been against this turning our army and navy into a kindergarten for Japanese inquisitiveness. There was the case of the steward on the *Oregon*, you know, who turned out to be a lieutenant commander in the Japanese-Russian war. There are Jap servants in too many officers' houses and sticking round the Army and Navy Club, to suit me. I've been in Japan, and I know they wouldn't allow a foreigner within a mile of a reservation or a dockyard. But you're off about invasion, Bruce. They wouldn't dare to tackle us."

"They wouldn't, eh?" replied Grahame grimly. "I'd like to show you a book called *The War Between Japan and America*, published by the Japanese League for National Defense. The first edition came out in 1915, with a million copies sold. The war is seriously proposed on account of 'inhuman treatment of the Japanese immigrant and the hostile legislature of the United States.' It says that Japan ought to occupy California, Hawaii, and the Philippines. Look here, here's a literal translation of a paragraph." He took a typewritten slip from a pocketbook, and read it as the two stood by the car of the *Aërolite*.

> The hearts of sixty million Japanese are inflamed with courage, and are stormy like the strong winds of the heavens, insisting that a war be begun against the United States which will prove to the bluffing Americans that the Japanese people do not know defeat, and that her soldiers cannot be beaten.*

"Strong language," said the major. "Sounds to me suspiciously like bluff in itself, Grahame. Japan's financially on the scrap heap."

"Did it ever occur to you that some other nation might finance them in return for certain possessions—the Philippines, for example? I tell you, major, every time that alien immigration bill comes up in Congress, I can see the Japanese fleet getting up steam in their boilers."

---

* From Boston News Bureau published in New York, Philadelphia, and Chicago papers, January 1916.

"You've got too vivid an imagination, Bruce. What do you propose doing?"

"I'm neither the president nor the head of the army or navy," said Grahame, "but there's one thing I can do and intend to. I'm going to try and unite all the aviation clubs of the Pacific coast into an aërial militia."

The major whistled.

"You *are* in earnest, aren't you? Minutemen of the air, eh? But you'll have to get state permission, Bruce. Probably federal."

"I'll get it," said Grahame grimly. "Want to take a trip, major?"

"Not I," laughed the major. "The C.O. would have me court-martialed. Better let him cool off before you make your next call, Bruce."

He stood watching as the great propellers whirred to the petulant explosions of the engine, and the *Aërolite*, gliding along the ground, seemed to leap into the air and went aloft in a great spiral, climbing fast and high, the Stars and Stripes still waving in the breeze.

II

AT ATASCADERO

Atascadero is in San Luis Obispo County, California, not far from the resort at Paso Robles Hot Springs, between the Coast Range and the Salinas River. Every little while a military city springs up overnight on its levels, and khaki-clad soldiers of Uncle Sam play at war and try to unite theory with practice while burning blank cartridges. They build pontoon bridges under imaginary fire, dig themselves in, charge trenches while imaginary shells burst above them, and machine guns rake them with imaginary bullets. The hospital corps binds up imaginary wounds, and occasionally makes itself really useful in case of a sprained ankle, or sunstroke. There is some smoke and some noise, and umpires stimulate their imagination to decide the victors of the sham attacks.

Of the horrors of real warfare, the nerve-shattering explosions, the raw wounds and dismembered bodies, the heart tests of shrapnel and cold steel, the exposures, the demoralization of physical defeat, the frenzy of victory, the decimation of companies—there is nothing. The soldier knows death and surrender only by the command of an excited umpire, and finds his slaughtered comrades safe again by the camp fire.

It is useful, necessary, like the shadow boxing of a pugilist. It is even to a certain extent inspiring, but it is not war.

The last day of the maneuvers was ended. The Reds had captured a hill and raked the enemy over a range furnished by the *Aërolite*, attached by special dispensation, hovering triumphantly above two limping, low-powered army biplanes of the Blues, either of which it could have annihilated with impunity in the first hour of the game. A week of marching had hardened—and tired—rank and file alike. The bulk of the command were camped ready to entrain the next day. Officers on leave had motored to Paso Robles for a dance or a hot mineral-water bath, according to choice or necessity.

The Rancho del Nido lay like the nest for which it was named in a little amphitheater of rolling hills, golden brown in the summer heat, dotted with great live oaks, beneath which grazed the pedigreed dairy herd of Mrs. Houston, General Lancaster's widowed sister. The rancheria itself stood in a grove of oaks and sycamores, a low, rambling dwelling of thick adobe walls, set with porches, roofed with old Spanish tiling, inclosing a patio garden filled with flowers about a central pool.

Here General Lancaster, with one or two of his staff, were pleasantly and conveniently quartered. Mrs. Houston played hostess, assisted by her niece. Ogden Kirby, whose attentions since his introduction had been assiduous in cultivating the acquaintance of both the ladies with apparent impartiality, was one of the guests. There was a little lake not far from the house, and in it the *Aërolite*, moored fore and aft, rode on her pontoons like a great gull. The choleric general had forgotten or forgiven the incident at the Presidio. Grahame was an old friend of the family, and had done real service in the maneuvers. And the invitation was of old standing.

Grahame had seen little of Irene during the busy battle practice, and, when time had allowed, Ogden Kirby, for whom his instinctive dislike was being tinged by more personal feelings, usually monopolized her company.

Ogden Kirby had brilliant qualities. He was a man of good education applied to a wide experience, and his fund of information was apparently both unlimited and accurate. Mrs. Houston he had completely won over by subtle flattery, and the same general principles had been successful with General Lancaster, who had once published a monograph on ballistics when a captain of artillery. This, Kirby was not merely familiar with, but able to discuss intelligently. With Irene Lancaster he had established a basis on the subject of Japan and the Japanese people. The girl, out of sheer feminine delight in the establishment of rivalry, seemed to find especial pleasure in discussing with him all the good qualities he ascribed to the race, particularly in the presence of Bruce Grahame. There was an occasional rasp to the fencing of the two men that betrayed their antagonism and a hidden wish that the buttons were off the foils.

"I consider them a most courteous and charming race," said Irene, as the after-dinner coffee was served. "Aunt has had them on the ranch for ten years as house servants, so have we from time to time, and they are perfect. They are not generally understood, that is all. They have a pride that is sensitive, and resent being treated as too many of our domestic help is used, given poor food, worse quarters, and no appreciation."

"I agree with you absolutely, Miss Lancaster," said Kirby.

"Good Lord, are you off again on that subject?" groaned the general, in mock dismay, as Irene Lancaster looked expectantly at Grahame.

"I have no objection to them as a people, nor do I underestimate their capacities," said Grahame. "The fact remains, that the Japanese are in much the same position as were the islanders of Great Britain soon after they had benefited by the civilization of their neighbors across the channel, and had also demonstrated their own power as fighting men. Their ambitions were aroused, and their land was too small for their growth as a nation. They colonized. Japan has to do the same. The Pacific coast invites them by sheer force of fertility and climatic attractions. Restrictions have been placed on them which they resent. These may be just or unjust. The resentment is smoldering, ready to burst into flame. I say, we should be prepared for it. We are in possession of desirable land. It is needed by others. They are stronger than we are."

"Bah!" said the general.

"Stronger at present in aggressive possibilities than we are in defensive, sir."

"What do you suggest, Grahame?" put in a staff officer. "Give them free entrance?"

"I do not think they would ever assimilate with us," said Grahame. "If we are the melting pot of the nations, the Japanese represent a metal that will not blend into the alloy of Americanism."

"Japanese have married white women," said Kirby.

"White women have married negroes," retorted Grahame. "You would not consider that a generally desirable mixture. I have yet to hear of a white man who married a Japanese."

"There have been many Butterfly unions. *Lieutenant Pinkerton*, in Puccini's opera, is far from entirely an imaginative character." Kirby spoke with a repressed heat and an ironic quality in his voice that made the others gaze at him wonderingly.

"I was discussing international ethics, not doubtful episodes," said Grahame. "You seem to hold a brief for Japan, Mr. Kirby."

"I know them better than you do, sir."

Grahame passed over the sneer. "Possibly," he answered. "But you cannot ignore statistics. The general will correct me if I am in error. The ladies will tell me if I am boring them. I am going to leave the naval question alone.

"The peace army of the United States is under one hundred thousand. It has never been up to standard. It is doubtful if a fully equipped army of defense of more than thirty thousand could be gathered in an emergency. The Japanese peace footing in 1908 was over a quarter of a million. There are fifty-five thousand Japanese in California alone. There are more than one hundred thousand Japanese in the Hawaii Islands—more than half the total population, which includes almost as many Chinese as natives, and twice as many Portuguese as Americans. Many of these Japanese are reservists, men trained to modern warfare, soldiers of undefeated service."

He paused, and said impressively:

"It is highly probable that there are more ex-Japanese soldiers of the war with Russia in 1905 now living on the Pacific coast than the total available number of American soldiers."

Kirby laughed.

"Ranch hands, domestic servants, petty merchants!" he said. "Your theory is absurd, Grahame. And this is 1920. By your own statement, what ex-soldiers there may be are fifteen years out of practice and behind the times."

"I will prove differently," said Grahame. "And that inside of the hour, if you will give me the opportunity. I have seen Japanese drilling in modern tactics in the algarroba scrub back of Diamond Head, in Honolulu. Your bucolic ranch hands exercise almost nightly with wooden guns not ten miles from Fresno, and in a score of places in the San Joaquin and Sacramento Valleys—"

He broke off as Yamamato, Mrs. Houston's Japanese butler, entered the room unobtrusively.

"You like anything else?" he asked his mistress. Grahame thought his eyes roved furtively toward Kirby.

"Nothing more, Yamamato," she said.

The man was retiring, catfooted, as he had come, when the general spoke.

"Hold on a minute, Yamamato," he said. "Let's test this. Kirby, you're more liable to get the facts. Ask him if he was in the war with Russia, and if he is a reservist?"

Without any show of reluctance, Kirby addressed the servant in voluble Japanese. Yamamato affected no surprise at being spoken to in his own language. Once only Grahame imagined that the man halted an involuntary salute. Undoubtedly he treated Kirby with respect, and the conversation seemed longer than necessary. At last Yamamato bowed somewhat effusively and left the room.

"The man fought in 1905," admitted Kirby. "He was wounded. He has no desire to fight again, he says. Nor does he want to return to Japan. He is more independent here, less taxed."

"His arguments are largely those of the Australian and Canadian colonists," said Grahame, "none of whom is eager to return to the mother country."

"What about this proof of yours?" asked the general.

"There's a big colony of Japanese in the Pajaro Valley," said Grahame, "making fortunes out of apple lands."

"To their credit," put in Kirby.

"Because they have community labor, willing to work for wages that would not uphold the standard of living demanded by the American," retorted Grahame. "Pajaro's about a hundred miles away, as the plane flies. The *Aërolite's* outside. It's moonlight, and a light breeze, ideal for flying. I can't take all of you, but if you, general, with Irene and Mr. Kirby, will accompany me, I will prove my words and have you back here before half past ten."

"That's a fair challenge," said the general. "I'm not too old a dog to learn new tricks. Irene?"

"Surely," she said. "I've always wanted to take a flight."

Kirby looked at Grahame.

"How do you know these Japanese will be drilling to-night?" he asked.

"I have land interests near there," answered Grahame. "I am sure of my information."

"You seem to be a disciple of preparedness."

The sneer was again apparent in Kirby's tone.

"I believe in patriotism," said Grahame quietly. "And, at present, patriotism and preparedness seem to me one and the same thing."

III

THE PLAIN OF PAJARO

The triplane soared through the moonlit night, holding a course almost due north, guided by the silver ribbon of the Salinas River. In the floor of the car were observation windows, from which the rubber protection covers were removed as soon as the quartet was seated. Graham had dispensed with his mechanician, and was busy with his engine. The general sat beside him, with Irene Lancaster and Kirby behind them. Despite the closed car, conversation was impossible while the engine was running. The constant vibration, insufficient for discomfort, made them feel as if they were ensconced in the heart of some mighty monster of the air.

Their course lay along the Salinas Valley, between two spurs of the Coast Range. Fields and hamlets were a blur beneath them in their rapid flight, spurning the air with the speeding propellers. Twice a train, vomiting blotches of smoke, passed, one north and the other south, where the railroad followed the river. At Salinas, there was a sparkle of scattered lights, and they swung nearer to true north by the compass in the electric-lighted binnacle in front of Grahame. A chronometer and aneroid barometer hung on the instrument board attached to the forward wall of the car. As the former marked fifty-five minutes of flight from the lake, they approached a shoulder of the inland line of hills. Grahame angled his planes, moving a lever in a series of connecting slots, and the machine rapidly descended below the level of the brow of the hill ahead. A change of steel rods, and they glided over the obstruction as he shut off the engine, and the perpetual shudder and coordinated roar ceased. Over the hill they swooped silently as a hawk.

"I don't want to warn them," he said to the general. "Watch closely."

They were gliding above a cup in the hills, still at a tremendous rate. Manipulating rigid planes set vertically between the main wings, Grahame deadened the speed.

"Now look," he said.

Below them, like ants, were moving figures advancing across the plain in massed formation. These halted, split into companies, the companies dividing into broken ranks that advanced in open order; crawling swiftly over the ground, evidently obeying the orders of a group of men on a little knoll.

Above them swung the moon. The shadow of the triplane crossed the rise. Swiftly, like poultry under a threatening chicken hawk, the group clustered, gazing upward at the flying machine.

"Are they Japanese?" asked the general.

For answer, Grahame threw his engine into gear. The *Aërolite* leaped ahead, and, with banked planes, swerved in a great loop and swung back, hardly a hundred feet above the ground. The antlike figures were scurrying for cover. The aëronaut touched a pedal, and the ray of a powerful searchlight swept the earth. As it passed, the startled, upturned faces showed clearly with Oriental features carved in light and shadow, while the *Aërolite*, climbing, once again topped the hill and sped on southward back to the Rancho del Nido.

There was no more chance for talk until the machine, soaring like a swan, slid down the airways into the lake, and nosed gently to shore.

"You've opened my eyes," said General Lancaster, as they walked toward the rancheria. "I'm much obliged to you, Grahame. I'll have something to send to Washington."

Kirby was silent, apparently chagrined at Grahame's vindication. At the arch leading to the patio, from which steps mounted on either side to the outer verandas, giving entrance to the house, Grahame spoke to Irene Lancaster.

"Would you mind coming into the garden with me?" he asked. "There's something I want to say to you."

She gave him a swift, slightly troubled look, and went with him as the general and Kirby left them.

The patio garden was redolent with the perfume of roses and jasmine, pink and white oleanders, and a medley of old-fashioned flowers. Palms threw fanlike shadows, and here and there ripe lemons and oranges showed golden globes where the moonlight touched them.

They reached the broad curb of the central pool, where the fountain tinkled, and Irene sat down, idly scattering the petals of some carnations she had plucked.

"I think you know what I'm going to tell you, Irene," said Grahame. "I wish I could put it in more impressive language. I love you. I have always loved you, I think. There has never been any one else in the life that I ask you to share and make perfect."

She tossed the last fragrant petal into the pool before she looked up and answered:

"I'm sorry, Bruce. More sorry, because I did know what you were some day going to tell me, and I had thought that my answer might be different.

"It is not that I do not care for you very dearly, Bruce," she went on. "But I think I have come to demand more as I have grown older. I want a full share in the life of the man I marry, and I want that life to mean something."

She paused, then continued in a voice that held a hint of embarrassment, while Bruce Grahame surveyed her with steadfast tenderness.

"I admire you, Bruce," she said, "for many qualities—but—"

"But what?"

"I'll speak frankly. You were left a great deal of money, Bruce. I don't know what use you've made of it."

"I've doubled it, for one thing," he replied half humorously.

"But you had it to start with. You've got a profession, you don't practice it. You're clever, yet content to become the commodore of an air fleet, and run your own plane as the summit of your ambition. A man should have a definite purpose in life."

"May the defendant speak?" he asked.

She nodded gravely.

"I was left a great deal of money. Granted. It was rather a handicap than otherwise. Ever since it came into my possession, a great many ingenious persons, singly and combined, have persistently tried to take it away from me. I am a chemical engineer by profession, a title that means a good deal more than a lay man—or a lay woman—might suspect. By the exercise of that profession, I have largely been able to double my fortune, while retaining the original amount against all the efforts of burglarious financiers. As to my aircraft, I am on the eve of success with an invention, neither new nor my own, but so far unperfected, that will revolutionize—"

He stopped, wheeled, and darted through the shadows in the direction whence his quick ear had caught a sudden rustle. He came back in a moment.

"Some one listening," he said. "They got away through the servants' quarters."

"Did you see who it was?" she asked.

"I am not certain. Whoever it was, he is not likely to come back."

"I can't imagine who would be eavesdropping," she said, with vexation.

Grahame, practically certain that it was Yamamato he had surprised lurking in the shadow, forbore to mention it. He knew what Irene Lancaster considered his prejudices.

"Let us walk down by the lake," he suggested.

The water was bordered by a walk fringed with live oaks heavily bearded with moss. On the dark surface that was unsilvered by the moon, the *Aërolite* floated ghostlike.

"You call that the summit of my ambition," he said, pointing to the triplane, "and say I lack a purpose. It is, in a way, an emblem of what I am devoting all my energies to. You are the daughter of one of our country's guardians, Irene, a warder by profession, wedded to one branch of a service that is handicapped by being directed by so-called statesmen, who are ignorant or careless of its requirements. As such, you are accustomed, through personal pride and belief in the army, to consider the country safe, despite the wars that have recently racked the world. The majority of Americans share your convictions. Some of us do not. To my mind, there is no better purpose in life for a man than to be an effective patriot. I believe the nation, or at least the Pacific coast, in imminent danger. With Washington blind or indifferent to the peril, it is up to us of California, Washington, and Oregon to defend our own. I cannot tell you our plans, even in brief. I doubt if you would have the patience to listen to me. But the writing is plain on the wall. I have worked day and night; I shall continue to concentrate my life on this matter. You say I have no purpose. I hold this one ambition—to be a patriot in deed as well as word."

He spoke with an enthusiasm that kindled as he spoke. His head was thrown back, his shoulders squared. She caught the gleam of his eyes in the moonlight, and sighed.

"It is only a theory, Bruce," she said.

"Were those men we saw to-night merely part of a theory?" he asked.

"Do you think the United States should take fright because a few men exercise themselves in their leisure hours? Does it follow that they wish ill to us? You acknowledge they are reservists. Can they serve their country in case of recall only against us?"

"Apparently you consider Ogden Kirby's arguments sounder than mine," he said.

"They seem to me more reasonable, Bruce. If your theory is wrong, you are wasting your time. I do not share your dread of invasion, and I cannot be in sympathy with its plans."

She placed her hand on his arm.

"Believe me, I do not mean to hurt you. But there are so many more certain things you could do, it seems to me, to build up this great Western country of ours, that would be equally patriotic!"

"We'll dismiss the subject, Irene," he said. "It's getting late. Your father will be wondering where we are. I was forgetting the other guests. But if," he went on, as they walked back toward the house, "if my theory proves a true one—"

"I shall be the first to confess my mistake and ask your pardon," she said.

"That is all any one can ask," he answered. "Here we are. Good night, Irene. I'm not coming in right away. I shall smoke a bit outside."

She lingered at the door.

"I'm sorry, Bruce," she said, giving him her hand. "Good night."

He raised her fingers lightly to his lips. A moment afterward he was walking back toward the lake, his lips tight set about his cigar, his face hard with resolution.

"So she thinks I am a dreamer and a chaser of shadows," he thought. "It will not take long in the testing. Anyway," he tried to console himself, "the pursuit of patriotism leaves little leisure for love-making. I spoke too soon." And he knew in the back of his brain that it was the phantom of rivalry raised by Ogden Kirby that had hastened the issue.

The shifting moonlight had checkered the back of the *Aërolite* in black and white, and splotched the bank to which the airship was moored. Two men crossed one patch of light, and Grahame waited to see them appear in the next. Looking closely, he could just distinguish them as blotches in the shadow, standing with their faces turned toward the aëroplane. After a few moments, they emerged from the darkness, and crossed a strip of moonlight, walking around the lake in his direction.

Grahame slipped behind the trunk of one of the oaks, and ground the spark of his cigar out against the bark. The men came on, deep in confidential conversation. Soon he could distinguish syllables, though he could not understand them. But he recognized the rapid staccato of Japanese. Just beyond the tree he had chosen for his hiding place there was a space illumined by the full moon. He flattened himself against the oak, holding his breath as they came opposite to him, craning his neck cautiously to peer at them as they passed, unconscious of his presence, absorbed in their talk.

He remained without moving until the sound of their voices died away. Then he turned and hurried across the hill at his back, taking a short cut to the house. He was lolling in a rocking-chair on the outer veranda five minutes later, the end of his cigar prominently aglow, when Ogden Kirby mounted the steps.

"Good night, whoever you are," said Kirby.

"Good night," answered Grahame. "Been taking a moonlight walk?"

"Just a stroll round the garden," replied the other. "I'm going to turn in now. I didn't thank you for your trip to-night, Grahame. It was very interesting."

"Wasn't it? Good night.

"Now, I wonder," Grahame asked himself, as he finished his cigar, "just what your game might be, Mr. Ogden Kirby? Naturally, you lied about walking arm in arm about the lake with Yamamoto. To my mind, you speak Japanese dangerously well for a white man. On general principles, I don't like visitors who chum with butlers. And that works both ways. I've an idea Yamamoto would exchange his servant's jacket for a military blouse without regret."

IV

AT THE UNIVERSITY CLUB

In San Francisco, Grahame lived at the University Club. Its atmosphere was congenial, and there were a number of its members who were kindred spirits. Some of them belonged to his fraternity, some had been of his own year at the University of California. They had a table set apart for them at dinner, and generally forgathered daily. They were a clean-cut, efficient-looking crowd, none of them drones, unless Irene Lancaster's definition of Grahame's character was correct. When they talked together, it was of the vital topics of the day, and the conversation was apt to be tinged with expert opinion. Among them were transportation, light, and power men, chemists, lawyers, architects, engineers, doctors. Grahame was not the only wealthy one; there were others who managed their own affairs of considerable magnitude, big ranches, lumber, and shipping interests.

Nor were they all of an age. They ranged from twenty-five to sixty, bound together by common interests and a mutual impulse of friendship and respect. The rest of the members dubbed them the "Ultras," and accused them of forming a clique within the club, at which they laughed good-naturedly, and continued to prefer each other's society.

Grahame, dressing in his room for a farewell dinner to one of the Ultras about to leave for Europe, frowned at his half-shaven reflection in the glass, beyond which he could see in the opening door the Japanese valet, who had brought his freshly pressed dinner clothes. He had made it a point never to accept a position on the directorate of the club, as conflicting with his own affairs, but he had held points of difference with the board, one of which was the employment of Japanese, excused by the house committee on the grounds of utility and the scarcity of American help that would stay on the job.

There was little, as a rule, to be said about the efficiency of the Orientals.

They were deft, noiseless, and excellent servants. The valet's imperturbable face might have been carved out of ivory as Grahame swung upon him with a rebuke:

"Confound you, Ito! I've told you a dozen times not to come in here without knocking."

"I knock, sir. I think you no hear."

"Then wait next time till I tell you to come in. Now get out!"

The Japanese, his face still a mask, laid one of the suits he carried on his arm on the bed, and retreated hastily, as Grahame gestured impatiently toward the door.

Grahame was not in his usual even temper. His refusal by Irene Lancaster, while not final, had possibly upset his equanimity, but it was the sight of the Oriental that recalled his paramount grievance. He had made the trip from Atascadero in the *Aërolite* that morning, and only the rigid inspection with which he invariably overhauled the machine before a flight had saved him and his mechanician from a probably fatal accident. During the night, some one had half filed through several important guys close beneath their turnbuckles, where least likely to be noticed. He suspected Yamamato or one of the other Japanese servants at the rancheria, acting as an agent for Kirby, whom he shrewdly mistrusted as not all unwilling to do him mischief. It was merely suspicion, as far as Kirby was concerned, based chiefly upon intuition. The main fact was the filing of the wires, and the logical doubt that the butler would have acted on his own initiative. Kirby's reason for the attempted crime he did not set down entirely to rivalry. But Kirby, as a man confessedly intimate with transpacific international relations, was, to Grahame's reasoning, entirely too apt and specious in his defense of Japanese intentions.

He picked up the suit, saw at a glance that the valet had made a mistake, and threw them across the foot of his bed. Then he telephoned to the housekeeper.

Within a minute, Ito returned, knocking punctiliously. There was a shade of concern on his impassive features as he apologized.

"I make mistake," he said, with a deprecatory bow. "You please excuse. Here your suit, Mist Grahame."

"These wouldn't fit a man half my size," said Grahame. "Do you know who these belong to?"

He picked up the dinner jacket before Ito's quickly extended hands could reach it, and turned back the breast pocket to look for the name label.

"These belong to Mr. Kirby," he said, dropping the jacket abruptly, as he read the name below the tag of a Yokohama tailor. "Take them away."

The valet carefully picked up the offending suit and bore it away.

As Grahame stooped for his shoes, he caught sight of a glittering object beneath the bed. It was a piece of gilt board about an inch and a half square. On it was a Japanese ideograph:

"Must have dropped out of Kirby's pocket," he thought. "I wonder what it means?" He placed it in his own vest pocket, uncertain whether to offer it to its probable owner. Acting on a sudden thought, he took it out and made a careful pencil sketch of the character.

A man, tall and dark and thin, with nervous hands and brilliant eyes, met him as he stepped out of the elevator, and his words made Grahame temporarily forget the scrap of cardboard.

"Look here, Bruce," said his friend, slipping an arm into his in friendly fashion: "Here's news for you. Thayer came into our office to-day. He's up from Hermosillo. Closed out some smelter interests there. There's a projected branch of the Sonora Railroad to King Bay on the coast that's been nothing but a dotted line on the map for ten years. Now it's being rushed in a hurry. And the interesting part of it is that King Bay is opposite Tiburon Island, and Tiburon Island has been sold to the Japanese government by Mexico. The two are thick as thieves, anyway. Mexico needs the money, and Japan seems to have it."

"That means a naval base in the Gulf of California," said Grahame, "with access to a railroad only a hundred and fifty odd miles from the border of the United States at Nogales, Arizona. The head of the gulf is about seventy-five miles from Mexicali and Calexico, on the California line. There's a big Japanese colony there in the Imperial Valley. Thanks, Fred. That's in line with a rumor I got to-day from San Diego, that the Japs have acquired the Coronado Islands. Launches run over there from San Diego once in a while to view the sea gardens, like those at Catalina, and a tourist party was warned off by Japanese. The islands belong to Mexico. They're about ten miles from the big Hotel Coronado, on the peninsula by San Diego."

"What does that mean? A submarine base?"

"More than likely. I'll take a flight down there as soon as I can. They can't hide it from the *Aërolite*. Want to come?"

"If I can get away. Begins to look like business, eh, Grahame?"

Grahame nodded and pressed his friend's arm warningly as Kirby passed them.

"What's the idea, Bruce?"

"I don't fancy that chap, Fred. But I've got something of his I want to return to him. Excuse me."

Grahame hurried after Kirby, but the latter, his light coat over his arm, and his hat in his hand, had caught a waiting elevator and vanished.

Grahame's friend, Fred Thurston, an official of the telephone company, was waiting for him.

"What's wrong with Kirby, Bruce?" he asked. "I never liked him particularly. He was up with me at Harvard, you know. That's how he got his membership here. Queer sort of duck. Used to chum with a couple of Japs in his freshman year, I remember. Stopped him from making the frats."

"I'll tell you about him later," said Grahame. "Here comes the crowd."

The big room of the University Club has its eastern wall almost entirely taken up by a great window looking down from the California Street hill across San Francisco Bay, taking in a sweep from Alcatraz to Goat Island. After the dinner was over, and the guest had departed for his train, some of the Ultras sat smoking and gazing across to where the lights of Oakland and Berkeley glittered on the eastern hills of the mainland, like a diamond tiara set in platinum. The illuminated clock of the ferry tower in the foreground set the hour at ten o'clock. Across the water the ferries passed with their electrics doubled by reflection. From Alcatraz the lighthouse above the military prison showed an intermittent, wary eye.

The discussion fell upon defense, as it often had of late, and Grahame and Thurston related their news.

"They seem to be getting ready right under our noses," said Cox, a shrewd controller of the coast lumber trade. "It's certain they are after something in this neighborhood. It isn't Canada—they're friends by treaty. It isn't Mexico, or they wouldn't be buying concessions. That's two guesses out of three. And yet the Pacific squadron is a joke. Two out-of-date cruisers at Mare Island, and some torpedo destroyers that would shake to pieces if they went over twenty knots, a couple of submarines, and a collier. Some at Bremerton, a few at San Diego, the rest on Asiatic duty, and not one of them able to do better than from six to seven knots less than the same types in the Japanese fleet. Here's the finest harbor in the world wide open for attack."

"There are the land batteries," said another. "We've got the new sixteen-inch guns. The Dardanelles proved that dreadnaughts can't silence forts."

"That was a matter of trajectory," said Grahame. "The Dardanelles forts were too high for plunging fire. The Japanese have probably got the position of every one of our big coast guns to a nicety, as they've got every mud bank in all our harbors charted. They could stand out below the horizon in a moving battle line, with the range officers calling off the variations like a stock clerk chalking quotations, and pitch shells into our casements or knock the top off the Call Building at their leisure. As Cox says, our fleet will never worry them. But it's the back door, gentlemen, where the tradesmen deliver, that is our vulnerable point, I fancy, with fifty-five thousand Japanese in California waiting to make the call."

"It's a cheerful outlook generally," spoke up one of the Ultras. "The question is, what are we going to do about it? I say 'we,' meaning the people of the Pacific coast. Our senators have been thundering at the staves of the Washington pork barrel, but it's still intact. It's a question of individual property aside from general patriotism."

"What can Washington do? They might buy a few ships, ready-made, but you can't buy an army and navy overnight. We're outmanned, outstripped, outgunned."

"We might put up a pretty good fight," said Grahame quietly.

"How?"

"By giving the enemy nothing they could use as a satisfactory target."

"That's beyond me," said the elder man.

"I don't believe it's beyond the bounds of possibility," answered Grahame.

There was a quality of purpose in his tone that checked the general laugh.

"Well, Bruce," said Cox. "If the worst comes to the worst, you can count on the Ultras. Form us into an emergency committee, and tell us what to do."

"I will."

Again the earnestness in Grahame's voice carried a leaven of conviction.

"If the government won't or can't protect us," he went on, "we've got to do the best we can for ourselves, and organize a system of preparedness."

"Become the minutemen of 1920?" said Thurston.

"Exactly."

The group gradually broke up, with the air of seriousness that had tinged the talk still evident in their good-night greetings.

"I'm not sleepy, Bruce; are you?" asked Thurston. "What do you say to a run out to the beach?"

"That suits me," said Grahame. In a few minutes they were speeding through the city limits, through Golden Gate Park, and onto the wide boulevard that parallels the great rollers of the Pacific, pounding ceaselessly at the dunes of sand.

They passed the road houses, with their blazing electrics, and the occasional beach bungalows, one of a squadron of motorists out to enjoy the night according to their varying desires. From the gateway of a high board fence that surrounded a building, of which only the roof was noticeable from the road, a car emerged at slow speed, waiting its opportunity to take the road. The headlights of another car illuminated the faces of those in the tonneau, showing them plainly to Grahame and Thurston on the ocean side of the road from the house. The car turned in their direction, hastening to the southern end of the boulevard.

"That was Kirby, with a couple of Japs, and a Japanese chauffeur," said Thurston.

"And one of the Japanese in the tonneau was Yamamato," replied Grahame. "After them, Fred. They haven't seen us."

Thurston touched his accelerator, and soon they were following the car, which turned into the Ingleside Road for the city.

"Who's Yamamato?" asked Thurston.

"I'd like to find out," answered Grahame grimly. "He's apparently butler to Mrs. Houston, General Lancaster's sister, at their Atascadero ranch. I left him there this morning. Don't lose them, Fred. I think we're on the trail of something."

V
In Little Nippon

After the fire and earthquake of 1906, the Japanese colony of San Francisco sequestered themselves in a neighborhood of which the hub is at Fillmore and Geary Streets, turning the private houses of this unburned district into employment agencies, pool rooms, rifle galleries, photograph studios, curio dealers, and warerooms of kimonos and distinctive Oriental wares. Stores were built on the sidewalk levels, and every floor held its meed of Japanese, men, women, and children, brown and yellow and ivory, outwardly Americanized, but still a race apart, retaining their own language, doing their own banking, emphatically aliens in the community, a little Nippon in America.

Fillmore Street, close set with stores, is American, save for an occasional curio merchant. The side streets stretching eastward are, for some blocks north and south of Geary, emblazoned with the vivid signs of the Japanese. China has its colony many blocks eastward, nearer the bay. The car bearing Kirby and Yamamato followed the electric-car line down the smooth asphalt of Geary to Fillmore, with Thurston's roadster a block behind.

"Close up a bit, Fred," said Grahame. "There, they are stopping. Swing into Fillmore slowly. Stop outside that saloon. You'll find me round the corner."

He stepped off the low running board lightly and followed Kirby and the butler on foot across Fillmore, taking the opposite side of the street. At a house standing at the corner of an alley bisecting the block, they paused, looking up at a big sign emblazoned in gold Japanese hieroglyphics, to which were added the words in English lettering:

Takamaki
Photographer

The basement was occupied by a dimly lit employment agency, filled with lounging "schoolboy" help. A wooden stairway ran to the front door, behind which a light showed red, displaying on the fanlight a Japanese character that looked familiar to Grahame, even from where he stood across the street, apparently gazing in the side window of a store filled with porcelain dishes.

Kirby and the two Japanese mounted the steps. The chauffeur had remained with the car. At the door there was some delay. Presently it was cautiously opened part way, and a brief parley held.

The Orientals presented something to the doorkeeper, while Kirby appeared to be giving a voluble explanation, backed up by Yamamato, that finally admitted him.

Thurston came up as Grahame strolled across the street, holding the square of gilt card in the palm of his hand, and comparing it with the character on the fanlight. The two were identical.

"Come up to the corner, Fred," he said. "I want to show you something."

In a jeweler's doorway, still brightly lit for advertising purposes, though the store was closed, he displayed the square of cardboard.

"That's the admission card to some society," he said, after he had told how it came into his possession. "I'm going to take a chance at finding something out about it."

"They won't let you in. You can't talk Japanese well enough."

"I can try," said Grahame. "Come on back. You hang about outside."

He overruled his friend's protest. From the breast pocket of his overcoat he took out some closely folded blue prints he chanced to be carrying, walked briskly up the steps, and rang the bell. A wizened Japanese opened the door carefully, looking at him doubtfully. Grahame displayed his card.

"Yamamato," he said, tapping his packet of blue prints.

The man's face cleared. He took the gilt talisman of admittance, and tittered something in guttural Japanese, throwing up his head on his withered neck, like an old turtle in a gesture that Grahame interpreted to mean that he should ascend.

The stairs were dimly lit from gas jets in the halls. On each floor he paused, listening. Apparently the rooms were vacant or occupied by sleepers. He had noticed four stories to the house outside. As he mounted to the last landing, he heard the murmur of voices and saw a streak of light beneath a door on which was repeated the photographer's outside sign.

Grahame applied his eye to the keyhole. The limited vision revealed the interior as a photographer's studio. In the center was a group of Japanese, seated about a table. He distinguished Kirby's profile, and, beyond him, at the head of the company, a Japanese in a uniform that blazed with decorations, a man of evident authority, his face seamed with a scar on one cheek, the upper lip garnished with a stringy black mustache.

Grahame's keen interest in Japanese international affairs gave him instant knowledge of the identity of the man in the uniform as that of a high attaché of the diplomatic corps. He even recognized the order of the Golden Kite that he wore upon his breast above the other decorations. He was Hyozo Yamaki, the Wise Man of Nippon, Japan's prototype of Li Hung Chang, who had successfully poured oil upon the troubled waters of his country's diplomacy, and left the strategists and statesmen of Washington still guessing the drift of his suave arguments.

His presence in San Francisco was unheralded and unknown. His appearance in full uniform in the studio of an obscure photographer bespoke the occasion as extraordinary.

One of the Japanese rose and came toward the door, and Grahame shrank swiftly down the stairs, stopping for developments halfway in the flight. The door opened, and the man cast a rapid glance outside, then shut it again. Grahame resumed his breathing. The action was merely precautionary, not caused from any suspicious sound that he might have made. He crept upstairs once more, tip-fingered and tiptoed. A screen had been placed in front of the door, blocking his view.

He paused for a moment, then swiftly descended, treading cautiously. He had put the blue prints away in an inside pocket, and, as he passed the guardian of the door, he used the stock of Japanese he was rapidly acquiring in an airy farewell.

"*Aroyato. Sayonara,*" he said. (Thanks. Good-by.)

"*Sayonara,*" croaked the man carefully, closing the door behind him.

Grahame joined Thurston, pacing up and down, apparently waiting for a car.

"We've got to look into this," he said. "They are all in the photographer's, at the top of the house. It's an important meeting of some kind. There must be a skylight to the gallery. Let's see if we can't get on the roof."

In the alley they found the series of fire escapes prescribed by law, ending in a raised ladder, fifteen feet above them. The narrow way was deserted. There was a barrel for rubbish close to the wall. Grahame rolled it beneath the ladder, mounted it, balancing himself on its rim, and sprang for the rusty rungs, swinging himself upward, and securing a footing on the first stage of the iron emergency ladder. Thurston followed suit, with the ease of an athlete who had never entirely slumped in his training. They made their way to the parapet and across the roof beneath a mesh of clotheslines to the skylight, which was only partially covered with shades.

On the table beneath them a map made up of wedge-shaped sections of a circle was being fitted together. Hyozo Yamaki and Kirby stood watching the process with keen interest. As the man who performed the work stood back and raised his head, Grahame whispered to Thurston.

"That's Takeo, the Japanese aviator. And that's an enlargement of an aëro photo of San Francisco Bay."

The diplomat appeared to be extending congratulations to the airman. As he finished his speech, Kirby followed him in talk. The glass deadened the sound of voices, but the similarity of Kirby's mannerisms to the Japanese he was so evidently in league with was remarkable. He pointed out certain places on the circular map, and produced a sheet covered with ideographic inscriptions, from which he read fluently. As he concluded, there was a general manifestation of applause, and the faint sound of a united *"Banzai"* (Hurrah for Japan) penetrated to the watchers on the roof.

Hyozo Yamaki took from his neck the ribbon and gleaming pendant of the Golden Kite, and presented it to Kirby, who bowed in smiling gratification.

"The dirty traitor," ejaculated Thurston.

In the emphasis of his disgust, he forgot his caution, and leaned too heavily upon the glass. The weathered putty gave, and a pane smashed down upon the table. There was a second of consternation, then Kirby drew a pistol from his pocket and fired point-blank at the faces dimly seen through the skylight. The bullet sent splintered glass into Grahame's face. A second shot followed. Neither Grahame nor Thurston heard any report. Some of the Japanese had rushed to the door, headed by Kirby. The landing led to a window opening on the fire escape. Their retreat was cut off.

Grahame looked hastily about him and ran to the edge of the roof farthest from the street. To his right, the unscalable side of a brick building blocked the way. Below him was the top of a low building—a sheer drop of two stories. He leaped to the uprights that supported the clotheslines, and Thurston, guessing his purpose, sprang to his aid. With his penknife, Grahame hacked two lines free, while his companion did the same. Grasping the severed ends, Grahame swiftly fastened them to a short ladder leading to the top of a water tank, praying that the cords might prove strong enough to bear their weight. He hustled Thurston over the edge, and crouched low, watching him sway against the wall, striving to twist the slim cords between his legs for purchase, and at last reach the roof below, where he ran to a hatch and tugged at its ring.

Grahame followed as the head of the first of the pursuers appeared above the roof line at the top of the fire escape. He slid down to Thurston, careless of the scald of the ropes against his palms, and reached his side just as the hatch came open with a jerk. Two spurts of flame flashed from above, and a bullet thudded into the timber of the scuttle cover. Again there were no reports.

They leaped down the crude steps, expecting every moment to run into an ambush, but the house was vacant and unfurnished.

"Out the back way," said Grahame. They tore loose the rusty bolts of a door and burst out into a garden high with weeds and inclosed with an old-fashioned brick wall. The footsteps of the Japanese were already clattering down the bare stairs as they reached the open. The wall afforded no foothold. Escape seemed impossible.

Beating through the weeds with Thurston, Grahame heard the latter's foot strike against something that clicked, saw him stoop, and in one swift movement straighten and hurl an object that gleamed in the moonlight directly at a figure that appeared in the door through which they had just come. There was the impact of a dull thud, a smash of glass, and a chuckle from Thurston, as the man fell prone, and another close behind him stumbled over the body.

"Here's a door hidden in the weeds," said Grahame.

They wrenched away a thorny tangle and forced an exit, coming out into a paved yard, in which were piled cases filled with empty bottles and barrels that reeked of stale beer.

"In luck," panted Grahame. "It's the saloon."

They entered the rear door and found their way to the washroom, where they surveyed each other in gasping dismay. Thurston's coat was ripped from collar to hem, his dinner clothes were crumpled, his face smeared with grime and sweat. Grahame was in little better case, and his hands were bleeding.

"You're a sight," said Thurston.

"Look in the glass," answered Grahame.

They cleaned up as best they could with the primitive conveniences.

"Where's your hat?" asked Thurston.

"Some one put a ballet through it and knocked it off."

"They were using Maxim silencers," said Thurston.

"Noiseless cartridges, I fancy. Mercury mixed with a fulminate of some kind. What was your weapon, Fred?"

"I kicked an empty flask in the garden. I guess I haven't lost my pitching arm altogether, Bruce. I put it straight over the plate and beaned him. I think it was Kirby. I hope so. If it was, I marked him."

"One o'clock, gents. Closing up," said the bartender.

They eased his suspicions by the purchase of a round of drinks for the loungers, and reached their car. The motor that had carried Kirby and Yamamato had disappeared.

"We might have got its number," suggested Thurston.

"That would have done us no good. Do you realize, if we tried to do anything about this, we might be arrested as porch climbers? Laughed at, anyway, as clubmen out on a spree. We have no proofs."

The light behind the photographer's front door was out as they passed.

"At any rate, we've seen the last of Kirby," said Thurston.

"I'm not so sure about that," answered Grahame.

There was the sound of a motor car coming swiftly up behind them. Geary Street was deserted. Only the hourly owl street cars were running. Thurston kept to the curb at an even pace, not willing to dispute the road with what was probably a crowd of drunken revelers. The car came up beside them, almost scraping their running board.

Grahame turned in his seat.

"Look out, there!" he called. There was a noiseless flash, and the next second he had pitched forward, crumpled up at Thurston's feet, while the attacking car roared past them up the incline.

How Grahame's fears were verified and crystallized into an actual Peril of the Pacific will be told you in the next issue of PEOPLE'S.

The Peril of the Pacific

by J. ALLAN DUNN

Part Two: The Threat

Synopsis of Preceding Installment

Bruce Grahame, an expert in aëronautics, and a believer in preparedness, especially against a suspected Japanese invasion, is in love with Irene Lancaster, daughter of General Lancaster, chief of the Pacific division of the United States army, located at the Presidio, San Francisco. As the country at large refuses to be aroused over the Japanese peril, Grahame proposes to try and unite all the aviation clubs of the Pacific coast into an aërial militia. To prove his assertion that the Pacific coast Japanese, most of them veterans of the war with Russia, are drilling secretly at night, Grahame takes General Lancaster, his daughter, and Ogden Kirby, whom he suspects of a connection with the Japanese government, in his triplane, the *Aërolite*, to a valley in the Coast Range. There they find a large company of Japanese drilling on the open plain, in the moonlight. Upon the return he walks with Irene Lancaster in the garden, and declares his love for her. She rejects him on the ground that, being wealthy, he has no serious purpose in life. He declares that his purpose is to be an effective patriot, to wake the nation to the oncoming peril. The matter is left in abeyance. The next day Grahame and his friend, Fred Thurston, an official of the telephone company, who is in complete accord with Grahame's views, happened to see Kirby in an automobile with a couple of Japanese, and they follow. They trail them to a Japanese club, where are gathered several distinguished Oriental statesmen, in consultation over an enlargement of an aëro photo map of San Francisco Bay. Kirby enters into the discussion, making suggestions, etc., so that it becomes evident that he is in league with them. In the excitement of the moment Grahame and Thurston forget their caution and betray their presence. Chase is given at once, and Grahame is wounded by a revolver bullet, but they escape.

I

Discredited

BRUCE GRAHAME STAYED CLOSE TO HIS ROOM in the University Club for three days. The bullet from the automobile had evidently been fired from an angle slightly above and back of him, and the aim of the assassin had been diverted by the differing speed of the two vehicles. The missile had struck the base of his skull glancingly, the blow on the mastoid process being sufficient to render him unconscious and provide him with a splitting headache for the next seventy odd hours. The lobe of his right ear had been nicked. It was the flow of blood from this that brought Grahame back to his senses in time to prevent Thurston from taking him to a hospital.

One of the "Ultras," a close-mouthed, clever, comprehending surgeon who lived at the University Club, patched up the wounded man without asking questions. To the bleeding ear, Grahame had applied first aid at an all-night drug store with collodion and absorbent cotton. The generally dilapidated appearance of both of them, the sleepy night force at the club ascribed to an automobile accident, and Thurston, on Grahame's request, did not enlighten them.

"We don't know it was Kirby fired at us," he told his friend after the surgeon had left. "You didn't get the number of the machine. As for the affair at the photographer's, we were trespassing. The time isn't ripe to start anything public. This isn't a police affair. I'm going to get in touch with Washington about that map of the harbor, and I think we'll start work on that Emergency Committee. We might see the major and get the civic authorities interested."

"You take this pink stuff Shiels left for you and stop talking," said Thurston. "You are all eyes. You've bled more than you think. I'll see you in the morning. Do you want me to move against Kirby—in the club, I mean?"

"No. I've a notion he'll move on his own account. I think it was Hyozo's idea to get rid of us to-night before we cleared with any information we might have gathered. I'd give a good deal to know what goes on in that photographer's. They'll be looking for eavesdroppers after this. Look here, Fred, I saw a telephone in the room. Can't you make some pretense of installing a new style of phone and put in a dictograph? Your men could run the wires where they wanted to without suspicion. They may have to change several phones on a bluff. That empty house next door would be a good place. We could sneak an interpreter and stenographer in there through the saloon, if necessary. I can borrow an interpreter from the custom people."

"I'll fix the dictograph, if you'll take this," said Thurston, advancing with the bromide.

Grahame swallowed the salty mixture obediently. The next day he awoke with a raging pain in the back of his head which all efforts at coherent thought aggravated, while movement was a torture.

"You'll keep flat and still on your back for forty-eight hours or more," said Doctor Shiels, after an examination. "You've got an abrasion of the sternocleidomastoid, and some of your cranial nerves are a mite congested. Sleep. That's what you want. And quiet. I'll send up a prescription."

"What's the sterno what you may call it?" asked Thurston, outside the door. "It sounds awful."

A twinkle came into the Scotch surgeon's eyes. "I meant it to," he said. "Grahame's got to keep quiet. It's a muscle that runs from the occipital and mastoid bone to the sternum and also the clavicle."

"Thanks," said Thurston ironically. "I understand perfectly. If you'll give me that prescription, I'll see that he gets it—and takes it."

"And see that his friends keep out of the room."

So, that the third day found Grahame clear-headed, out of pain, save for a slight stiffness in the neck, hungry for the solid food that had been denied him, and eager for news of the outside world.

Thurston found him in a lounging chair, letters and newspapers to one side of him, his breakfast tray, well emptied, to the other.

"Well," said Grahame, "I see the annual fight is on to tie a Japanese exclusion amendment to the Burnett Immigration Bill. I'm afraid it'll bring matters to a head this time, Fred. There are a crowd of hot-heads who'll say things that are likely to start trouble. Part of the Atlantic fleet has to stay home from battle practice because they haven't enough men. And the commanding officer of the Canal Zone is begging the Senate committee on military affairs for the twentieth time for more land forces. The committee, as usual, thinks because they've got a big gun or two on the spot they've got the whole forty odd miles covered. It's the old story of putting laymen in authority. 'Modern guns can easily reach twenty-five miles,' says the scientist. 'They can't harm us,' says the man from Des Moines. We've got to get busy. You see that, don't you, Fred?"

"Surely. What are your general plans?"

"Get the municipal authorities of the main cities from San Diego to Seattle to organize committees for vigilance, protection, and relief. Perfect plans for a mobile auxiliary coast defense that will take in the railroads and private equipments of aëroplanes, fast launches, and motor cars. Get options on ammunition, establish ranges and bases of supplies. When the time comes, offer it to the government. If they won't work out these things beforehand, we'll do it ourselves. We can. Look at the 'Ultras' alone; we've got brains enough there to organize a practical defense. The power companies will come in, of course, and we've got to arrange effective wireless communications.

Your telephones are likely to be put out of commission on the jump. It can be done, Fred. It's got to be. It'll pay from a straight point of financial insurance alone, aside from patriotism. A patrol system and mobile defense. That's the meat of it. As for the offensive, I've one or two things in that connection that may work out all right if we can get the time. That's what I'm afraid of. It's our unpreparedness unfortunately that is our present immunity. Give them a hint we're getting ready and they'll strike."

"I'm with you, Bruce," said Thurston, fired by Grahame's convincing enthusiasm. "I thought you were a bit of a crank on the subject, but after the other night I'm wondering at my own blindness. Count on me from the start.

"By the way," he went on, as they grasped hands. "Kirby has given up his rooms in the club. Ito quit at the same time. We're well rid of them."

"Read that," said Grahame, handing over one of the letters he had been reading. It was on paper of good quality, faintly perfumed, and the writing, that of a woman, indicated breeding and education, if not firmness of character.

> I can give you valuable information regarding the actions and affairs of Ogden Kirby. I shall call you up at your club on Thursday morning.
>
> One who is no longer his friend, but may be of service to you.

Thurston read the note aloud.

"Unsigned," he commented. "Do you think it's a trap?"

"We'll see. This is Thursday morning. She hasn't rung up yet. Did you get the dictaphone in at the Japanese photographer's?"

"Yes. Without any trouble." He had plunged into a description of the installment when the room phone rang.

"A lady to talk with you, Mr. Grahame," said the club operator. "Doctor Shiels said we might call your room. Do you want to speak to her? She says you are expecting the call."

Grahame looked meaningly at Thurston and took up the receiver, answering his communicant with brief monosyllables.

"She wants me to meet her in the palm room of the Palace Hotel this afternoon at five," he announced. "That doesn't sound much like a trap. She hints at a quarrel with Kirby."

"Going?"

"Yes. It's evident Kirby is in touch with the heads of Japanese authority. It'll pay to keep an eye on him."

"Well, I hope the lady proves good looking and the information valuable. When are you going to start work on the Emergency Committee plan?"

"To-morrow. We'll talk it over tonight, Fred, at the end of the evening. I've got to make a call first. See if you can get Cox to come—and Hanchett and Fee. I want men of their type—executives."

"I understand. I'll do the best I can between now and then."

At five o'clock, Grahame was in the big lounging room of the Palace. The place was a hive of conversation from the scattered tables, blending with the strains from the galleried orchestra. Grahame, nodding to acquaintances here and there, passed down an aisle of tables on the side of the men's grillroom, according to the arrangements made over the phone.

The unknown, whose voice had held a quality of culture, had said she knew him by sight, and he walked slowly. At a table midway of the rest a woman sat alone. She was dressed in the height of the mode in a fashion that was the latest on Fifth Avenue, New York, and ultra on Grant Avenue, San Francisco, too conspicuous for absolute taste. She was a decidedly good-looking brunette, whose hair bore a tinge of henna and whose face an unnecessary suggestion of make-up. She had already attracted the attention of several men to the apparent, if covert, displeasure of their escorts. Grahame casually sat her down as an actress not unappreciative of publicity.

Then she smiled and nodded at him, and he realized that here was the woman he had come to meet.

"I'd almost given you up, Mr. Grahame," she said as he stopped at her table.

Her voice, with its assumption of arch reproof, was in accord with her general individuality. It was vibrant and rich. Grahame felt an uneasy sense of being the cynosure of all eyes.

"I think I am absolutely on time," he said quietly, his voice purposely crisp to offset the suggested familiarity of hers.

The woman's eyes roved from his for a moment, and an attentive waiter came promptly to their call.

"What may I order for you?" asked Grahame.

"The same I always have. A quart of Cordon Rouge, and two glasses. And make it cold," she called after the waiter.

Grahame was uneasy both in the present situation and an intuition of what might follow. The woman's words seemed to accentuate an intimacy already established between them that he was neither anxious to countenance nor cultivate. Already people were looking in their direction with raised eyebrows.

"I would suggest," he said in a low tone, "that if we are to exchange confidences we had better go to some place where there is less chance of being overheard."

She leaned forward with a confidential air as he spoke, and he mentally kicked himself for the soft voice he had used.

"Is it too public for you here?" she asked, with a glance of blandishment.

The wine came, and the waiter displayed it with a flourish, opened it with eloquent care, and set it down again in its icy bed in the silver-plated holder with ostentation. Grahame's brows were creased in annoyance as his vis-à-vis pledged him.

"Here's to both of us. Bottoms up!" She held out her empty glass to be refilled. "Don't be stingy," she said, with a laugh.

Grahame began to sense the nature of the trap that had been set for him as the woman began to grow audibly and visibly tipsy. She helped herself for the third time, insisting upon wasting the foaming liquid upon his untasted glass. Suddenly her eyes took on a defiant glare.

"You ain't ashamed of being here with me, are you?" she demanded truculently.

Trying to placate her, Grahame sought to catch the attention of an attendant. To his relief, he saw one of the assistant managers hastening toward him. The man spoke first, while the people close by obviously strained to hear.

"You'll have to take this person out of here, sir," said the hotel official politely, but firmly. "There's been a complaint to the desk, Mr. Grahame."

He rose, vexedly conscious of his reddening face.

"Get me a taxicab quickly."

"Yes, sir." The assistant manager, glad to be freed of the situation, hurried ahead. Grahame turned to the woman.

"Come," he said. "I've sent for a cab."

She rose willingly enough and swayed slightly, catching at the back of a chair for support. "Why, how ridiculous," she said, with a hiccup. "The thingsh absurd. Give me your arm."

Furious at the false position he was placed in, Grahame escorted her through the long room astir with the sensation of something out of the ordinary while she made caustic comment about the Puritanism of the hotel regulations. The cab was waiting, and he placed her inside.

"Where to?" asked the driver, and he repeated the question.

"Tell him to drive to the ferry," she said. She had suddenly regained control of her voice, and her eyes held a mocking light. Grahame thrust some money into the chauffeur's hand and reentered the hotel.

"Now, then," he asked angrily of the assistant manager, "who made this complaint?"

"I'm sorry, Mr. Grahame," he began. "If it hadn't—"

"Never mind that. Who was it?"

"The gentleman brought the complaint from the lady with him, he said, sir, and backed it up himself."

"Do you know him? I'm not blaming you, man!"

The hotel man seemed relieved.

"Of course not, sir. There they are now."

Turning out of the palm room into the main corridor of the hotel Grahame saw Irene Lancaster escorted by Ogden Kirby. He hurried toward them. Kirby glared at him superciliously. The general's daughter looked both at and through him as if he had never existed. Grahame stood impotent. To make a scene was impossible.

"It was a clever move, Kirby," he said to himself. "But mine is the next one."

II

THE ALIEN IMMIGRATION BILL

Washington was in a turmoil. Not since the anxious days when the United States Congress, represented by President Wilson, strained every resource to preserve a neutrality that should comport with the honor and dignity of the nation had there been such a ferment in the capital city, a ferment that leavened the entire country with unrest.

The Alien Immigration Bill, or, rather, its amendment relating to Japanese exclusion, was the cause of the unrest. Urged by deputations and petitions from the Pacific coast states of California, Oregon, and Washington, backed by representations from labor organizations, the House of Representatives had passed the amendment after heated discussions. The Senate chamber saw a yet fiercer fight. The bill was sent back, approved, from the Committee of Foreign Relations, and its final passage seemed imminent until a strongly supported attack by the champions of preparedness brought visions of a compromise in a possible agreement to submit the matter to the state department.

The secretary of state received, at this juncture, a citizens' committee from California, introduced by the senator of their state, and made up of men from various political parties who had sunk their differences in the earnestness of the present issue.

For an hour the secretary listened with grave attention to a synopsis of the helplessness of the Pacific coast against alien attack.

"The Pacific coast is a separate country by sheer geography," said the spokesman for the committee, "shut off from the continent by the Sierra Nevada and Cascade Mountains, with a climate of its own, fifteen hundred miles of practically unprotected sea-coast, perhaps the most fertile strip in the world. If this matter is put up to you, Mr. Secretary, I beg of you. in the name of the people of not only the Pacific coast, but of all America, to bring to bear all your influence to delay, if not entirely offset, this matter until we are prepared to defend invasion."

"I think it will hardly come to that, gentlemen," replied the secretary, with a pretense of assurance that did not accord with his troubled brows. "And the matter has not yet been referred to me. I shall do all in my power to avert any danger that may seem to threaten, although I do not share your views as to either the imminence of invasion or adequacy of defense. There have been many additions made to our coast protection of late."

"Perhaps, sir, we who live on the frontier see hints of trouble that are lost sight of in Washington."

The secretary rose. The audience was over.

"I recognize my responsibilities, gentlemen," he answered. "There is always war and rumor of war. I am glad to have met you all." He bowed and dismissed them. As they left, and he prepared to give audience to his next visitor, the creases of worry deepened in his face. He made a strong effort to dismiss them as the Japanese ambassador was announced.

Count Kato's face, the color of old ivory, was destitute of any expression as he bowed low in response to the greeting of the secretary of state. Only his eyes, like black opals, showed shifting flashes of light. He was less than six inches over five feet in height, and his general physique suggested a frailty that the secretary knew was nonexistent as regards his mentality.

There was the pause of a few seconds as if the two men were measuring each other's strength, as fencers, having given the salute, pause before the cry of "On guard!" provokes their engagement. Then Count Kato, laying a portfolio on the secretary's desk, proceeded directly to his affairs.

The secretary listened, shading his eyes with one hand. Through the screen of his fingers he at once watched the representative of the Japanese imperial government and shielded any traces of perturbation that might betray his own state of mind. It was not the first visit of the count upon this mission. The secretary feared it might be the last. For Count Kato, in placid, perfect English, was delivering what was to all intents an ultimatum, a threat veiled only by the polite terms of diplomacy.

"Equal privilege is all we ask," he said. "Merely that. To accord to us what is given to peoples that have no greater claim for nationality than a language. Of America, land of liberty, to whose shores flock Finns, Poles, Slavs, the skimmings of Europe, assured of welcome, of a voice in the land, of the possession of property, we, the sons of an empire acknowledged as a world power, ask similar rights. We are willing to accede to an immigration head tax, to conform to the illiteracy regulations. Upon this issue depends the future welfare and prosperity of one hundred and fifty thousand Japanese on the Pacific coast and in Hawaii.

"We are becoming overcrowded at home," he went on. "There is pressure there. Already there are over sixty millions of us. We seek an outlet on your coast; we wish to bask in the far-reaching rays of your liberty that enlightens the world. We have been patient."

He stopped. The secretary removed his hand.

"You know the temper of my nation, count," he answered. "You understand the feeling that between the Japanese and the other nations from which America is being built up there is an inseparable barrier."

"You give citizenship to black men," said Count Kato. "Is the Malay—if you will, the Malayan—Mongoloid, less than the negroid race? Is yellow a deeper stain than black? There are many Chinese in California whose children, of both sexes, vote and hold property rights."

"That is a restricted matter."

"Yet they vote. So can their children's children. There is no lack of ability or willingness on the part of the Japanese immigrant to assimilate. It is Americans who set up the barriers. Religion and brotherly influences can surely change these conditions. The doctrines of your church and government cover such cases, surely. It is our constant hope that Japanese immigrants, particularly those who have already secured a foothold upon the Pacific slope, may be permitted the privilege of American citizenship. They have proven their utility to the community. And we have been patient—under pressure. I fear I take your time. In this portfolio is the official communication that I trust you will do me the honor to set before your government for a speedy consideration."

"And if we cannot accede to your request, count?"

The eyes of both men, black opal and gray flint, met in open gaze. Count Kato bowed once more with ceremony.

"I fear," he said, "we shall be compelled to ask for the passports and safe-conducts of the various representatives of his imperial majesty's government, of which I have the honor to be ambassador."

The closely clipped syllables suggested the click of steel against steel. It found an echo in the secretary's tone:

"You will allow us ample time to prepare an answer? The question is a grave one."

"The question, as you say, is a grave one. We must trust it can be soon answered. But I can hold out no promise of modifications."

The secretary of state watched the slight, dwarfed figure of the Japanese, walking with the precision of mechanism to the door, and the lines returned to his forehead. They deepened as he opened the portfolio left by the Oriental and began to read.

The news broke that night. It was rumored that the hint came from the Japanese legation. There the reporters met with neither affirmation nor denial. The Washington papers published accounts that contained phrases startlingly close to those in the portfolio left by Count Kato, now transferred with its burden of care to the desk of the President of the United States.

And north, south, east, and west, the story girdled the world. Cables were busy, and translators overworked, while editors stayed late at their desks to word the message that thrilled the civilized world the next day. Japan had delivered an ultimatum to America: "Free Entry or Forcible!" That was the key of the black-lettered headings.

At the White House, there was anxious council. In the Senate, after stormy sessions, the matter was placed in the hands of the nation's chief executives. And, while the Japanese legation and its consulates waited for their reply in seeming patience, a flame of resentment ran through the land like wildfire, fanned by the words of those who believed in their patriotism and those who wrote and spoke from the impulse of jingoism or the animus of political ambition and opportunity.

Day by day the tension grew. There were anti-Japanese riots in California, Washington, and Oregon. The fuse was sputtering. The voice of the people called for an answer from the president, and the head of the nation and his aids, conning the future, knowing the present, spent anxious hours in which the minutes were marked by the reports from the heads of citizens' committees and the yet more pregnant reports on naval and military supplies, the lack of men and transports, of coal and colliers, of field guns and ammunition. There was not enough of the last to serve the admitted insufficiency of the artillery for forty-eight hours of constant fighting.

And all this information, thanks to an avid press, all the world knew. Of the strength of Japan some guessed, none were certain. But Japan was knocking at the gate.

III

THE EMERGENCY ASSOCIATION

On the evening following the delivery of Count Kato's portfolio to the secretary of state, forty men were assembled in the directors' room of the Southern Pacific Railroad about two long tables placed end to end. There were a few vacant chairs for the lack of occupancy of which Bruce Grahame, presiding over the first meeting of the Emergency Association, asked excuse.

"They will join us in a little while," he said. "They are attending the mayor's meeting, also called for to-night."

The countenance of every man present bore the stamp of executive capacity and experience. Back of them stood the authority of their respective organizations. Here were the representatives of railroad, of light and power and water companies and the important factors of public service. Experts in architecture, engineering, chemistry, and surgery were present, controllers of big private interests, bankers, men versed in commissary details, a commissioner of police who was also the head of a big hotel system, the commodore of the San Francisco Motor Boat Club, the president of the California Automobile Association, Grahame as chief officer of the Aëro Squadron, aside from the main factor of his presence as organizer of the committee. Human dynamos, all of them. Men who could think and act, and, above all, who could listen and effect quick judgment.

Most of them were older than Grahame; but ability, not age, was the qualification necessary; and as, with the aid of a great blackboard, he outlined his tentative plans, they sat in appreciation of his abilities as designer and leader of a plan their attentive silence approved. Their mutual interests were pooled for the emergency that had called them together, their united intellects concentrated upon the broad lines of Grahame's scheme, ready to grasp the maze of details and reduce them to a working system later.

"It is not to be supposed, gentlemen," said Grahame, "that use will not be made of the Japanese reservists already in California. Junction of these with any landing force must be prevented. We may be able to intern them—providing they are unarmed. I think it most likely that they have a base of supplies the location of which I hope to discover. Action, if it comes, will be swift. The aërogram from our senator at Washington this evening states that the question cannot be delayed many days. He considers a month the limit of diplomatic postponement. Japan will not consider discussion by correspondence. The president does not wish to sacrifice California, but he cannot ignore the will of the majority. What we can expect from government defense stands there"—he pointed to the blackboard, where rows of figures accented his words.

"Excluding troops in insular possessions and on permanent coast defense or noncombatant duties, we have a mobile regular army of about thirty thousand officers and men. And an army reserve of—*sixteen* men. National guards, on paper, show one hundred and twenty-seven thousand—half of them trained. Call it sixty thousand, partially trained and equipped. Less than one hundred thousand fighting men, all told. And these will take many days to muster on the coast. The Pacific squadron is not up to date, lamentably insufficient to cope with any one of Japan's three battle fleets. The Atlantic fleet is in—the Atlantic. Our government aëroplane service is insignificant, less than that of Chile or Brazil.

"The conquest of California, if such a catastrophe should occur, will be a question of hours."

A mutter of assent ran round the table.

"When the blow strikes, it will be swift and heavy. If the Japanese representatives are handed their passports, we are bound to see those assurances made valid. You will find little delay, I think, on the part of the Japanese to depart. Practically every ship bottom of importance plying between here and the Orient belongs to Japan at this moment."

Another murmur of appreciation manifested itself.

"The faster they leave, the less time we have to prepare. And you may well be sure that they are ready for their offensive.

"If this plan of mine, fortified by your suggestions, is finally approved, it should, I believe, be offered to the government, but it should be in such practical shape that our share of it can go into instant operation. And that share will be the largest.

"Gentlemen"—Grahame paused and looked around the table at the serious, intent faces—"I have outlined our weakness, well known to you already. Let me tell you of our strength.

"Given thirty days, we can organize a defense that will leave the enemy baffled. Japan has done wonders in the last quarter of a century. She has absorbed many things, but she *has not yet caught up with American inventions.*"

Involuntary applause filled the room with echoes, then abruptly subsided to attention to the speaker.

"I propose to face the enemy with a mobile, elusive system of defense that will give them no tangible objective. We will play hornets to their tiger. Let me split this defense into three parts: air, water, and land. To the first I bring the helicopter, to the second the Hammond torpedo, the third the Ferguson dynamite gun.

"The Ferguson gun is smokeless, noiseless, and without recoil. It can hurl a dynamite bomb from a twenty-pounder twenty-two miles. It is operated by compressed air. It possesses two vital factors: cheap and swiftly made ammunition, and lack of recoil. It can be mounted on and fired from flat cars. A large portion of the shore of California is patrolled by the Coast Line Railroad. And landing places are few. It is up to you railroad men, that problem.

"The Hammond torpedo needs no submarine. Only a base for launching and wireless for its guidance. That is the problem of the power men, here, and of the motor-boat men.

"And now we come to the helicopter. It has long been foreseen that the dirigible has reached its limitations, and that the aëroplane is in the same predicament. The one is merely an improved balloon, the other a glorified kite. The air machine of the future is the helicopter, the machine projected by Jules Verne as he prophesied the submarine, independent of air currents, rigid, powerful, capable of rising and descending directly to or from the ground and of hovering in a fixed spot against a mile-a-minute gale, or moving at a speed of a hundred miles an hour in either direction.

"It lifts not by planes, but by screws revolving on horizontal axles in opposite directions, set in pairs. It moves forward or backward by screws in vertical action. It has the facility of the humming bird or the dragon fly.

Any man who can run an automobile can handle it. It is perfectly stabilized. A machine weighing thirty-five hundred pounds can carry fifty-five hundred pounds above its own weight, including gasoline for ten hours with a range of a thousand miles, bearing a crew in a boat body, wireless, machine guns, bomb tubes, and a peritelescope.

"With such machines, a mile up, stationary or hovering at will, giving ranges by wireless for the mobile guns or the Hammond torpedoes, there should be little difficulty in preventing a landing or of making a sieve out of the enemy's battleships, without, in return, presenting an appreciable target."

"You call these 'machines of the future,' Mr. Grahame?" asked the shrewd traffic director at the other end of the table. "Can they also be machines of the present?"

"They are," said Grahame. "I have perfected an engine that will give over twelve pounds thrust per horse power with a total motor and propeller weight of less than two pounds, or ten pounds surplus thrust or lift. I can put ten helicopters in the air within the next two weeks."

There was no applause, but each man nodded to his neighbor in a silent tribute to the speaker.

"All this is to be backed up, of course, by the special work of the civic committees to offset and repair damage to municipalities, by commissary and hospital service; expenditure for ammunition from the supplies left in the factories established during the late war, by the auxiliary aid of swift motor boats to harass submarines, destroy their periscopes, or pierce their plates with rapid-fire guns before submergence; by coöperation of the aëro clubs of the coast, also in armed machines, all of which matters can be taken charge of by the committees which inevitably suggest themselves and their personnel. I can furnish a number of maps, drawings, and aërophotographs that I have prepared during the last five years, guided by the advice of military and naval officers and those of our coast marine. You will find them available as aëroviews of important railroad points, of possible bases of supply, of the few available landing places for a hostile army, together with the trajectories and ranges for artillery fire in connection with these spots.

"That is, I believe, all that I have to set before you as one mind of many. I suggest that we take up a discussion of general feasibility, and, if so approved, an immediate selection of committees."

He sat down amid congratulations. The traffic manager voiced the sense of the meeting:

"We—the nation at large—is to be congratulated, Mr. Grahame, upon the vivid sense of preparedness you have displayed. You make me, sir—and I think most of us—ashamed of our blindness. I speak briefly, but no less sincerely. I move that we go into executive session after a rising testimony of thanks to Mr. Grahame as the man of the hour, and I move, moreover, that he be appointed permanent chairman of the Emergency Committee he has brought into being."

The door opened, and those who had been delayed at the mayoralty meeting appeared in the door, backed by the eager faces of reporters. Grahame addressed the latter.

"I am sorry to have kept you waiting so long, gentlemen," he said. "But the matters discussed have been necessarily of the most private nature and not yet made determinate. We will issue a statement in time for your city editions and make it as ample as we can. Will that do?"

There was a general shrugging of shoulders.

"It will have to be ready by ten-thirty, Mr. Grahame," spoke up one of the newspaper men.

"It shall be. How many copies are needed? Are you all here?"

"The *Clarion's* man left an hour ago. He'll be back, though. Seven altogether, including the Associated Press."

The reporters settled back in their chairs in the anteroom, accepting the inevitable and mitigating it by a liberal use of the cigars provided by Grahame.

In the directors' room, the newcomers were given a brief review of what had taken place, and in short order a discussion was in progress, with opinions given in crisp terms by the experts along the various lines of the general project. One after another spoke incisively, while the rest listened in grave and attentive comprehension.

"These invaluable maps and photographs of yours, Mr. Grahame," asked one of the men who had arrived late—"are they immediately available?"

"They are in the safe in my office. I shall be—"

He broke off in his speech and leaped for the window. The night was warm, and the sash had been raised. Grahame flung it upward and leaned out, swiftly withdrawing his head.

"There was some one listening," he said. "On the ledge. He's gone that way. Get through the rooms and cut him off!"

The police commissioner had already raced the length of the room and was hurrying through the connecting offices. Others followed his example, stopping at different windows to open them and trace the flight of the eavesdropper. It was the twentieth floor. Below the windows ran a cornice of stone nearly three feet wide. Upon this the spy had evidently crouched, listening through the gap between sash and window until Grahame had caught an unguarded movement for relief that had betrayed him.

"Get back in there! Get in, or I'll shoot!"

It was the voice of the police commissioner, at the far end of the office suite that ran the full length of the building. A figure appeared outside one of the opened windows and was dragged in by half a dozen volunteers. The man stood with a sullenly defiant air amid the ring of his captors as Grahame and the commissioner came hurrying up from opposite directions.

"Ah, ha!" said the head of the police department. "So you're the sneak, Fenton! Trying to get a scoop for the *Clarion*?"

"There's no crime in that."

"Not with any other paper, perhaps."

Every one present understood the innuendo. The *Clarion* was the yellowest of journals, pro anything that might pander to popularity, its columns notoriously purchasable and untrustworthy. Fenton showed no consciousness of stigma in his attachment.

"We can't trust him," said the commissioner to Grahame. "The only thing to do is to hold him until his paper is out."

"You can't do that," protested the reporter.

"Oh, can't I?" retorted the commissioner grimly. "Well, I'm going to. The *Clarion* gets scooped for once. And I think these gentlemen have got influence enough between them to stop anything they want kept out of even your rotten sheet."

Fenton glanced about him. A request once placed by men of such prominence would unquestionably have its weight with even the irresponsible policies of the *Clarion*. Though, if he could have got in his story without interference, it would have meant an extra, and for him praise, a check, and the laugh on the men of the other papers who were not overkeen on acquaintanceship with the *Clarion* staff.

The traffic manager touched a button, and a watchman appeared.

"See that this man stays in that room till further orders," he said, indicating one of the smaller offices, leaving one room vacant between it and that of the directors. The watchman locked the farther door and prepared to lock the other, Fenton sitting by the window, now closed and locked, his heels on a radiator, smoking defiantly.

"He'll not get away, sir," answered the stalwart guardian.

The interrupted meeting took up its session. At a few minutes after ten, Grahame dictated a brief statement for the waiting newspaper men, and they dispersed, with thanks. In less than five minutes, they were back again, demanding an audience. Several copies of the *Clarion* were in their hands.

"Look at that!" One of them thrust a newspaper at Grahame. "They've got out an extra on us. It's been on the street for half an hour!"

Grahame looked at the glaring headlines:

EMERGENCY COMMITTEE PLANS NOVEL DEFENSE
GRAHAME TELLS OF RANGE MAPS
Three Inventive Triumphs to Offset Superior Strength

IV
KIRBY CAPITULATES

Grahame glanced hurriedly down the page. The story was jerkily written, but in fair detail.

On a common impulse, the Emergency Committee members sought for Fenton. The reporter was sitting where they had left him, the watchman close by. Fenton's eyes gleamed when he caught sight of the sheet, and he grinned at the police commissioner.

"I turned the trick," he said. "I couldn't hear, with the window shut, whether it was on the street or not. The *Clarion* doesn't get scooped so easy, you see, after all.

"Want to know how I did it?" he asked vaingloriously. "It was easy. I saw, early in the evening, you were going to hand us a statement, and while those boobs sat down and waited I got busy. I left for the office and came back with another man. I got out on the ledge from the lavatory and left him there. He was still there when you got onto me and I drew you off in the other direction. But ten minutes later he was down at the *Clarion*, giving out copy. In between the lavatory and the room you were talking in, those chumps who think they are newspaper men jollied themselves with your cigars. I was on the ledge, with a string in one hand that led back to a little device we doped out in the office a long time ago. Did you ever make a ticktack when you were a kid, commissioner? That worked the trick for us. I ticktacked all you said, in Morse, to my pal sitting snug in the lavatory taking it down as fast as I could send it in case you got onto me, as you did. Some foxes, I guess!"

"Have you any idea what you've done?" asked the traffic manager. "You've given the Japanese inside information of our secret plans for defense!"

Fenton only grinned.

"You can't muzzle the free press," he retorted. "I've committed no crime. You can't touch me."

"You ought to be hung for a damned traitor."

Grahame was talking to the police commissioner.

"It mentions the keeping of my range maps in my office safe," he said. "There are other papers there, too—helicopter plans. The safe is fairly strong, but—"

"I'll send in an alarm. Have you got your car downstairs?" The commissioner was already at the telephone. He got his connection.

"What's the address?" he asked.

"Crocker Building. Tenth floor. Ten-forty-three to ten-forty-eight. We'll be there first."

A swift order issued, they caught the elevator, and barely a minute later were in Grahame's car, speeding eastward down Market Street.

The Crocker Building occupies the head of one of the many gores formed by the slant of the side streets north of Market with that main thoroughfare. The entrance runs through from Market to Post Street. As the swift car neared the building, another came from Post Street into Market. The lights of the safety station illumined the faces of the occupants as the machine crossed the street to the proper side for ferry-bound traffic, and slowed down to avoid a passing street car.

"That's Kirby!" cried Grahame. "This is not a coincidence. If they've broken into my safe, he's got the papers."

The car ahead of them picked up speed. The face of Kirby, looking backward as if in fear of pursuit, espied Grahame at the wheel of his machine. He tossed a word to his chauffeur, and the automobile fairly leaped ahead, regardless of the protest from the night traffic policeman who started to ride after the limit breakers. As Grahame set his foot to the accelerator, the officer rode beside them, ordering them to stop. The commissioner leaned from his seat.

"Never mind that, Kelly!" he shouted. "Follow us down to the ferry. Get his number if you can."

It was a short ride, but a furious one, with the homeward-bound amusement seekers in the street cars and on the sidewalks watching the two motor cars roaring from their open exhausts and the policeman galloping behind.

Kirby's car swung off to the right when it reached the Embarcadero, and Grahame followed, scarcely fifty feet behind. The leading machine slowed up as it reached a slip landing, where public launches plied for hire. Kirby sprang from the running board and leaped down the ladder to the float, where a launch was waiting, moored only by a boat hook in the hands of a squat man who looked, in the brief glance Grahame was able to bestow upon him, like a Japanese. As he sprang across the gunwale and took the wheel, the man touched a self-starter, and the launch spurted from the slip. It was of hydroplane model, and slid away on the surface of a smother of foam at a forty-knot clip.

"Over to the next slip!" cried the commissioner. There they found the police boat waiting, its crew alert for any alarm along the water front. The commissioner flashed a golden badge, and the launch captain saluted as he sprang aboard, Grahame hard at his heels. The traffic policeman drew his revolver and arrested the chauffeur of Kirby's machine.

"Follow that boat!" ordered the commissioner, as they cleared the slip and surged into the open bay. "They've got the speed of us," he said to Grahame, "but they may have a breakdown with those multiple engines of theirs. Clear that gun forward!"

Two men sprang to his bidding. The fleeing launch was rushing away from them, making almost two knots to their one as the policeman attached a cartridge belt to the quick-firer and prepared for action.

A Key Route ferry swung in between them and their quarry, and the commissioner swore fluently. As they cleared the public boat, the machine gun started a sputter of fire and bullets. Grahame jumped forward.

"Elevate!" he ordered the man at the lever. "They are increasing the range every second."

The hydrolaunch utilized its superior speed in steering a zigzag course to baffle the aim of the quick-firer, still managing to forge ahead of the slower police boat.

"They are making for Alameda Creek," said the commissioner, handing Grahame an extra pair of binoculars. "If they can get through the draw ahead of us, we'll lose them."

Grahame nodded. There were scores of dismantled hulks rotting along the banks of the Alameda slough, and it would be hard work tracing the runaways if they once gained shelter amid the maze of moorings.

Gliding over the surface, the hydroboat was soon so rapidly diminishing a target that the rapid-firer was stopped from throwing its useless hail of bullets.

"It looks like a get-away," said the commissioner. "There's no doubt but what they've got your papers by their actions."

Grahame, peering through the night at the fast-disappearing object of their chase, straightened up with an exultant chuckle.

"We're gaining on them," he announced. "They are having engine trouble. I was hoping for that. We'll get them yet. I don't mind the helicopter prints so much—it takes time to build engines of that type—but the loss of the range maps would be almost vital. And we can get Kirby on a criminal charge."

"Surely. The police have found evidence of burglary in your office by this time. You know what's been stolen. If we find it in Kirby's possession, he'll go to San Quentin the next trip he makes across the bay. And we've got that chauffeur, too. Oh, we can make it interesting for Kirby!"

The police boat was rapidly overhauling the other. They could hear faint sounds borne across the water as the fugitives worked over their stubborn engine. The members of the patrol got their revolvers ready, and the two men by the rapid-firer waited for orders.

"No use murdering 'em in cold blood," said the commissioner. "It's a different matter when they are trying for a get-away. Damn—"

The expletive came like the crack of a pistol. With a sudden volley of explosions, the hydroboat once more shot ahead, darting right and left, shuttle fashion. Both boats were now close to the head of the navigable creek that makes an island out of the popular suburb of Alameda. Vessels of all types lined the shores by factories and warehouses. Ahead loomed the drawbridge of the electric-train service. As the police boat shot between the piers, only a quarter of a mile behind, though losing rapidly, the rattle of the quick-firer started up once more. They had passed a series of boat-building yards, and were approaching the section where the old whalers and outworn ships lay rotting side by side. The channel was narrowing, and the hydroboat was forced to a more direct course with the line of fire, well within the radius of the machine gun's arc of control.

"If they don't quit, we'll riddle 'em like a sieve," said Grahame.

A glare of light lit up the dark water and the bare spars of the dismantled ships. With a loud report, a burst of flame broke from the cabin of the fleeing launch. Two figures, their arms wrapped about their heads, darted into the open, silhouetted against the flaring fire. One of them shrieked as he leaped into the water. The other stooped and groped with desperate haste about the cockpit.

"That's Kirby!" said Grahame. "He's blinded with the explosion. Trying to find the maps!"

Another flash came from amidships. With the report a tongue of flame licked out, and the groping figure shrank as if seared, hesitated, stumbled to the rail, and dropped into the water as the police boat came alongside the flaming hydroboat.

Grahame's eyes saw the flat bundle that Kirby had failed to find beneath the seat that ran around the cockpit.

"Hold on to her!" he cried, and jumped into the launch while a police mariner held to the gunwale with a boat hook. Within five seconds he was back again, his clothes scorched, his hair singed, but unhurt, the plans and maps in his arms.

"That was touch and go," said the commissioner, as the patrol boat was pushed free from the menace of the flames that now wrapped the hydroboat from stem to stern. "We must have put a bullet or two in her gasoline tank."

They cruised about, with eight pairs of eyes searching for traces of the men who had jumped overboard, their search aided by the fire. There was no sign, not a ripple on the quiet water save that of their own wake.

"Engineer probably breathed in flaming gas and sank like a stone," said Grahame. "That last explosion may have done for Kirby. But I'll swear he was never born to be drowned."

"Then he must swim like a loon," replied the commissioner.

They kept up the search long after it was hopeless. The hydroplane burned to the water's level, drifting sluggishly on the slack, intertidal current, and sank at last with a hiss in a smother of steam.

"Everything there?" asked the commissioner, as Grahame rapidly ran through the rescued package.

"Everything."

"Then we'll get back to San Francisco. I fancy we've seen the last of Mr. Kirby."

"I wish I could feel satisfied of it," said Grahame. "But I've got a hunch we're not through with him yet."

As the police boat sped once more beneath the railroad draw, a pale and tortured face showed beneath the midnight stars as its owner dragged himself painfully from the slime of the margin of the creek onto the bank and lay there, panting. Presently the figure moved, rose to uncertain feet, and, with eyes seared by flame, staggered along the footpath to where a tumble-down house boat, apparently untenanted, was linked to the shore by a rough plank drawbridge. The man tottered across the boards and knocked upon the door three times. It opened. A Japanese holding a shaded lantern appeared.

"You've got them?" he asked, in his own language.

"No!" answered Kirby, with a curse. "Get me flour and oil, quick!"

The other deftly administered relief.

"Yamamato?" he asked, as he completed his task.

"Dead!"

Kirby, still writhing in agony with every movement, lay down on a cot. The Japanese extinguished the lantern and sat beside him, motionless, long after Kirby's groans had ceased with the unconsciousness of sleep and exhaustion. His face was a mask set in a fixed expression of resolution, and its lines were the features of the Oriental diplomat who had rewarded Kirby with the order of the Golden Kite in the photographer's gallery on Geary Street.

V

THE CHRYSANTHEMUM CLUB

Three nights after the recovery of the plans, four men who had separately entered the saloon at the corner of Fillmore and Geary unobtrusively passed into the washroom and thence through the saloon yard and the gate of the weed-grown garden of the vacant house next to the building occupied by the Japanese photographer, and assembled quietly in the back room of the ground floor. These were Bruce Grahame, Fred Thurston, head of the telephone company, Gaffney, Japanese interpreter of the custom service, and an expert stenographer.

The room was unfurnished save for a broken chair and three empty boxes from the saloon yard. The window was boarded. Over the planks newspapers had been pasted. The flash of an electric torch revealed a thin wire leading athwart the wall and ending in the vulcanite receiver of a dictaphone concealed from a casual gaze behind a flap of the peeling wall paper. The interpreter clamped this to his ear with a telephone attachment and sat down upon the chair. The stenographer fastened to the wall by a rubber vacuum disk a hooded bulb fed by a storage battery and seated himself close to Gaffney. Grahame and Thurston took the remaining boxes and completed the little group.

"Nobody there yet," announced Gaffney, in a low tone. "They put over their meeting the night before last till nine to-night. We've ten minutes to spare."

"The Chrysanthemum Club. That's the name?" asked Grahame.

"Yes. That's the meaning of the sign on the fanlight at the entrance."

"And the same that was on the card of admission Ito gave me, Fred."

"I've heard of it before," the interpreter went on. "A political organization of some kind with all the Japanese bigger merchants and bankers in it. Branches in all the coast cities, I understand. They are starting to come in now," he said. "Better get your notebook ready. I won't get the chance to translate it literally, Mr. Grahame. They don't use many pauses. But I'll give out the meat of it."

The stenographer opened his book conveniently on his knee, ready to record, and the little group sat silent. The lamp threw a circle on the notebook and the stenographer's hand holding his pencil ready. Outside the ring of light, the room was black.

"Of course I can't identify them by voice," said Gaffney.

"That won't matter," answered Grahame.

"Now, then!" The stenographer poised his pencil, and they sat almost breathless in the suspense. "Man named Kirby laid up, badly burned from an accident," said the interpreter presently. "They are worried about him and his failure to deliver certain information."

"I knew my hunch was right," whispered Grahame to Thurston, as Gaffney ceased talking.

"One man's doing all the talking now," said Gaffney. "Patriotic dope about Dai-Nippon being the land of the gods and the mikado the direct representative and descendant of the sun goddess. Shinto stuff. Telling them what great soldiers they are and what bluffs we are. Says they are the coming race. Nothing can resist them. He's got the spread-eagle style, all right. Ah—"

The stenographer's pencil made its swift symbols, and all bent closer at the hint of importance in Gaffney's exclamation.

"News is expected from Washington to-night, he says. The ambassador is to be in conference with the secretary of state this evening."

"That's more than the evening papers knew," whispered Thurston to Grahame. The latter pressed his friend's knee as Gaffney went on again:

"He says Japan will not change a word of her demand. That if the United States does not concede them full privilege of citizenship, passports will be asked for. That means the return of American representatives from Japan and China. In the meantime, the local Japanese are not to leave the coast, but to report to their various headquarters when the signal is given. They are to be ready at any moment in case of any movement to intern them."

He stopped speaking.

"Get it all, man," said Grahame. "Don't lose any of it."

"They are all talking at once and cheering," said Gaffney. "Now they are quiet again. All the Japanese in San Francisco will leave the city by the means already provided. The leaders—that's the crowd upstairs, I take it—are to wear chrysanthemums in their buttonholes as a badge of authority. The contingent in the San Joaquin Valley will assemble at—some place in the hills—he didn't name it. This man Kirby is to command them. They are to march north to join the Sacramento Valley force."

"Where?" demanded Grahame.

"He doesn't say. According to later orders determined by circumstances. The club is not to meet again until there is definite news. The word will be passed in the usual way. They are to receive special instructions as to their duties within the next forty-eight hours.

"Now he's piling on the patriotic bunk again. Here's some one else talking. It's a man with the message from Washington. Here it is."

The stenographer, with his pencil hovering above the paper, waited while Grahame and Thurston sat with every nerve vibrant for the news.

"Japan refuses to concede the suggestion of long land leases in place of actual ownership, and insists on absolute citizenship. The secretary of state is to submit the question to the cabinet for a final decision. They are cheering again. They are going to break up the meeting. He is telling them to go round the city and caution all the Japanese against any display of enthusiasm. They are to spread a belief in a peaceful settlement among Americans. That's the end of it."

The four men, imbued with the gravity of the news they had learned, filed out quietly through the garden and the saloon and met six blocks away on the western side of Fillmore Street, where Grahame's car was waiting.

"Talk about German preparedness!" said Thurston. "They've got every detail down. And think of their spy system! What are you going to do, Grahame?"

"Send a transcript of this to Washington and the civic committees. Call the Emergency Committee together and double up speed. And one of the first things I'll do is to send the *Aërolite* over the hills of the San Joaquin Valley for an observation trip. I've a notion it may uncover a Japanese base of supplies. We've got no time to waste. The cabinet will hold off as long as they can, but it's close to a show-down. Call it a fortnight, then another for safe-conduct of the Japanese representatives. They should hold off until our own get back if they observe the rules of the game. But you can't tell what they'll do except that they'll strike when and where we least expect."

There were crowds about "Newspaper Corners," at the junction of Market, Kearney, Third, and Geary Streets. Great bulletins were pasted in the windows. They did not need to read the news. It had already been told them through the dictaphone. The last move had been made in the international chess game by the Japanese expert. The United States could move and lose, or could play to a stalemate, sweep the men off the board, and prepare for the final tournament—the game of war, with living pieces on the hazard of the board.

VI
CHECK!

The days that followed were filled with suspense for the Americans of the Pacific coast. To most of them the admission of Japanese to citizenship was a thing to be dreaded, one that prefaced financial disaster. And war foreshadowed the desolation of the fair land they had made their home, to which many of them were native born.

The civic committees busied themselves with measures of protection. The wide-branching departments of the Emergency Committee worked night and day. General business was at a standstill. The public utilities were run by subordinates, while their heads labored to make Grahame's plans bear fruit. Already the auxiliary fleets of airships and motor boats were assuming flexible shape. In the railroad yards, cars were being secretly armored and prepared for the cannon that were already bought by private subscription, and, with ammunition, on their way from the East by expedited freight. Twelve helicopters were on the point of final assembly.

There was no panic. The people to whom an earthquake only acts as an incentive held their spirits strong and their heads level. Washington was still silent, and the press suspended prophecy, while practically united in their announcement that the army and navy was adequate for defense. With few exceptions, they seemed to hold the Japanese lightly as adversaries.

The government had not signified its acceptance of Grahame's plans, submitted in detail, but the preparations for coöperation went on by private enterprise, and, as the reports began to show actual progress, the belief mounted among the minutemen of the Pacific coast that they could hold their own until the nation awoke. One thing was assured: they would not tamely retreat beyond the Sierras and wait for a tardy victory, or, at the worst, the price of an enormous ransom to restore to them the Pacific slope.

It was the first of January, 1921, that the New Year saw the threat turn into a live menace. All negotiations were declared at an end, and the Japanese embassy asked for passports, turning over their affairs to the representatives of Great Britain, to act as their treaty allies, if not as active partisans.

The answer of the United States to their request, following the issuance and exchange of safe-conducts, was a silent one that thrilled the hearts of every American as they read on bulletins and headlines the pregnant words:

THE ATLANTIC FLEET LEAVES FOR PANAMA CANAL AND THE PACIFIC

On the evening of the same day, another dispatch assumed the right of place and paramount attention:

PANAMA CANAL CLOSED BY EXPLOSION AT MIRAFLORES LOCKS
Landslide Blocks Ocean to Ocean Waterway. Atlantic Fleet Must Go
Through Straits of Magellan or Round the Horn.

The national representatives of Japan were on the high seas. Although Yokohama was ten days' travel from Vancouver or San Francisco, they were to all intents already in their own country, for not only were all the transpacific steamships Japanese bottoms, but they had the heels of any of the American war vessels. Yet, until the ambassadorial and consular attaches were actually on Japanese soil, the safe-conducts of the United States government held good.

But American officials to Japan, having had no great stretches of country to cross to reach shipboard, were already halfway across the Pacific, and were due to reach American soil from four to five days before the voyage of the Japanese attaches was concluded. Thus, while the hands of the American state department were self-bound by diplomatic courtesy for ten days, the Japanese, knowing their own safe-conduct promises fulfilled, might take advantage of the five days' leeway.

Those were days filled with anxiety. It was the lull before the storm. The dwellers on the Pacific coast could already hear the mutterings of the gale, brewing back of the sunset, and wondered where it would break.

In the interim of the delay, the local Japanese attempted, in the public press and by private utterance, to emphasize the fact that they were anxious to remain undisturbed in what they termed their "chosen country."

"Here we are free men," they stated. "If we return, it is a feudal community where we will be bound by the rules of caste and subject to heavy taxation. Even if America restricts us, as she did the Chinese, we hope that we, like them, will be permitted to remain."

The Japanese employment agencies would supply no help, and none was asked for. Holders of regular household positions gave them up. It was generally believed that a quiet, but steady, exodus of Japanese from the cities was in progress. Their stores still kept open, announcing enormous reductions in prices.

Editorial writers of the American press raised the question whether the time had come for another revolution in Californian history. They pointed out how the Latin race had taken the rich territory from the aborigines in the Spanish occupation, how the Slav had threatened invasion but had retired, and how the Saxon had wrested the land from the Latin. "Was it now the turn of the Malay?" they asked.

The civic committees, organized and under the leadership of the men composing them, citizens of large accomplishments, soon achieved efficiency and resourcefulness with carefully thought-out plans for safety. They had feared at first incendiarism and rioting, but so far had been called upon only to suppress disturbances incited by their own citizens against the Japanese, who seemed to be making strenuous efforts for neutrality. Fire they still feared from sea and sky, in the case of a bombardment; and, profiting by the disastrous San Francisco fire and by the examples of European cities in the great war, they prepared for sudden calls for aid, dividing the municipalities into zones, storing provisions and hospital supplies, planning for the possible horrors of a siege.

San Francisco's committee, headed by the mayor, consisted of such men as W.H. Crocker, the banker; President Sproule, of the Southern Pacific; John A. Brittin, head of the Gas & Electric Co.; Henry T. Scott, of the telephone system; W.B. Bourn, of the water supply; Thornwell Mullaly, of civic transportation; Allan Pollok, of commissariat expertness; Doctor Ainsworth, of the railroad hospital service—all men of wide executive experience in public service. Other members included, ex officio, the heads of the police and fire departments.

Los Angeles promptly followed San Francisco's lead, choosing their men along the same lines, with such a personnel as: I.W. Hellman, junior, W.H. Huntington, A.L. Corey, Harrison Gray Otis, E.L. Doheney, and J.A. Whittier.

Then came Portland with C.W. Phalen, Eugene Selby, J.M. Lewis, Patrick Bacon, W.H. Clark, and H.A. Henshaw. Seattle, Tacoma, Sacramento, San Diego, and all the important community centers chose similar committees from the most prominent and efficient men among their citizens.

The man of the hour was Bruce Grahame. His duties were those of a generalissimo, burdened with personal inspection of certain prime details. The chance of national protection seemed almost ephemeral, but the plans went forward with precision. The Emergency Committee emphatically considered it their immediate duty to effect preparedness. Fundamentally they were patriots. Primarily they were the defenders of their own homes.

Much had been accomplished. Ammunition, secretly forwarded in the refrigerator cars of the Fruit Association, was on hand. The dynamite guns were mounted on the armored cars and held in readiness under heavy guard in the railroad yards. The Hammond wireless torpedoes were stored in their magazines. Nine helicopters formed the backbone of the big air fleet. The speedy launches had been outfitted with rapid-firers. Options were secured—in the lack of government enterprise—upon dreadnaughts owned by Brazil and Argentine. Funds were arranged and specie secured by private subscription without thought of final recompense.

The project of Grahame, finally reduced to a working basis and outlined on a great map of the Pacific coast that hung in his quarters, was comparatively simple. The task had been made easier by the lack of landing places. Tacoma and Seattle, in Washington, had the natural and fortified protection of the Juan de Fuca Straits and the inland waterways of Puget Sound. The one was eighty, the other a hundred miles directly inland from the coast. Their chief menace lay in British territory. Portland, in Oregon, lay far up the Columbia River. The northern coast line was rock-bound; the unimportant harbors were guarded by treacherous sand bars. From Cape Flattery to the Bay of Monterey, the landing of troops would be naturally defended, save San Francisco Bay itself. And from there southward, where grim cliffs did not drop sheer into rock-fanged waters, the breaking of the great rollers upon shallow sand beaches was supplemented by the wide belt of kelpweed. Special surfboats alone could achieve a slow landing of troops. A swift concentration of bomb-dropping airships would create havoc. Los Angeles was twelve miles from the coast, and its comparatively shallow harbor at San Pedro.

Seven strategic points were set aside for special defense by mines, torpedoes to be propelled from shore by Hertzian oscillation or launched from the air fleet, backed by the armament of the government coast defense plus the Pacific fleet. These were the entrances to Puget Sound and the Columbia River, San Francisco harbor, Monterey Bay, the range of Santa Barbara Channel inside the islands—where defense stations were established—and the harbors of San Pedro and San Diego.

The entire coast line was divided into sections for aërial patrol. Hangars and repair stations were improvised or built. Six of the helicopters were assigned to as many squadrons. Each station had from one to three seaplanes and their crews, and was equipped with a wireless apparatus, powerful glasses, and a microphone. To each, where sea facilities permitted, was given a proportion of the auxiliary launch flotilla.

So was planned a reconnoitering patrol reaching fifty miles offshore, tied up by radio communications, capable of instant transmission, of the approach of hostile vessels, their strength, and apparent destination, so that the mobile coast artillery of dynamite guns and the sub-sea batteries of wireless torpedoes could concentrate.

California was eminently the main objective, and the Californian coast offered the greatest facilities for landing. The railroad ran from the northern portal of the Golden Gate to Eureka parallel to the coast, and temporary spurs were laid to bring the guns to closer action. Hidden batteries were planned in the great redwood forests. From San Francisco south, a road followed the surf line, broken for a while at Monterey Bay, where the cliffs absolutely prohibited a landing; but, reaching the shore again at the end of the Santa Lucia Range, and continuing to Ventura at the southern end of the Santa Barbara Channel. From there a short breach occurred to Los Angeles, but thence the rails were again available to San Diego.

Grahame feared less a frontal coast attack than the dangers of the Mexican border at the south and the Canadian line to the north. More than all, he feared the Japanese in California. He planned a patrol of the power lines by airships, though such work could at the best be incomplete. For his torpedo patrols, local power plants were in readiness, but the problem of guarding them was a hard one.

His main factors—concentration and mobility—were handicapped by the great area he had to cover and the lack of men for interior watchfulness. No order of internment could be expected until the safe-conduct term expired, and he tried to grapple with the uncertainty of where the first attack would be delivered by the Japanese reservists by striving to find their base of supplies he knew to be hidden somewhere in the coast ranges. If that could be destroyed, the sting of at least the San Joaquin contingent would be rendered harmless. But, as hour after hour of the fateful days slipped by, his searchers brought no word. In Washington, the shadow of British cooperation with their allies still dominated Congress. The time was pregnant with war. Mars was supplanting Liberty.

The wireless signaled the landing of America's Japanese representatives in California within twenty-four hours; and that moment, Grahame believed, would see an outbreak of the Pacific coast Japanese in California.

The news came to him at the University Club, still the noon rendezvous of the "Ultras," all now enrolled in the defense committees.

Grahame rose.

"That's our bugle call, gentlemen," he said. "Government is bound in honor not to act for five days until the steamers with the foreign attaches reach Japan. Then they can order the coast Japanese interned. That the troops now here and at Monterey can handle that problem I doubt.

"It is significant that the Japanese have made no attempt to leave in the face of this imminent action. Their suggestion that they may be allowed the same restricted privileges as the Chinese is manifestly absurd, seeing that they have no official representation in this country. Their expressed belief that Japan will not declare war and that they will therefore not be considered war prisoners and at the worst must face exportation is, as we believe, a threadbare attempt at hoodwinking us into apparent security.

"The outbreak is imminent. To-night the Emergency Committee will order all our units to be ready for instant action. Unless I am greatly mistaken, we cease to be peaceful citizens from the moment our representatives set foot upon the landing pier."

No applause followed his speech. All left their unfinished luncheon in a grave silence, their faces hardened with resolve. They implicitly believed in Grahame's warning, avowed his genius, and were themselves fired by its inspiration. To the wise men of California, Grahame was their Napoleon, and a Napoleon was sadly needed. Rumors came from Washington that the Atlantic fleet was to be recalled in the fear of an attack on the eastern coast line by some ally, as yet unrevealed, of Japan. And the rumors grew to assertions that England and Canada—under the terms of a treaty amended in the last stages of the European war for special aid rendered by Japan at a desperate moment in Great Britain's Asiatic affairs—would respond to Japan's summons for men, munitions, and money, the three essential M's of warfare. And Canada had a veteran army of over a quarter of a million men, ready to pour across the border.

Grahame feared that already Ogden Kirby might have secured the services of white men, probably British. If such was the case, the question of mischief to be wrought by spies and plotters in the workshops of the Emergency Committee became an issue of the gravest apprehension. Because of the racial characteristics of the Japanese, it had seemed easy to eliminate them from interference, but if white men were involved it would be hard to distinguish the incendiary among the thousands of workmen employed, many of whom, particularly in the engineering departments, were admittedly British by birth.

In the meantime, there was no state of war existing. The withdrawal of ambassadors is not necessarily a declaration of war. Only once in its history, in 1812, against Mexico, has the United States ever actually declared war. It has recognized in Congress that a state of war existed. But such was not now the case. Japan had committed no overt act. The landslide that blocked the canal might have occurred from natural causes. On the other hand, the Zone engineers joined in the shrewd suspicion of the army and navy that Japanese, working from their base at Tiburon in the Gulf of California, had landed a force that might readily have disappeared in the jungle, unnoted by the scanty members of the canal patrol. There for weeks they could have labored, secretly preparing great bores in the earth to be filled with high explosives and at the crucial moment touched off, to form the initiative of a great slide of the shifty strata of the Zone region which would culminate in the blocking of the waterway.

Proof was practically impossible. And, without overt act, unless the United States forced the issue, there was no excuse for interning the Japanese on the coast. Grahame's proofs of conspiracy, submitted to the government, were not accepted as such. While military and naval affairs were active, diplomatic Washington made no move. The majority in Congress demanded that the bulk of the insufficient defense of the nation guard its most thickly populated and wealthiest portions, and no troops were sent to supplement those on the Pacific coast. A guarded approval of Grahame's plans had been issued from the White House, followed by newspaper comment that seemed inclined to use this citizen preparedness as a basis for lack of supplemental aid. The bugaboo of British interference seemed to induce a martial paralysis.

Was the United States no longer to be united? Was it no longer a continent open to two oceans? Or was the pusillanimity of pork-barrel politicians to prevail?

The answer to this grave question, and how the terrible blow fell upon the Pacific coast, will be told in the next issue of PEOPLE'S.

The Peril of the Pacific
By J. Allan Dunn

Part Three: The Blow

Synopsis of Preceding Installments

Bruce Grahame, an expert in aëronautics, and a believer in preparedness, especially against a suspected Japanese invasion, is in love with Irene Lancaster, daughter of General Lancaster, chief of the Pacific division of the United States army, located at the Presidio, San Francisco. As the country at large refuses to be aroused over the Japanese peril, Grahame proposes to try and unite all the aviation clubs of the Pacific coast into an aërial militia. To prove his assertion that the Pacific coast Japanese, most of them veterans of the war with Russia, are drilling secretly at night, Grahame takes General Lancaster, his daughter, and Ogden Kirby, whom he suspects of a connection with the Japanese government, in his triplane, the *Aërolite*, to a valley in the Coast Range. There they find a large company of Japanese drilling on the open plain, in the moonlight. The next day Grahame and his friend, Fred Thurston, an official of the telephone company, who is in complete accord with Grahame's views, happened to see Kirby in an automobile with a couple of Japanese, and they follow. They trail them to a Japanese club, where are gathered several distinguished Oriental statesmen, in consultation over an enlargement of an aëro photo map of San Francisco Bay. Grahame steps into a trap that has been set for him by keeping an appointment with a woman who claims to have incriminating information against Kirby. In order to talk with her he meets her in the Palm Room of the Palace Hotel, where she and Grahame become the cynosure of all eyes when she becomes suddenly and very ostentatiously inebriated. Japan delivers an ultimatum to Washington, the context of which is "Free Entry or Forcible," practically threatening war unless Japanese immigrants were given the same right of entrance as other immigrants. In default of immediate protection and assistance from Washington the Emergency Association of the Pacific Coast meets, presided over by Bruce Grahame. Grahame outlines plans for defense. Kirby steals the plans from Grahame's safe, but is caught by Grahame after a long motor-boat chase in which Kirby escapes, but the papers are recovered. By means of a dictograph Grahame and Thurston overhear the Japanese plans at the Chrysanthemum Club. Suddenly the Panama Canal is blocked by an explosion, leaving the Atlantic fleet on the wrong side of the continent.

I

THE SHAPE AGAINST THE STARS

THE UNION IRON WORKS, where many of the United States warships have been built and launched, including the *Oregon*, famous for its Round-the-Horn trip in the Spanish-American War, was one of several centers of activity in creating the armament for defense promulgated by the emergency committee. Its work was typical of that being turned out in factories and railroad shops at Portland, Seattle, Sacramento, and elsewhere on the coast. From the public-utility corporations and from private establishments the best mechanics had been concentrated in such places.

There were twenty pattern makers to take the place of one, and so, in casting shop and lathe rooms, through all the processes of machinefacture, expert draftsmen, foundrymen, electricians, and their kind jumped the work from start to finish with two score pair of hands for every one that had represented the ordinary force.

Here the helicopter engines were made with all the foundry parts of the new heavier-than-air machine. Two hundred men bent every energy of a furious twelve-hour drive to each airship. Then they were taken out to Tanforan to be assembled in buildings hastily constructed for that purpose in the center of an abandoned race track.

Grahame bent every effort to such time as he could spare from the manifold duties of an executive upon the completion of his machines, hoping to finish a dozen of them within the same twenty-four hours. The great triplane had been sent out on patrol duty to find a Japanese base of supplies, but there were many places in the mountains where a machine of that type could neither approach the ground closely enough for satisfactory survey nor land for inspection. But the helicopters would be able to dip and rise into every hollow of the range where arms, ammunition, equipment, and commissary supplies would be likely to be concealed. And that somewhere the Californian reservists of the Japanese army had such a base seemed a foregone conclusion.

At Tanforan the open plain of the race track helped to safeguard the machines from possible damage from marauding Japanese. Armed guards patrolled the outer fence, and, with other sentries on the track itself, a cordon was formed impossible for the unauthorized to pass. Two powerful searchlights were manned at nightfall, their rays constantly sweeping the great inclosure, ready at any moment to concentrate upon any given spot from which an alarm was sounded.

On the evening of the day that the superintendent in charge of the assembling of the machines telephoned Grahame that three of them were practically ready and within twenty-four hours at least one-half of the helicopters would be complete, there came a bolt from the blue. The machines were built in rigid construction. The chassis consisted of the cantilever framework of the hull, boat-shaped for marine use, shock-absorbing buffers to take up the impact of descent, the powerful motive machinery, eight pairs of propellers on vertical shafts with horizontal axes, and one pair, larger, at either end of the craft, which had neither proper stem nor stern, revolving vertically for forward or backward propulsion. The hull was sheathed in aluminum, decked with cedar on which were mounted quick-firers and fitted with a floor equipped with the wireless apparatus, the bomb-dropping compartment, steersman's quarters, and the engine room equipped sparsely with conveniences for the comfort of the crew. A circular stairway of perforated metal led to the deck.

Three helicopters had been passed to the inspection shed awaiting Grahame's approval. The building was a hangar of wood construction. The aviators for the twelve machines, men chosen from survivors of the European War, were assembled about the flyers, watching the painting of their names upon their sides, dulled with acid to a nondescript gray. *Saturn*, *Mercury*, and *Mars*—the titles were affixed with gold leaf. Grahame was expected momentarily. There was to be a brief christening with bottles of salt water filled from the Golden Gate, a ceremony to be attended by such heads of the emergency committee as could spare the time from their well-filled schedules.

As the launching party, in two motor cars, sped through the sparsely settled suburb of San Francisco, night had settled down. The moon was almost due to rise. Meanwhile the sky was sprinkled closely with glittering stars. A mile from the track, Thurston, next to Grahame, who was at the wheel of his machine, called his attention to a whir that sounded faintly far above his head.

"There's an aëroplane up there, Bruce," he said.

Grahame nodded. He, too, had caught the sound. Advancing his spark, the motor picked up its last reserve of speed. An attack from the sky had entered the possibilities in Grahame's mind already, but the danger had seemed remote from the apparent scarcity of Japanese aviators. He knew of but one, the man who had secured the aëro map of the fortifications of San Francisco Bay. At the track, the identification of Japanese would-be visitors on foot was an easy matter; in the air, there seemed practically only the one to be feared in that vicinity, and he knew that the biplane of the Oriental airman was practically dismantled for repairs at that moment.

But, taking no chances, he raced for their destination. Night flying was not popular with aviators as a rule, though the members of the now combined Aëro Clubs of the Coast had been practicing after-dark flights of late.

The sound passed and they reached the gate, passed the sentries, and sped around the track to the entrance opposite the main aërodrome. As they halted a whistling noise stopped them from rising in their seats. Something unseen hurtled earthward and struck the ground close to the hangar where the three helicopters awaited approval. There was an explosion and a burst of flame. Figures ran out from the building and gazed upward, as Grahame, followed by Thurston and the rest of his party, ran toward the group.

"Scatter!" cried Grahame. "Get apart, men!"

The groups separated as another bomb dropped from the void, striking the hangar squarely on the roof and plunging through to detonate inside.

The wooden walls fell outward, and, in the glare, the three helicopters were seen dissolving into a tangled mass of metal. Fire leaped among the ruins and licked greedily at the timbers. The beams of the searchlights on top of the main building lifted their shafts skyward, seeking for the enemy. Between them, a dim shape among the stars, Grahame saw the blur of a biplane, like a night hawk soaring in a great circle. Twenty spurts of quick fire followed by rifle reports testified to the vigilance of the guards as they fired uselessly at the raider.

"Shut off those lights, Fred!" shouted Grahame, as he rushed toward the aërodrome. "They help him—not us."

His superintendent met him at the door of the main building, consternation on his face. Grahame grasped him by the arm, bearing him inside.

"Fill up those tanks," he said, pointing to the nearest of the helicopters, a skeleton of framework, but equipped to the point of hull completion and the mounting of her guns. Thurston came up with two of the aviators as the two men hurried to the gasoline supply.

Grahame swung on the two pilots.

"You, La Rue!" he called, choosing a man medaled for bravery and efficiency in the French corps, a man he had chosen for his head instructor. La Rue clambered into the frame, followed by the second aviator, eager to act as mechanician. The floor of the hull was roughly boarded over, the engines had been tested and were ready oiled. As they rapidly made ready

Grahame turned to the superintendent, who held a rifle taken from a guard, while Thurston handled another.

"Keep your gun, Fred!" he snapped. "Quick, Williams! Get me some charges, the half sticks, short fuses."

He lit a cigar as the superintendent raced off to where the dynamite used in blasting foundations was stored, returning on the run and working desperately to affix caps and fuses.

La Rue and his assistant stepped from the helicopter, the double doors were opened, and the machine wheeled outside just as another bomb, ill aimed, exploded in the center of the inclosure. Then they remounted, followed by Grahame and Thurston. The engine broke into a volley of action under the thrust of the self-starter, the horizontal propellers roared in compensating directions, the metal body vibrated, and the helicopter sprang from the ground, gaining velocity as the blades bit the air, mounting, like a released balloon, straight upward. The building shrank, the circle of the track contracted, as they rose, the pressure of the lightening air forcing itself upon eyeballs and eardrums. Speech was impossible, but the four brains were concentrated upon one thing, the position of their quarry.

At six thousand feet they hovered, swung, and darted in the direction of the fleeing biplane, a dark shape beneath them, beating across the southern arm of the bay toward the mainland shore and the foothills of the Mount Diablo range. Fast as it flew the helicopter gained, always above, the wind of its going singing through the framework, the crew clinging as best they could with their free hands.

The biplane was a speedy one. The helicopter was capable of a hundred miles an hour at its best, but the engine, while not missing a revolution, was not yet attuned, and there was less than five aërial knots an hour between pursuer and pursued.

The marauding aviator was a master of his profession. Finding himself being gradually overhauled, he banked his planes, seeking to double just as the moon came up above the hills, silvering his upper planes to the semblance of a gull. They were across the bay now, making southward over the valley of Sunol, a stretch of sand and gravel where the subterranean lakes of the city's water supply lay deep beneath the surface.

The fugitive's move was his undoing. The after propeller of the helicopter automatically locked its blades in a horizontal position, and the other driver whirled into play. The helicopter darted backward, angling across the arc of the other's loop. La Rue, at his levers, slackened speed, and, as the biplane came directly beneath them, skillfully gauged his flight to keep them above it, flying foot for foot.

Grahame, kneeling on his rude platform of boards, lit the short fuse at his cigar. He had weighted the short sticks of dynamite with bullets attached with cord. He motioned to La Rue, the horizontal planes changed their note, and the helicopter settled slowly down. A hundred feet above the biplane, Grahame tossed his sputtering death down to the gleaming planes beneath. It missed the mark, but exploded in mid-air, the concussion making the biplane swerve. A second attempt failed, but the third charge fairly hit the target. The helicopter seemed to lunge upward as the lifting propellers picked up high speed once more.

Peering down, they saw the flaming wreck of the biplane falling like a comet, smashing at last far below on the sands of Sunol.

They followed, dropping leisurely, alighting on their buffers half a mile from the destroyed machine. Fifty yards from the biplane lay a shattered body sprawled shapelessly, half in, half out of the shallow creek. La Rue turned the body over in the moonlight. The face had been protected in some measure by the outstretched arms. The Frenchman bent in sudden curiosity, then knelt and lit a match.

He came back to the trio who were looking at the remnants of the biplane.

"Of what nation did you figure him?" he asked, jerking his head backward.

"Why, Japanese, of course," said Grahame.

La Rue shrugged his shoulders.

"The man had gray eyes," he answered. "There's something that fell out of his pocket."

It was a pocketbook. There were bills amounting to a hundred dollars, some papers that Grahame set aside for later investigation, and, stained, like the rest of the contents, with the blood of the dead aviator, a visiting card. The name on it was "Ogden Kirby."

II

KIRBY REAPPEARS

Ogden Kirby had disappeared. No trace could be found of him by detectives, and it would have been a comparatively easy matter for the Japanese colony to harbor him.

The swift course of events had left Grahame little time for thought of the strained relations existing between Irene Lancaster and himself. He had no intention of allowing the trick played in the Palace Hotel to separate them. On the other hand, the girl seemed equally determined to make the breach a permanent one. Her snub was repeated on two occasions when she maintained an attitude oblivious of Grahame's presence.

He forced a wedge of two hours at last into his multitudinous duties, resolving to repay them by contributions from his meager sleeping time, and motored out to the Presidio. General Lancaster was hastening back on a transport from an inspection at Honolulu. His sister chaperoned his daughter and maintained the household at the San Francisco reservation.

The maid took Grahame's card and returned with the answer: "Not at home." He knew the girl well, and she faltered before his keen gaze of inquiry.

"Where is she?" he asked.

"I don't know, sir—out to dinner—maybe—I think."

"Then I'll wait," answered Grahame.

The grim determination of his voice dominated the maid.

"I'm sorry, sir," she said. "Maybe there is some mistake."

She disappeared through the door of the Lancasters' reception room. When it reopened the clear voice of Irene Lancaster followed the exit of the servant.

"Tell the gentleman," she said, with evident intention that the sentences should reach Grahame's ears, "that I am sorry he could not understand my first message. Tell him that I am engaged."

Before the door could close Grahame replied:

"Tell your mistress," he said firmly, "that I have but little time of my own, and ask only ten minutes of hers. But for that favor I feel I have the right to insist."

The maid hesitated. Then Irene Lancaster stepped into the hall.

"Since you insist, Mr. Grahame," she said, with chilling emphasis, "I will submit this once to your pertinacity. My aunt and I leave in the morning for Del Monte."

She swept by him and entered a front room used as the general's library. Grahame followed. Irene Lancaster stood pale and palpably annoyed. He faced her.

"It seems to me, Irene," he said, without preface, "that I am entitled to the opportunity for explanation, even to demand one from you for the sudden removal of your friendship."

"There is none. I am perfectly aware of your relations with that—creature. Let us not discuss it. I have seen positive evidence, and I am not sufficiently interested in the matter to discuss details that are, to say the least, degrading."

Grahame bowed. "The evidence—which we will not discuss—was presumably furnished by the man with whom I saw you, a man against whom I consider it my duty to warn you."

"Behind his back!"

"In which I only follow his example. The man has proven himself to be a thief and would-be assassin. It is not as my personal enemy I ask you to regard him, but as the enemy of your country in the service of which your father holds a high position. Even now he—"

"Stop!" Irene Lancaster's eyes were blazing. "Whatever Ogden Kirby may have said it would have been spoken just as readily in your presence if he had possessed the opportunity. Would you say these things to his face?"

"Assuredly."

"Then do so."

She flung aside the folding doors between the library and the drawing-room. A man came forward, hesitated for the fraction of a second, then confronted Grahame, a smile that was more than half a sneer upon a face scarred on the brow and one cheek with half-healed burns.

It was Ogden Kirby.

III

"TRAITOR OR—"

For a moment Grahame stood amazed at the temerity of the man, fully aware, as he must be, that he was wanted on serious charges, yet daring to make a social call in the very heart of the enemy's country.

"Mr. Grahame has made certain charges against you, Mr. Kirby," said the girl. "As my guest, I demanded that you hear them."

"I should like," said Grahame coolly, "to hear Mr. Kirby repeat any accusations he may have made against *me* in my absence."

"There have been none," said the girl. "The evidence I spoke of was not obtained from him, but from an even more reliable source."

Grahame shrugged his shoulders. His brain worked rapidly over plans by which he could insure the capture of Kirby. He had been announced at the Chrysanthemum Club meeting as the leader of the Japanese reservists of the San Joaquin Valley. Aside from all other crimes, he must not be permitted to carry out any such plan. Obviously the first step in the matter was the disenchantment of Irene Lancaster's belief in the man.

"What are these charges?" asked Kirby.

"I pass up your first effort at murder by weakening the wire stays of the *Aërolite* and your second attempt when you shot at and wounded me," said Grahame, "but I charge you with conspiring against the peace and safety of this country; with stealing valuable maps and plans to that end; and with inciting the destruction of life and property at the Tanforan Aërodrome."

Kirby's sneer increased.

"And your proofs to these cock-and-bull stories?" he asked.

"Yes, the proofs," echoed the girl.

"Ask him where he got those scars on his face? Ask him if he knows where this came from?"

He held out the bloodstained card that had been taken from the dead aviator bearing Ogden Kirby's name in engraved letters, and, beneath it, a penciled address. Kirby took it nonchalantly and looked at it, then handed it back to Grahame.

"It is my card," he said. "But I do not know where you obtained it. I have given away a great many of them. I would like to ask you, Grahame, whether the motive that impels these violent accusations against me is a political or a purely personal one?"

Grahame clenched his fists as Kirby looked at him mockingly.

"The fact is unalterable, sir, that if the police were aware of your presence in this house you would leave the Presidio reservation under arrest and certainty of conviction."

"The commissioner of police is a great friend of yours, I believe," said Kirby. "Why don't you telephone to him?"

"I intend to."

As Grahame stepped to the door the girl forestalled him and stood with her back to the exit.

"You seem to forget that Mr. Kirby is my guest," she said. "Even did I believe all that you have said of him, he is still entitled to the sanctuary of my father's house."

"This is the house of the nation," answered Grahame. "It can hold no such sanctuary, nor would your father desire that it be used to harbor a traitor. It is my duty to see that this man pays the penalty for what he has done and is prevented from further crimes against our country."

"You shall not use the telephone in this house. Do you think I would allow Mr. Kirby to be taken from here as if from a trap?"

"Then I shall be forced to alarm the military authorities or make the arrest myself."

"You would not dare."

"The moment he leaves your premises."

Irene Lancaster glanced from the resolute face of Grahame to the impassive countenance of Kirby. A shadow of irresolution passed over it.

"You have not answered him yet," she said to the latter.

"No. Then I will. I swear to you that—" He stood with lifted chin, his short stature at its utmost, the fire of an ardent spirit in his eyes. "I swear to you, Miss Lancaster, by all I have held, now hold, or hope to hold dear and sacred, that I am no traitor to my country. The time will come when I can prove it."

The man's voice was eloquent with truth. There was no question about its utter sincerity even to Grahame, who knew that somewhere there must be a solution to the apparent riddle.

"Are you a British subject?" he asked.

"I am not. Your insistent attempt to place me in a false light amounts to paranoia, Grahame. I am not a subject of any nation that is allied, or likely to be, with Japan. And I am no traitor."

Again the words rang true.

"I believe you," said the girl. "I want a word with you alone, Mr. Kirby."

She stood aside and crossed the hall, opening a door that Grahame knew was the dining room, beckoning to Kirby to enter with her. Grahame pointedly stood in the hall by the front door as they passed him. He waited for a minute or two, then tried the door through which they had gone. Irene's voice answered the attempt. In a few moments she opened the door, transferring the key to the outer lock and turning the bolt.

"He has gone," she said simply.

Grahame's eyes grew hard as steel.

"You don't know what you have done, Irene," he said.

"He spoke the truth. He was my guest."

"He has tricked you. I only hope that you will never have to repent your action in your own person."

Grahame opened the front door and stood for a moment on the threshold.

"It did not occur to you," he said, with cutting emphasis, "that if he was not a traitor he had nothing to fear from arrest!" With the last word he had sprung down the steps and was running toward the quarters of his friend the major. Within five minutes, long before Kirby could possibly have reached the nearest gate, the sentries had been alarmed and a special patrol sent out after the fugitive.

"If you catch him he is not to be allowed to speak," said the major, adding to Grahame, as the squad sergeant saluted and left: "We must keep Miss Lancaster's name out of this."

But no search revealed Ogden Kirby. No one remotely answering his description had passed the sentries. But an hour later, a short, active figure that had doubled and dodged along the woodland paths found a steep trail that led to Baker's Beach. Down this he crept like a slowly shifting shadow, foot by foot, a blur against the cliff. Presently from the shelter of a clump of rocks, flashes from an electric torch given at marked intervals brought in a softly paddled rowboat that worked its silent way out to a launch in mid-channel just holding its own against the ebb.

Ogden Kirby climbed aboard, the dinghy was taken up, and the launch headed for the open sea at a twenty-knot clip. As the moon rose it passed the Golden Gate and sped southward.

In General Lancaster's quarters, Irene Lancaster asked a question of her image in the glass:

"Can I have been wrong? Yet I know he spoke the truth when he said he was no traitor."

IV
LUCILLE L'ESTRANGE

Thurston met Grahame as the latter stepped into his machine outside his headquarters.

"I'll ride with you," he said. "I think I've got a tip as to that base of supplies."

Grahame's face lightened.

"Good!" he said. "From the Chrysanthemum Club?"

"No. They haven't had a meeting since the night we listened to their plans over the dictaphone. This sounds vague, but it's a clew. Six months ago a Japanese syndicate bought a lease on the quicksilver mines in the Pumacles Country."

"Vancouver's Pinnacles, near Soledad, wagon road from Tres Pinos. Yes?"

"I've just had a talk with our foreman, who has been erecting a special line of poles in that region. He tells me that lots of wagons have gone up to the mine in the weeks they've been working, but all of them came back empty. And I also happen to know that you can't get any mercury from them. They claim they are getting ready for bigger operating. The way things have looked lately, that's pure bunk."

"I've the committee meeting this afternoon," said Grahame. "So have you. But I'm going to take a trip to the Pinnacles to-night. It's a rough country. I'll figure on getting there at dawn. We'll take the *Ariel*. Want to come along? I think you've found the spot."

"Will I come? Why ask me?"

"Then meet me at the aërodrome at three o'clock. We'll start about four. It's a bare hundred miles. It's just the place for a base. Fine work, Fred. Getting out here?"

Vancouver's Pinnacles were first noted by the brilliant, but short-lived, discoverer at the close of the eighteenth century as one of the wonders of the western world. The government has inclosed them in a national reserve, but few save local picnic parties know the Doré-esque place of carven cliffs and great monoliths of stone, standing in red and gray solemnity as if they were remnants of the worship of some mighty, prehistoric race. Above the ground, the rock formations assume the shape of the façades of temples, the bas-reliefs of which have been nearly obliterated by the centuries, with cavernous doorways, pillared galleries, dome and spire and fretted pinnacles. In the amphitheater formed by these stand single stones, two hundred feet from base to crumbling summit, like mammoth dolmens. Underground, the rock is mined by water and exploded gases into a labyrinth of rifts and caves. Time has tried to smooth the ruggedness with vegetation, but the trees and shrubbery are futile to mitigate the weirdness of the spot. Some day a moving-picture manager will win fortune by staging there some scenario of L'Inferno or a preadamic romance. Once it was the stronghold of California's most famous bandit, Valdez, who perished with his stolen paramour on the brink of one of its subterranean pools. It is still remote. The railroad at Soledad, in the Vale of Solitude, where the wind scatters the friable adobe of the old mission walls still haunted, so the Indians say, by its last priest, who died there of starvation, is thirteen miles away. The trail thence to the Pinnacles admits only of foot passengers through the narrow gateway where Valdez held off the sheriff's posse for three days. From Tres Pinos and Hollister, a fair road winds up to the fastness. Over it the picnic parties and the employees of the mercury mines travel. The barren rocks hold but the one precious metal, cinnabar, or quicksilver, the excavation of which is perilous through the poisonous exhalations of the uncanny mineral.

The *Ariel*, flagship of Grahame's helicopter flotilla of the air, darted southward from San Francisco in the quiet hour that precedes the dawn, when the wind rests and the stars retreat from the ramparts of night. The machine, a gray cloud flying against the sky, was fully equipped. Its engines were muffled. Only the rhythmic whir of its propellers hummed high above the sleeping towns. It showed no light. Its windows were blanketed. It sped with the unerring flight of a projectile, eight thousand feet of progress for every minute of its journey, two thousand feet above the sea, guided by speed and compass.

The curtain of the sky was shaken and an orange glow was trembling in the east as the *Ariel* drove above the winding course of the San Benito River and hovered over the riven rocks of the Pinnacles, slowly settling eastward as the pilot peered down to find a landing place amid the mass of stone. It was a perilous landing. There were barely ten acres of comparatively level ground amid the ravines and slopes among which towered the monoliths. And these acres were for the most brush covered. A little stream, gleaming in the growing light as if it was quicksilver flowing from the mines, marked a space beside a roadway that seemed to offer a chance for descent. The mines were in a cañon where the ribbon of another dusty road stretched midway of the cliff.

Grahame ordered a circuit of the rim of the cliffs. Shadowless, the *Ariel* drifted as a hawk might scour the air on breakfast bent. The matchless engines ran like a clock, the fore and aft propellers gave the engineers absolute control.

"It will be some job to locate the actual supplies," said Thurston. "The place is undermined with miles of hiding places that have a score of entrances tucked away in rocks and masked by shrubbery. I suppose they are guarded."

"Yes," assented Grahame. "I hardly expect to make any definite discovery. But if I can find proof that there is a base here for ammunition and provisions, one bomb-dropping helicopter can easily block the outlet. The road to Tres Pinos and Hollister is the only exit. They may have rifles and possibly some machine guns, but not any anti-aircraft artillery."

He was gazing downward through an observation window in the floor as the *Ariel* soared slowly on, sinking gradually as the dawn light crept down from the verge of the cliffs and the rising sun shot golden lances of light through the deeper gorges. He scanned every inch of the shifting panorama. At the mouth of one of the ravines the face of a great slab showed flat. It was rent its length by a fissure running east and west, swept clear of shadow by the slanting sunbeams. Within the crevice something moved, pale in the depths.

Grahame spoke through his telephone to the engineer:

"Back slowly. Hold above the big stone and lower."

It was a face he had seen there for a second's space. Just a triangle of gray, accented by two smudges that were eyes, yet in that swift, vague look something stirred reminiscently in his brain. It was the face of a woman.

On slackening propellers, the *Ariel* drifted down like thistle seed. Suddenly the face showed again. Then the helicopter touched the surface of the big granite slab and the pliant, powerful springs of the absorbers took up the shock. The door in the side of the hull opened, a side ladder let down automatically, and Grahame and Thurston quickly reached the verge of the split in the massive boulder. The crevice was some three feet wide at the top, gradually narrowing in its depth of some twenty feet, its sides with their clean cleavage offering no chance for escape.

As they gazed the pit seemed empty. Then, like the swift play of a lizard from a crevice, a shadowy figure appeared from some side fissure in the rock, and the face looked upward. A voice, weak, appealing, the voice of a woman in distress, floated up to them.

"Help!" it said. "Quick! They are coming!"

Grahame had been swiftly knotting a loop in the rope they had brought. This he lowered to the prisoner. "Get a couple of men, Fred," he said.

Thurston got two of the crew ready to haul on the rope as Grahame called down to the woman:

"Put your feet in the loop!" Then he uttered an exclamation. "She's fainted," he said. "Lower me away."

At the bottom, he found the senseless form lying on the rubble that floored the crevice, close to the triangular opening of a cavity that seemed to run far back underground. As he swiftly fastened the rope about her he could hear the scramble of feet and the echoing sound of excited voices rising from the mysterious interior. The inhabitants of this underworld spoke Japanese.

He gave the signal to haul away, and the limp figure was carefully drawn to the surface. Grahame watched its ascent for a few seconds before the closer approach of footsteps warned him. Standing to one side of the tunnel mouth, he fired two shots from his automatic into the dark throat. There was a howl of pain and surprise and the footsteps halted. A flash in the darkness was followed by the dull splash of lead upon the wall opposite the cavern. The voices and steps ceased. Then upon the portals of the tunnel glowed the crisp light of an electric torch. Grahame fired again. As long as he was an unseen menace he felt that they would be cautious in rushing him.

The rope came snakily down the steep sides and dropped beside him. With his automatic hanging from his wrist by a thong and the ring attached to the pistol, he set his foot in the loop and nodded the signal to hoist, kicking himself clear with one foot, clinging to the rope with one hand and keeping the gun hand free.

He was halfway up when, looking down, he saw the circle of light suddenly switched from the cliff to swing upward. Three figures tumbled out of the tunnel, hindered from free action in the narrow pass on the shifting rubble. A bullet whistled upward, just missing him as he kicked out from the rock. Thurston's cap came fluttering down, brushed his shoulder, and sailed to the bottom as Grahame fired. His bullet found a mark. Apparently it penetrated the Japanese at the collar bone and ranged through the length of his body. The man collapsed instantly under the smashing impact, and his fall thrust his fellows into confusion. The next second Grahame stood on the surface of the rock. The woman had been carried into the hull.

"Aboard!" cried Grahame. "We've roused a wasps' nest. Here they come!"

As they sprang up the ladder a score of figures appeared at the entrance to the ravine and opened fire from rifles while the great propellers whirred and the helicopter lifted. At the head of the gorge, more Japanese showed on a ledge high up the precipice and scattered in both directions, prepared to rake the *Ariel* as she reached the level.

"Gunners on deck!" shouted Grahame, leading the way. The rapid-firers were protected by three-sided shields of armor steel over which the gun servers pulled out a roofing of steel slats working on the principle of a roller top to a desk.

It was all over in a few seconds of suspense while a few well-aimed bullets penetrated the light hull, fortunately missing any vulnerable spots and others spattered on the metal deck. The propellers gripped the air; then, as the engines raced at top speed, the *Ariel* leaped upward. Two machine guns viciously sprayed the ledge as they shot by it, and in a moment they had topped the gorge and darted out of range, leaving a group of gasping, shattered figures prostrate on the shelf of rock.

As they soared they could see men running from every direction, springing up from the ground like ants, or, as Grahame had said, like wasps from a disturbed nest. Tiny spurts of flame marked the discharge of a hundred rifles, they could hear the faint rattle of the reports echoing among the gorges above the hum of the propellers while the *Ariel* darted here and there like a shuttle, disconcerting the aim of the infuriated Japanese, mounting swiftly up to five thousand feet, then speeding north.

The woman was lying on the floor of the hull, still unconscious. Her hands and wrists were almost those of a skeleton. Her cheeks were hollow, her throat thin from emaciation. But the gaunt, strained features were those of the once beautiful woman who had made the decoy appointment with Grahame in the Palace Hotel.

He knelt beside her, administering restoratives. For a while it seemed as if life had left her. Neither heart nor pulse beat was discernible. Grahame forced the clenched teeth apart while Thurston chafed her wrists, and a few drops of brandy trickled down her throat. Her eyelids fluttered, and Thurston felt a throb of vitality beneath his fingers. She opened her dark eyes for a moment. As they gazed into Grahame's face they filmed with fear and closed again. But she gulped down a little of the liquor, and a flicker of color came to the sunken, waxen cheeks.

They propped up her head and shoulders with pillows improvised from their coats, and Grahame poured some of the contents of a thermos bottle into an aluminum cup.

"Drink this soup," he said. "It will do you good. Don't be afraid. You are among friends." Then, as she refused to look up: "I know who you are, and I still say *friends*."

Her eyes opened, holding an almost animal gratitude in their brown depths. Grahame held the cup to her lips, supporting her against his knee, and she supped at the invigorating broth.

"Not too much at first," he said. "Now rest and don't talk. You're safe, and there's plenty of time."

"You're good," she murmured. "And you know who I am?"

Grahame nodded.

"I guessed it even before I found you at the bottom of the cleft."

"And you didn't leave me there." She tried to put his hand to her lips.

"You are not to talk," said Grahame, and laid her down again.

"Nearly starved, poor devil!" he said to Thurston as the *Ariel* sped through the awakening day. "Evidently she's at outs with Kirby. There's all the information we want, I imagine. Thanks to your tip."

In fifteen minutes a man came forward and saluted.

"She seems all right now, sir," he said. "I gave her more soup as you ordered, and she's sitting up."

The woman, a pitiful wreck of the fascinating creature who had made the breach between Irene Lancaster and Grahame, essayed a smile.

"There's only one way I can thank you," she said. "That's by trying to undo what I have done and telling you all I can. I wish I knew more, but he kept his secrets to himself.

"My name is Lucille l'Estrange," she went on. "I met him, Ogden Kirby, when he was at Harvard. I was playing in *The Pleasures of Folly*, and he got an introduction to me. He was different from other men I had met that way. He fascinated me. He was masterful, and there was a mystery about him. For a while he was very kind to me. He took me from the company." Her face flushed a little. "Most people would have called me his mistress. It was rather that he was my master. I never really knew him, but he knew me, and I was absolutely under his influence. I never knew who he really was, but I soon found out he was devoted to a secret mission. Sometimes he brought men to my apartments—Japanese mostly—and they talked over maps and papers sometimes until daylight. He never threatened me, but he knew my fear of him would keep his secrets. My fear *and my love*. He didn't reckon on that part of it, smart as he was, and when he killed my love"—her eyes flashed—"the hate that took its place was stronger than my fear.

"He took me to Japan and to Honolulu, and then to San Francisco. I was his stool pigeon. He used me to attract men he wanted to get acquainted with—not to make money out of them, he had plenty always—but to get information from. It was all political and big and secret. I know now what it was, of course, though even now I know nothing of his plans. But when the Japanese have conquered California he is to have his great reward.

"He hates you and he fears you, Mr. Grahame. He made me trick you by making the public think you were close friends with a woman who—who was disreputable and a drunkard. It was the first time he had ever made me do anything like that. I did it because I knew he was growing tired of me, and, like a fool—and a woman—I tried to hold him by making a slave of myself. I did not know there was another woman in the case.

"That is why he hates you—because of Miss Lancaster. He fears you because he thinks you are the chief obstacle to his success. But he hates you because he loves Miss Lancaster. And he used me—his cast-off love—to help him win her and belittle you.

"He did not deny it to me. He told me he was tired of me when I pleaded with him. Then when his sneers roused me to threaten him he took me to that place and kept me prisoner. I was kept in a dark cave guarded by Japanese. One of the brutes, Yamamato, tried to make love to me. When I spurned him he starved me. He said Ogden Kirby did not care whether I lived or died. He put me in another cave—the place is honeycombed with them—where there was a passage that led out to the crevice where you found me. I could look up at the sky and sometimes see a bird or two, but I couldn't climb the sides, and Yamamato taunted me. 'Look at the sky,' he would say. 'When you like to see it closer, let me know?' Then you came in the airship. It was like a god descending from heaven. I fainted."

Grahame nodded reassuringly.

"You're safe now," he said. "We'll look out for you."

"And you forgive me?"

"Surely. Don't cry." The woman, in the swift revulsion of her feelings, was sobbing hysterically. "Come," he said. "You can help me more."

She made a strong effort to regain composure.

"Did you see anything of any supplies back there in the caves. Or in the mine?"

"They took me in through the mine. I was carried in, bound, from the automobile, but I know a lot of heavy boxes were being stored when we arrived. And as they took me through the passages underground I noticed many more piled up in the different caves. There are a great many men there. More every day, for they come to look at me as if I was some strange beast. Yamamato would not let them touch me. He was in command."

"He isn't now," said Thurston. "Yamamato was the Japanese with Kirby the time we followed them to the Chrysanthemum Club, wasn't he? Butler at the ranch for General Lancaster's sister at Atascadero?"

"Yes," answered Grahame. "What of it?"

"He was the chap you plugged from shoulder to sole leather in the crevice. I fancy he's resigned from his duties by now."

"I should have liked to have killed the beast with my own hands," said the woman. "But I'll save my revenge for Ogden Kirby."

Her fingers worked convulsively, and her features were drawn in the snarl of an angry tigress. "That isn't all," she added. "Perhaps you will not forgive me when you know."

The *Ariel* was flying up the southern arm of San Francisco Bay. "We'll talk that over presently," said Grahame. "Mr. Thurston will see you comfortably lodged." The helicopter hovered above the aërodrome for its landing. "Thank you. And don't worry. Our scores are wiped out. I'll promise to take good care of Ogden Kirby."

"Take good care of Miss Lancaster, if you love her," warned the woman. "I do not know which Kirby wants most, her or the success of his ambitions. Both in one, I believe. And he is as ruthless as he is resolute and resourceful. Remember that, Mr. Grahame. Ogden Kirby is powerful and not easily thwarted. Keep a close watch on Miss Lancaster!"

V

THE FIRST BLOW FALLS

It was three o'clock the morning after the rescue of Lucille l'Estrange and the discovery of the Japanese supply base before the emergency committee dissolved their meeting. They had been in active session for seven hours, all the while in wireless communication with the various units of the defense plan from the entire coast. The reports came in unceasingly until after midnight, among them an occasional message from the helicopter that Grahame had assigned to duty at the Pinnacles, reporting no activity in that direction.

After the mass of reports had been sifted by the committee heads, the announcement was made by Grahame that the defense machine was ready to move. Every man was in instant touch with his superior, every item of armament was prepared for action. The motor-boat fleet was armed, fueled, and provisioned, the crews waiting on the word. So with the aëro flotilla, and with the mounted dynamite guns on the armored cars. At the power houses where the main depots for the wireless torpedoes were maintained at the seven most vulnerable points, everything was at the limit of preparedness.

After the executive session, General Lancaster, arrived that afternoon from Honolulu by transport, addressed the meeting. To some extent his speech cleared the atmosphere.

"I have been empowered by the state department," he said, "to inform the president of the emergency committee that his plans have been carefully examined. While it is not believed that affairs have reached a crisis that calls for such extreme measures, the department declares its appreciation of the patriotism and generosity of the members of this committee. The plan is generally approved, and I am empowered upon my own discretion, *subject to any hostile action*, to accept such portions, or the whole, of your plan and equipments as may seem to me advisable in coöperation with the senior officer of the Pacific Squadron, in the name of the United States government."

He paused for the sudden, eager expressions of satisfaction to subside.

"This I received in code while yet at sea," the general continued. "Also a radio message of general confirmation from Rear Admiral Freeman. I have been granted certain powers, one of which enables me to secure for the nation the services of Colonel Bruce Grahame under especial commission as my chief of advisory staff."

There were no cheers. The men of the emergency committee were not the kind to waste their emotions, but Bruce Graham rose and bowed silently in response to the thrill that ringed the long table in a bond of martial magnetism.

"These dispatches are, of course, secret to the public," went on the general.

"One other piece of information I may also disclose—that Great Britain has informed the state department through its ambassador that their terms of treaty with Japan do not call for active assistance unless their Oriental ally shall be in actual peril of disaster. The ambassador moreover intimated that Great Britain, aside from its blood bond and generally friendly relations with this country, would be inclined to consider any attempt at invasion in the face of the restriction laws of the United States as a warfare outside the pale of legitimacy and the rights of humanity, opening at least an opportunity for a lengthy debate before Great Britain reached a decision in favor of Japan—*if she ever arrived at any conclusion before the close of the war.*

"Moreover, in the event of any irregular act of hostility by Japan, such as might be offered by the Japanese reservists upon the coast, who would by such action register themselves as *francs-tireurs*, it is more than probable that Great Britain would consider such movement a pretext for their righteous withdrawal from the responsibility of treaty provisions.

"That means, gentlemen, that the Atlantic fleet is on its way to the Pacific Ocean. In point of fact, its voyage has never been interrupted, and it is now close to Cape Horn, the fastest vessels constituting an advance squadron steaming at top speed.

"It means, moreover, that with the withdrawal of apprehension from an attack upon the Atlantic coast or across the Canadian border, troops are now hastening to our aid as fast as special trains can haul them."

A mighty breath of relieved tension came from his listeners. If they could hold out against any immediate hostilities, they were sure of support that would at least reduce the odds.

A messenger entered with radio dispatches. He delivered all but one of these to Grahame, the other to the commissioner of police.

Grahame's face grew grave as he rapidly read the messages.

"The general purport of these from Portland, Seattle, Tacoma, and Los Angeles," he said, "is to the effect that the Japanese are believed to have entirely vacated these cities."

The police commissioner rose. "Here is mine from the central station: 'Japanese wearing chrysanthemums appeared in neighborhood Fillmore and Geary an hour ago. Since then many automobiles filled with Japanese have left city. Reported bound for county line, traveling southward, observing speed limits. Shall we arrest? Fear armed resistance.'"

Grahame spoke rapidly to General Lancaster, who nodded.

"Until internment orders come," he said, "we have no actual authority for arrest. It would place us in the position of commencing hostilities. I shall order an air squadron to follow the general movement and report any assembly. At the first display of arms the county authorities will act, backed by the military which now includes our organization. Now, gentlemen, let us take our posts. We are forearmed and forewarned."

Morning brought confirmation of the exodus of the Japanese from the cities. Their houses were vacant, their stores closed. The conditions of the exodus in California prevailed in modified degree in Oregon and Washington. There had been no display of arms. The Japanese had gathered where their countrymen held the leases of ranches in colonies of sometimes considerable size. These main rendezvous were in the vicinity of Fresno, principal city of the San Joaquin Valley, in the Santa Clara and Pajaro Valleys, on certain islands of the Sacramento River, and, in the south, in the Imperial Valley, close to the Mexican line and in touch with their colonies in Mexico. The news was ominous despite the fact that all the movements were, on the surface, pacific. Dotted over all three of the states were many smaller holdings, impossible to watch. No alarm had come from local ranchmen of American citizenship, but many of these small Japanese farms were far away from neighbors. It was impossible to predict from which quarter danger might threaten.

The aëro patrols were sent out to the sea limit and to cover the coast railroad, precious for the use of the mobile artillery. There had been many Japanese employed by the various railroad lines, but they had long ago been dismissed at the suggestion of President Sproule of the Southern Pacific, while the remaining employees were enrolled as guards in addition to their other duties. The power-line patrols were urged to greater watchfulness. Headed by nine helicopters, five hundred armed airships covered a sky strip from the Sierra to a fifty-mile limit from shore. Their wireless spread a net above the threatened community. All that could be done for watchfulness was accomplished. The minutemen of the Pacific counted the seconds for the call to arms.

The storm broke. At noon Oriental strategy had achieved a coup unprecedented in warfare—the segregation of perhaps the richest section of a powerful nation without the firing of a cartridge. It was a universal movement, decisive, complete. The news came through the aërial land patrols. All other means of communication were, one by one, broken. At General Lancaster's headquarters the situation was summed up in a series of catastrophes.

The big dam at Crystal Springs on the peninsula back of San Francisco had been blown up, presumably by long-established mines fired from a distance. The watchmen had seen no evidence of local action. The great pipes that ran beneath the southern arm of San Francisco Bay from the other source of the city's water supply in the Sunol Valley had been similarly destroyed. San Francisco was waterless. The power lines, despite the inevitable limits of air patrol, had been cut in many places.

Los Angeles was in the same predicament. The long aqueduct that supplied the city from the Owens Lake district had been blown up, all traffic stopped with the shutting off of the power.

Portland's water from Mount Hood was running to waste. So with Seattle and Tacoma, San Diego, Sacramento, and Fresno. The main water systems were ruined. With those cities directly in touch with rivers and natural freshwater sources the case was not so desperate as with Los Angeles and San Diego, cities set in a seaside desert, and with San Francisco, on a peninsula of sand, the Sacramento River, the nearest stream of importance, many miles away. These had the very lifeblood of their existence draining from them. Thirst and pestilence threatened, aside from minor evils.

The sudden loss of the electric power taken from the mountain waters held the land in the grip of paralysis. Even this was forgotten for the moment in the news of fresh disaster.

The snow sheds of the Southern Pacific were in furious conflagration in a dozen places. The tunnels of the Western Pacific had collapsed. The Santa Fe bridge across the Colorado River between Drennan and Parker was a wreck. Tracks and tunnels on the Los Angeles and Salt Lake and other overland connections were destroyed by the same invisible hands. The passes through the mountains were useless. The Southern Pacific Sunset route was closed by the annihilation of the bridge across the Colorado River at Yuma. There it was suspected that the Japanese had connived with the Indians of the reservation with whom they were known to be on friendly terms. In a sentence—California was cut off from the nation. The gateways for the ingress of the military were closed. Across the northern boundary at Grant's Pass in Oregon the bridges and tunnels had been put out of commission, all within a few hours. Blown-up spans across the Columbia River barred the passage of the Northern Pacific trains. The Pacific coast was no longer a part of the United States. It had been segregated by unseen blows. And, while none doubted the source of the outrage, yet none could point to the actual agents.

Within the separated territory one main artery was yet intact. The vigilance of the watch kept upon the Coast Line tracks since the inception of the emergency committee had preserved it from destruction. By day and night trackwalkers, their ranks augmented by private guards, had walked its ties and guarded the tunnels of the Santa Lucia division. The defensive operations were still intact. The big problem of keeping apart the interior forces and those of a costal landing was still capable of a desperate solution.

The afternoon brought fresh terrors, the greater for the meager details accompanying them. From Hawaii the wireless radiations bridged two thousand miles of ocean and told of the surrender of the fortress of Corregidor in the Philippines, where the United States still exercised a protectorate over their late possession. The cable from Guam had relayed the news to Honolulu and closed with the fateful message that "Unseen Japanese warships demand surrender by wireless." And, at sunset, while General Lancaster expressed his fears for the Hawaiian Island, where a hundred thousand Japanese held the vast majority, a last radiogram, half finished, told of a rising of armed Japanese, of massacres, of valiant fighting against frightful odds, of a bombardment by great guns far below the horizon whose range made the mortars at Diamond Head mere noisy popguns and—*silence.*

While the stunned populace were exhorted by the proclamations of the civic committees as to what actions for help and safety should be taken, General Lancaster, with Grahame, made their preliminary moves in the great chess game. The sea patrol sent in no news of an approaching fleet, the land patrol found no evidence of a gathering army.

"They will wait till night for any massing movements," said Grahame. "When our aëro fleet is least able to help us."

"That," said General Lancaster explosively, "is the hell of it all! We've got to wait. There's no place to strike definitely. I'm cooped up here with my men like a blind mule that feels the whip and don't know where to kick."

"We've got the Pinnacles base fairly bottled, anyway," said Grahame. "And once our eyes are opened we can fight."

"It's the suspense that's the deuce of it," said the veteran. "The whole reservation's on edge with it. I'm afraid to read a dispatch. What's this?"

An orderly saluted and withdrew. General Lancaster brushed flat the radiogram on the table, his tanned face blanched to putty color as he motioned to Grahame to read.

"My God, man!" he cried hoarsely. "My God!"

The news had come across the continent by Federal wireless. Grahame's hand trembled a little as he set down the paper.

> Atlantic fleet practically destroyed near Straits of Magellan by overpowering Japanese fleet assisted by many submarines from supposed hidden base near Tierra del Fuego. United States ships outmetaled, outmanned, and outfought. Lack of range and speed cause of disaster.

VI

THE BLUE-EYED JAPANESE

Telephone communication between San Francisco and its outlying suburbs had been destroyed, but on the evening of the day which had chronicled so many crashing disasters, swift private cars racing cityward brought news of the destruction and looting of the palatial homes of W.H. Crocker and other millionaire residents of Burlingame. Word was also brought in of the kidnapping of the mayor of San Francisco. A prime member of the civic committee, he had hurried to his home in one of the city's residential parks, to assure himself of the safety of his family, at the earliest moment, only to be trapped. Details were confused, but confirmed by a note signed: *"Ogden Kirby—in command Japanese Reservist Army Corps"* and left upon the table of the official's library. It stated briefly that the person of the mayor had been apprehended as "hostage for San Francisco in coöperation with similar captures in other cities, the dispositions of such persons to be a matter for later adjustment."

Rumors, some of them too soon established as to their truth, flew far and fast. The governor of the State of Oregon was a prisoner. Every city of size had lost some important man, generally of financial or political prominence, and the abductions showed skillfully carried-out plans. In many cases Japanese were known to have been previously employed as house servants.

In the midst of these alarms, no less startling because of local interest, a summons came to Grahame from General Lancaster. He found the commander in chief awaiting him with all the military rigor of his bearing broken down, his face seamed with suffering.

"What is it, sir?" asked Grahame.

The general's voice was hoarse with emotion as he held out a letter.

"Irene, my boy," he gasped. "I supposed she was at Del Monte. Her aunt was ill, and she sent me a wireless that she would not meet me at San Francisco when I landed. This—I only just opened it, I've had no time for personal affairs—says that Mrs. Houston wanted to go home to the ranch. She had rheumatism and thought the warm springs would help her. I can't get word through. They've got Jap servants there—they've kidnapped the mayor and—"

Grahame's mind outstripped the general's utterance. Lucille l'Estrange's warning rang in his brain. As with the general, the swift sequence of public crises had placed personal matters in the background. He had not dreamed of Irene being in jeopardy.

"I'll start in the *Ariel* at once, sir," he said. "I've held her for emergencies, thank God!"

"We can't both go, Bruce," said the general. "My first duty is here. You'll go—"

He stopped. A glance at Grahame's set face assured him that all that was humanly possible would be done.

"There may be no cause for our alarm," said Grahame, "but I'll bring both of them back if they are still there if I have to shanghai them."

The laugh he forced with the words was a grim one. Within the minute he was in his car speeding for Tanforan.

It was a two-hundred-mile flight to his destination. At Tanforan the track inclosure was swathed in fog, the lights of the aërodrome invisible from the outer fence. But the waiting crew obeyed his crisp orders without comment. The *Ariel*, her self-adjusting carburetors unaffected by the moisture, mounted through the swirling gray wreaths and, at her flight level of two thousand feet, sailed beneath a jeweled sky above a shifting sea of mist covering the ground like a quilt of cotton wool.

Above the fog the breeze that had driven it in from the sea blew briskly, but neither wind nor fog had present power over the *Ariel*. Aneroid barometer, compass, chart, and established speed set their course as truly as the movement of parallel rulers across the map. The only trouble lay in the discovery of their landing place. The Rancho del Nido was set in a cup of the hills a little over twenty miles from the coast, and Grahame did not think it probable that the fog would reach that far inland. But never before had he seen such a wide expanse of condensation. A waning moon, slowly sinking toward the surface of the sea of vapor, silvered its rolling billows with opalescent radiance. He ordered the *Ariel* lifted to the height of nearly a mile, and saw the great bank of fog stretching far to the north and south, its landward border clearly marked, but the seaward verge lost where it blended into indivisibility with sea or sky. Grahame wondered how his patrols were faring as he marveled at the immensity of what was to be known as the "Great Fog of 1920" and play so important a part in the fortunes of California and the Pacific coast.

The ranch lay in a rolling country between two parallel spurs of the Coast Range. The western ridge fought valiantly against the fog that had surmounted its crests and was creeping on across the valley, broken by the lesser hills. The figures on the dial board, checking up with the revolutions of the driving and traction propellers fore and aft, registered the required mileage that Grahame checked off with ruler and dividers on his chart. The helicopter hovered, dropping steadily while Grahame anxiously scanned the hills for familiar landmarks. The insidious fog was tentatively feeling its way in the immediate vicinity of the ranch house. Slowly it flowed on, intangible, but irresistible, hugging close to the earth in its advance. The low hills were dotted with live oaks, and one by one the trees in the line of advance were gripped about the trunks and wrapped silently in the woolly vapor.

At five hundred feet Grahame caught the dull gleam of a small lake. The moon had sunk, and it dimly mirrored a sky in which now the stars were obscured by invisible, high-flying streamers of mist blown from the main fog bank.

"Ten minutes more and we'd never have found the ranch," said Grahame, as they sank gently to the surface of the water, the boat hull resting easily as, with the after propeller at quarter speed, they glided to the little wharf.

He left half of his crew on guard and, with eight men, ran across a hilltop to the rancheria. Already the trees that surrounded it were being shrouded in the mist. There were no lights burning, and Grahame's fears mounted. Their powerful electric torches lit the way as they mounted the veranda and searched the apparently deserted house.

In the long drawing-room that gave upon the inner patio, the rays disclosed a figure bound to a wicker lounging chair. The face was covered with a cloth that served as a gag, above which a tumbled mass of gray hair showed.

Springing forward, Grahame freed the indignant figure of Irene's aunt, Mrs. Houston. For the first moment as they unbound the ropes that held her she made only inarticulate sounds of concentrated rage. Then she found her voice in sudden protest.

"Ouch! Be careful, young man!" she admonished. "That's my rheumatic leg. Bruce Grahame, a nice time you've been coming. You'll find an oil lamp in the kitchen. The electricity's cut off, like the telephone. And bring me some water. I'm choking."

Grahame waved in the direction of the kitchen, and two men hurried off, returning, the one with the lamp, the other with water. Meantime four men had been dispatched to sentry duty. One of them reported that the house was surrounded by fog. Grahame nodded curtly. He had already seen its ghostly approach in the patio garden through the long windows where the blinds were still undrawn.

"Unless you know which way they went, Mrs. Houston," he said, "there's little chance of tracing them in this mist."

"You should have come sooner," snapped the lady, her face twitching with pain as she essayed to rise. Grahame gave her his arm, but she finally sank back amid the pillows.

"I broke my stick over one of their thick heads," she said. "It dropped him, but he evened matters by thrusting that rag in my mouth. Pah!"

"What happened?" asked Grahame.

"Happened? Ogden Kirby has carried off Irene to make her the Queen of New Nippon! I'm not demented," she said, in answer to Grahame's look. "I heard that California was captured. Is that true?"

"Not yet. But Irene—"

"Your anxiety is a bit late to be practical. Don't fluster me. I'm an old woman and a sick one, and I've been upset. Literally," she added, with a wry smile. "It happened about dusk. First we tried to get San Francisco on the phone to get in touch with the general. There was no connection, but we paid no attention to that.

"Tanaka and Iwagami served dinner. It was my fault we kept them, though Irene agreed with me they were faithful. After Yamamato left us they told us he was a bad man, but they were different. And I believed them. They said the Japanese did not want war, and I believed that, like the superannuated fool I am. In the middle of dinner we heard a sound of feet marching outside, and I sent Tanaka to see what it was. He said it was men driving cattle, and I believed that, too. A machine stopped outside. Tanaka went out again. Some one was making a speech in Japanese gibberish, and there was a big cheering of their heathen shout, *Banzai*. Then *he* came in with Tanaka—Kirby, I mean. He had an air like the conqueror of the world. He was alone, but a hundred or more Japanese armed with rifles had swarmed into the patio and stood on the veranda, looking in. Some of the doors were open. They looked like a flock of monkeys with their sly black eyes and quick gestures.

" 'What does this outrage mean?' I asked. I had never liked that man. He took no notice of me, but he threw an order at the men on the veranda, and they backed off. I suppose the flowers are ruined— Well, he spoke to Irene, his eyes glowing like blue lamps. 'I told you I was no traitor,' he said. 'The day has come to prove it, as I said I would.'

"Then the unspeakable blackguard told his story that he took so much pride in. He is half Japanese. 'My father lied to my mother,' he said, 'but I am true to her and the country of my birth.' He is the son of a naval officer and his tea-garden inamorata. He came to America as a spy—he thought it the most honorable of callings. He was at one of the big colleges, and he has had military training in Europe—he is the commander of the Japanese-Californian forces. He says California is to be the New Nippon, and for the work he has done he is to be made governor or shogun or whatever they call it.

" 'There is no height to which I may not rise,' he said. 'I have given Dai Nippon the desire of her heart.' And then, the half-bred, yellow dog, he had the audacity to offer to marry Irene, to make her the mistress of New Nippon.

"I jumped up despite my rheumatism, but those two ungrateful curs, Tanaka and Iwagami, held me back.

"And Irene?" asked Grahame hoarsely.

Mrs. Houston, her eyes flashing, a crimson flag in each cheek, laughed at the recollection.

"She slapped him across the face. It sounded like the pistol shot it should have been. 'How dare you!' she said, and slapped him the second time.

"I shouted 'bravo!' and he gave me the first hint he had shown of my presence. He gave an order, and they bound me where you found me and gagged me. I was dumb and helpless, but I could hear.

" 'Since you will not come with me willingly,' he said, 'I am going to take you along and give you the chance to change your mind. I'm going to own you, my beauty!' he cried, 'if all the powers of Shinto stand between. And if you will not share the fate I offer you, at least I can avenge my mother.' "

Grahame's teeth gritted. "If he is alive when I find him," he said, "I think I can make him sufficiently regret that."

"Irene screamed once as they took her away. I couldn't see anything. I don't know where they have taken her. I'm a wretched, broken-down old woman."

Mrs. Houston collapsed amid her cushions, her spirit broken for the time, helplessly hysterical. Grahame tried to calm her. "We'll take you to San Francisco in the *Ariel*," he said. "I can't leave you here—"

A man entered. It was the wireless operator of the *Ariel*.

"Message from headquarters, sir," he said. "General Lancaster states that armed Japanese are reported ascending the San Joaquin River in launches. He asks you to return immediately to your duty, regardless of circumstances. Those were his exact words, sir," he added, as Grahame bent an earnest gaze upon him.

"To return to my duty," repeated Grahame slowly. He knew how necessary his presence was. Yet Irene— If General Lancaster could set duty above fatherhood, then surely he could place it above the desire of his heart. He turned to the man, snapping out the syllables of his order:

"Get in touch with the helicopter *Polaris*. Tell them to make every effort to locate and prevent any outward movement of supplies from the Pinnacles. We go to San Francisco."

"The fog, sir—"

"Damn the fog, sir! Hurry!"

The blow had fallen! The Pacific coast was at the mercy of the Japanese. How Grahame and his associates met the emergency will be told you in the next number of PEOPLE'S.

The Peril of the Pacific

by J. Allan Dunn

Part Four: The Struggle

Synopsis of Preceding Installments

Bruce Grahame, an expert in aëronautics, and a believer in preparedness, especially against a suspected Japanese invasion, is in love with Irene Lancaster, daughter of General Lancaster, chief of the Pacific division of the United States army, located at the Presidio, San Francisco. As the country at large refuses to be aroused over the Japanese peril, Grahame proposes to try and unite all the aviation clubs of the Pacific coast into an aërial militia. To prove his assertion that the Pacific coast Japanese, most of them veterans of the war with Russia, are drilling secretly at night, Grahame takes General Lancaster, his daughter, and Ogden Kirby, whom he suspects of a connection with the Japanese government, in his triplane, the *Aërolite*, to a valley in the Coast Range. There they find a large company of Japanese drilling on the open plain, in the moonlight. The next day Grahame and his friend, Fred Thurston, an official of the telephone company, who is in complete accord with Grahame's views, happened to see Kirby in an automobile with a couple of Japanese, and they follow. They trail them to a Japanese club, where are gathered several distinguished Oriental statesmen, in consultation over an enlargement of an aëro photo map of San Francisco Bay. Grahame steps into a trap that has been set for him by keeping an appointment with a woman who claims to have incriminating information against Kirby. In order to talk with her he meets her in the Palm Room of the Palace Hotel, where she and Grahame become the cynosure of all eyes when she becomes suddenly and very ostentatiously inebriated. Japan delivers an ultimatum to Washington, the context of which is: "Free Entry or Forcible!" practically threatening war unless Japanese immigrants were given the same right of entrance as other immigrants. In default of immediate protection and assistance from Washington the Emergency Association of the Pacific coast meets, presided over by Bruce Grahame. Grahame outlines plans for defense. Kirby steals the plans from Grahame's safe, but is caught by Grahame after a long motor-boat chase in which Kirby escapes, but the papers are recovered. By means of a dictograph Grahame and Thurston overhear the Japanese plans at the Chrysanthemum Club. Suddenly the Panama Canal is blocked by an explosion, leaving the Atlantic fleet on the wrong side of the continent. The factory where Grahame's helicopters are being built is blown up in a night aëroplane raid. The Japanese withdraw from the big cities and gather at the ranches held by their countrymen. Suddenly the Pacific coast is segregated from the rest of the United States by the destruction of bridges, tunnels, railroads, telegraph, telephone, light and water supply. The Atlantic fleet, on its way to the Pacific coast, is destroyed near the Straits of Magellan by an overpowering Japanese fleet. The Mayor of San Francisco and Irene Lancaster are kidnapped.

I

THROUGH THE FOG

THE ADVENT OF THE FOG, CRAWLING STEADILY INLAND, capturing seaward spur after spur of the coast range, halted only by the main ridge that formed the western border of the San Joaquin Valley, seemed as uncanny as its limits were unusual. It extended from far below San Diego, northward, unrolling a sluggish veil averaging fifty miles in breadth, half on sea, half on land. It seemed as if born of the Kiroshiwo, the black current of Japan. Nature itself for the moment appeared in sympathy with the Oriental invasion.

San Francisco Bay was shrouded in a pall that mocked the efforts of the lighthouses and the bell buoys swinging on the tide. Mare Island and its navy yard were smothered. Far up past Benicia Straits, and the delta of the Sacramento and San Joaquin Rivers, the ghostly fingers of the fog obliterated channels, sloughs, and marshes.

At sea, the night detail of the aërial patrol, keeping flying sentry go beyond its outer edge, was cut off from the shore. Inland, the air flotilla was practically useless, save back of the main lift of the coast range in the San Joaquin and Sacramento Valleys, and southward, in the Imperial Valley, close to the Mexican border. The eyes of the defense were blindfolded. Like submarines, their night work was always curbed by darkness, and wherever the fog ranged, they were literally *hors de combat*.

Through the night, under cover of the mist, the Japanese reservists

were feeling their way. Above a great relief map of California, compiled
from the surveys of the hydrographic office, Grahame, General Lancaster,
and Admiral Freeman bent in anxious consultation. Roads, railroads, and
waterways were marked in various colors. Power stations, garages, supply
depots, with a concise layout of the villages, towns, cities, and important
private holdings, were all indicated.

"It seems evident, then," summed up Grahame, "that the main desire of
the enemy is to effect a junction of forces, and, by stealth or force, entrench
themselves in a position to cover a landing of troops from transports. From
the reports, they have left the northern side of the Sacramento River, and are
now ascending the San Joaquin. We know there are considerable bodies of
them in the San Joaquin Valley and also in the lower Santa Clara and Pajaro
Valleys. The main ridge of the coast range"—he ran his forefinger along the
raised surface of the map—"forms the western border of the San Joaquin
Valley. This ridge breaks down to lesser hills at this fork, in which is Mount
Hamilton. From there to the Sacramento, with the exception of Mount
Diablo's solitary rise, there is a break. The San Joaquin River bends about
the comparative levels of Contra Costa County. If the men now proceeding
up the San Joaquin were to debark near Stockton, they would cross country
naturally by Byron Hot Springs, Livermore, and Pleasanton, westward.
The Fresno contingent would join them in the neighborhood of Livermore.
From Niles they would proceed south, via Irvington, Milpitas, and San Jose,
down the Santa Clara Valley, augmented by forces in that neighborhood,
and supported by the supply trains from the Pinnacles via Tres Pinos and
Hollister. Thence their way lies through the gap in this seaward spur at Pajaro,
where still more men will await them. A march through Watsonville leads
them to the sea at Monterey Bay. Whether their objective will be Monterey
or Santa Cruz is in doubt. The former has the better landing, but the vicinity
of the Monterey Presidio inclines me to believe they will choose Santa Cruz.
All this is based, of course, upon my theory that Monterey Bay is the logical
landing place of the troops from their transports."

"In which we concur," said Admiral Freeman. "San Francisco harbor
would offer too much resistance from artillery and mine defense. I think your
reasoning is sound, Colonel Grahame. If this infernal fog lasts, it will not
only serve to cloak their movements, but hamper ours. I have no intention of
having my force, such as it is, bottled up in the bay. The first move, general,
is up to you. Colonel Grahame and myself, by sea and sky, are for the present
mist-bound."

General Lancaster paced up and down the big room, his hands clasped
behind him, his brows knitted. Then he halted, turned to a blackboard, and
rapidly chalked the salient features of Grahame's theory.

"They have apparently some twenty thousand men all told," he said.

"Roughly, five thousand each in the four divisions of the Sacramento, San Joaquin, Santa Clara, and Pajaro Valleys. We have not a tenth of that number. We don't know their equipment. With the exception of our field guns, we will assume their equality with ourselves. Without doubt they are attempting a night march under cover of the fog. It delays their progress, but they have time, with motor transit, to travel most of the distance before the sun can dissipate this fog, which will not be before ten o'clock at the earliest.

"From what meager information is at hand, they are commandeering motor cars right and left. I dare not split my forces, save as they are now divided at San Francisco and Monterey presidios. The Monterey troops must handle the Pajaro situation. I propose to allow the enemy to conjoin their forces from the San Joaquin, Sacramento, and Santa Clara Valleys. I will send my men from the presidio here by special train, to advance slowly southward, my endeavor being to come in contact with the enemy at some point south of San Jose, and, if possible, deliver a smashing blow.

"The fog—" He lifted his arms in a gesture of resignation. "It all depends upon the fog, gentlemen. It may prove friend or enemy. It has robbed us of the aid of the air flotilla for the present. With them in action there would be little to fear. As it is, we are literally fighting in the dark against big odds. If the fog lifts at the right time, we can scatter them like sheep with Colonel Grahame's bomb-dropping brigade. If not—we must do the best we can. And so, gentlemen," he ended, stretching a hand to his colleagues, "in God we trust!"

Subsequent events soon proved the correctness of the theory promulgated by Grahame and his associates. A fleet of launches, gunwales low with their loads of Japanese, had literally felt their way up the San Joaquin River, powerful searchlights keeping them out of trouble in slow but steady progress. Once landed, they pursued the same tactics as their other contingents. From every town, village, ranch house, and resort that harbored motor cars, they impressed them into service, showing an absolute knowledge of the whereabouts of automobiles that proved the effectiveness of a long-established spy system. And there were no lack of drivers, expert mechanics who had no trouble about the various types of cars secured. Northward from the heart of the mist-clear San Joaquin Valley they sped swiftly past indignant citizens, powerless to do anything but protest, and, swinging by Livermore, disappeared in the fog belt.

Frightened farmers and villagers vaguely saw the great procession of motor cars moving through the mists, with headlights twisted so that ahead and on either side the roadways were faintly but sufficiently illuminated by the rays. Word of the hostile progress filtered in gradually to General Lancaster's headquarters, and was relayed to the slowly moving special train, and there sifted down to some vaguely definite idea of the situation.

Logic was at the base of Grahame's theory. The Japanese must inevitably land an army. The reservists would be most useful in covering that landing and give the fleet opportunity for demonstration elsewhere. If they could wipe out the United States military force during the operation, so much the better. The bulk of the reservists centered naturally in a neighborhood comparatively close both to Monterey Bay and San Francisco. A success at the first place could be swiftly followed up by a change of base to the second.

That the date was definitely set seemed certain from the news elsewhere on the coast and the concerted exodus from the cities. But Ogden Kirby was playing in luck. He had most to fear from the airships, and they were idle. At the Pinnacles, where Grahame hoped to block the exit of munitions, observation was now impossible, aside from offensive.

In a private steel car of the last section of the special troop train, that, split into four divisions, was moving slowly down to striking distance, Grahame and General Lancaster tried to piece together the puzzle of the reports that came constantly through the wireless attached to the car. Far to the south the Japanese had crossed the Mexican border. What that presaged they hardly dared to think. Resistance from the insignificant number of regulars and the available militia might save Los Angeles and San Diego, if attacked, but the obvious method of conquest of those cities was from the sea, a project that could be carried out almost at will by the superior numbers of the Japanese fleet. That problem was left for the time to Admiral Freeman.

It was five o'clock in the morning, the land still impenetrably swathed in the secretive cloak of fog, when the military special crawled into San Jose, forty-seven miles south of San Francisco. The men were in armored cars, built in the yards of the Southern Pacific, some of them constructed from open trucks and holding machine and field guns. Ammunition was plentifully supplied.

From San Jose, southward, every furlong held the peril of a sudden flanking attack from the cover of the fog, and the car wheels turned slowly. Pilot engines felt out the way, ready to hoot a warning and return at full speed on the first hint of alarm. Every man was on the qui vive born of the desperate situation. Back of the regulars came another train, bearing the militia, all too few and ignorant of actual warfare.

Out of the jumble of messages, Grahame and the general reached a fairly definite belief that the Sacramento and San Joaquin battalions of the enemy had joined issue and were proceeding southward, some few miles ahead. Whether they had succeeded in making a junction with the main body of Santa Clara Valley reservists or their ammunition trains from the Pinnacles was doubtful. Such frightened observers as they got in touch with had only been able to guess at the numbers and character of the movements they barely sensed through the dense mist.

"They are probably well supplied, in any event," said Grahame. "They have held leases on the delta islands for years, and have had every opportunity for burying stores of arms against to-night."

General Lancaster assented moodily. In both their minds, sternly set to the task in hand, subconscious reaction occasionally forced the recollection of the plight of Irene Lancaster, alleviated only by the probability that Kirby, in the stress of his command, had placed her in some remote spot, and that so far no harm had come to her. But the uncertainty of her fate was a hidden spur to the father and the lover, unnecessary as such urge was to their efforts.

"It's a question," said the general, "whether they will ambuscade us or press on until they get through to the coast. They probably feel they can afford to despise us under these circumstances. Whoever dreamed of such conditions for a fight, groping through this damnable fog?"

"With their superior numbers it may be a blessing in disguise," said Grahame. "If it lifts, and we can get them massed, I can bring up six helicopters and a hundred biplanes, inside of an hour. Kirby must have a general idea of our power in that direction. That is why I think he'll keep straight through to the coast without offering a fight, hoping to get entrenched. The naval squadrons, he figures, will make diversions enough elsewhere to keep our air fleet busy. The thing I'm most afraid of is that they'll destroy the track or try to blow up culverts as we cross them."

As mile after mile was covered, the conviction grew that the enemy's aim was to press on to the coast, if possible, without a fight. Apparently they had some definite schedule upon which to perform their work as a covering party. The main road now closely paralleled the rails, and, unless the Japanese were making much faster progress than the trains, some evidence of them was momentarily to be expected. The tension of this weird warfare with an unseen foe became almost unbearable. At way stations, huddled groups of citizens told of the passing of the motor-borne host only an hour before. Still no word came from the pilot engines.

At Coyote, sixteen miles farther on, reached at seven o'clock, the land, still in the swirl of vapor, showing no appreciable sign of day, a radiogram told briefly that scouts from the Monterey presidio had located the Pajaro contingent of the enemy at Watsonville Junction, close to the coast, and midway between Monterey and Santa Cruz. There had been a clash with the Japanese outposts, and the American forces were now entrained and moving on Watsonville Junction to engage.

Two hours later, at Morgan Hill, the fog seemed less dense. It held color now, a gray monotony of opaque vapor from the daylight that strove to penetrate it, but there was no sign of the sun.

"We've got to catch them before they get through the gap," said Grahame.

"We'd better close up the divisions and get in nearer touch with the pilots."

"It's risky—if you can increase a hazard like this," said the general. "Best thing to do, though." And he gave the orders.

At ten o'clock they were approaching Gilroy, eighty-one miles south of San Francisco. Grahame hurried in from the rear platform of the car. Beads of mist clung all about him, jeweled in the electric lights. His face bore a look of relief.

"The fog's shredding, sir," he reported. "It's lightening toward where the sun ought to be."

General Lancaster hurried to the platform. The mist was in motion from some impulse of wind or sun, or both.

"The air fleet's been in touch with us all through the trip," said Grahame, with a ring of hopefulness in his voice. "If we can only get into action—"

The shriek of a locomotive, followed instantly by a score of others, broke through the heavy air, coming rapidly nearer.

"By God, sir, we're in touch with them at last!" cried the general. "They're afraid the fog will lift too soon for them. Come on, Grahame."

"I'm going to stay here, general, if that's a real alarm."

General Lancaster whirled and looked at his advisory aid with his eyes blazing.

"What do you mean?" he challenged sternly. "You want to stay here?"

Grahame's returned gaze was level and steady.

"The air fleet will follow the railroad as soon as they can see anything, sir," he answered. "My flagship, the *Ariel*, will pick me up on signal. I can do more good in the air than on the ground."

"I beg your pardon, my boy. For the moment I—" Grahame bridged the broken sentence with a handclasp.

"If you can hold them for an hour, general," he said, "I'll drop in on them in a way they won't fancy. It's clearing every second."

The fighting face of the old soldier lightened with a grim smile.

"An hour!" he said. "I'll hold them till hell freezes and they're sliding on the ice."

II

THE BATTLE OF GILROY

The screaming of the engine's whistles ceased, and the sputter of desultory firing ahead took its place. The train slowed down, and the sections closed up. The fog was appreciably less dense. Long lines of abandoned automobiles, some of their lights still burning, could be dimly distinguished on the road to the right of the track. Beyond them the faint shapes of low hills formed in the mist. To the left lay flat fields of sugar beets, with Pajaro Creek, bordered by trees, a quarter of a mile away, still hidden in the fog.

Grahame, working his way to the end of the militia train, ordered held in reserve, heard a burst of firing, the volleys of rifles, and then the rattle of machine guns. The first section was engaged.

The commanding officer of the militia grasped him by the arm.

"What's the idea, Mr.—Colonel Grahame? Are we going to make a stand? The odds must be frightful."

"They'd be greater if we retreated. It's one thing or the other."

The noise of guns fired in earnest had brought home the danger of the issue to all the militiamen, young men from the cities most of them, many of whom had never even pressed trigger. The gravity of it all sat upon their countenances and showed in their silence as they fingered nervously at cartridges and weapons, resolved to do their best, and realizing, in a moment, all their unpreparedness. Under the electric globes their faces looked ghastly white but determined. Their women were behind them, in San Jose and San Francisco. The leaven of patriotism was spreading through them.

"Very well, colonel," said the officer. "We'll do the best we can. We're in reserve at present."

Both men saluted, and Grahame passed on, climbing to the roof of the last car.

Ahead of him, flashes of light showed lazily. The roar of light-calibered artillery was incessant, echoing from the near-by hills. The armored cars had passed beyond Gilroy, to the small depot at Miller. He could just make out the buildings. The next station, at Sargent, was but three miles away. About two-thirds of the distance the wagon road crossed the tracks close to the buildings of the Sargent ranch. There was a fairly steep slope alternately to right and left before and beyond the crossing. He knew the country well. Back of the ranch, low hills mounted, covered with brush.

About him the fog swirled like a tide, from which objects gradually emerged, the railroad fence first, then the road parked with automobiles of every description, then uncertain shapes of cattle gazing wonderingly toward the firing, that steadily increased in fury.

The trees by Pajaro Creek began to loom up. Above them a pallid suggestion of a glow was hinted at rather than revealed in the sky.

"An hour will do," muttered Grahame, as he swung down to the track and hastened back over the ties. The railroad curved about the shoulder of a hill, and the sound of firing was deadened. At the first outbuilding he stopped, leaped the fence, and investigated. It was a barn half full of hay. Some of this he loosened, and then applied a match. In five minutes the interior was well alight, and Grahame retreated to the fence, where he watched the development of his appointed signal to the *Ariel*.

The sun had strengthened to a golden shield that drove against the flying mist. The landscape cleared like scenery gradually revealed behind up-drawn curtains of gauze. The distant sputter of firing kept up as Grahame anxiously scanned the lightening sky above him. For the moment he was inactive, and the personal problem for which he had found no solution came up once more to vex him.

If Ogden Kirby was killed, he took the secret of Irene Lancaster's hiding place with him. Somehow he had to be taken prisoner and then forced to talk. It was not an easy task.

At the front, General Lancaster was hard beset. The armored train was between two fires. A veritable hail of bullets beat against them from both sides of the track, and told of the host of their enemies. Had he deemed it expedient, a descent from the protection of the cars would have been disastrous. If the Japanese had possessed field guns of even moderate caliber, the fate of the train would have been settled within five minutes of their getting the range.

He was fighting men skilled in modern warfare. As the fog first lifted, there were no visible signs of the enemy. But from the hills the bullets poured down at a dangerous tangent, while from the creek others came thickly as swarming bees.

The shells that he replied with, spent their explosions with little effect against an infantry widely scattered over a long line, firing at will with apparently unlimited supplies of ammunition. The armor of the cars was pitted, and the impact of the high-powered bullets from the unseen enemy sounded a distinct note above their own firing.

Presently they could see hundreds of figures advancing individually by short rushes through the beet fields, coming on in the perfection of open-order warfare. In the open gondola cars, with the field and machine guns, men were falling rapidly from the aim of marksmen hidden in the brush on the hills, coming closer with every clip of cartridges discharged. The hundreds of creeping foes grew to thousands. The rushes were automatically timed and precisely executed, each gain covered by a tornado of bullets. On the nearer slopes, machine guns were coming into action. The engines were perforated and rendered useless. Inside the cars, foul with the powder gases, the men dripped with sweat as they fired their overheated weapons. The gun crews were decimated, halved, quartered. The militia's attempted advance was stopped by the destruction of the engines, and the two trains were isolated.

Against the armed hordes that relentlessly closed in, the united fire of the American troops seemed as futile as garden hose against a prairie fire. Sheer force of numbers must inevitably overwhelm them. Once let enough men get within hand throw, and a few well-tossed sticks of dynamite would utterly wreck the cars and compel their defenders to a wild sortie, a stand, a few scattering rallies, and then—annihilation!

There were gaps in the fog now, high patches of blue amid the gray that the general watched anxiously. Grahame had asked for an hour. Three-quarters of it were gone, and the end could already be reckoned by minutes.

There was an explosion in the forward car. A too well-sped bullet had reached an ammunition box. The interior was a silent shambles, filled with fragments of humanity.

Suddenly, flying low, lost in vapor one moment, a swift speck against the open sky the next, appeared a helicopter. It swung above the hills, weaving back and forth, a thousand feet up, pouring death from down-pointed guns on its deck, hovering for a moment, regardless of the hasty upfiring from the brush, to vomit bombs from the tubes in the bottom of its hull. Explosion after explosion followed their contact with the earth. Fires sprang up in the scrub, following the clouds that marked the miniature craters of the bursting missiles. From staffs on its deck flared the Stars and Stripes and the ensign of the aërial navy.

From all quarters, like vultures gathering to a feast, came the air fleet. The *Polaris*, from the Pinnacles, was the next helicopter to appear. Within ten minutes four more had arrived, and soon a hundred biplanes soared above the panic-stricken Japanese, ringing in a field of death which they literally sowed with missiles. The moist earth spurted under them as the bombs detonated, and the biplanes sailed in wheeling squadrons back and forth above the huddle of men desperately seeking safety, their weapons tossed aside. The helicopters formed an outer circle, from which there was no escape. The soldiers in the train ceased firing. Japanese gathered in clusters, their arms up-thrust in token of surrender. Resistance was ridiculous against these bolts from the blue. Dead men, singly, in groups, shattered many of them out of the semblance of manhood, lay thick as stones on a New England hillside. The battle of Gilroy was ended.

At a signal from the *Ariel*, two of the helicopters darted westward over the hills, followed by three squadrons of biplanes, twenty-five machines in each, rushing to the help of the American forces at Watsonville. The remainder patrolled the sky, literally herding the survivors into two great groups of beaten, dispirited Japanese, speedily surrounded by the regulars and militia that issued from the trains.

The *Ariel* dropped lower, skimming the hills, descending close to the flats in a constantly narrowing circle, seeking for Ogden Kirby. Suddenly it rose and fled south. Along the road toward Hollister a car was racing at the full drive of twelve cylinders, spurning the dust at almost a hundred miles an hour, rocking, as it went, with desperate speed, in the hope of reaching the shelter of the underground maze of the Pinnacles.

Fast as it sped, the *Ariel* followed faster, its inexorable shadow gliding along the road, closer and closer to the car. At Tres Pinos, it overhauled it. Little puffs of smoke showed from the car where Kirby, in the tonneau, fired uselessly at the pursuer from his swaying seat. Heading the car, the *Ariel* adjusted speed to that of the motor. A bomb dropped and blew a pit by the side of the road. It was obvious that the flying machine could drop one in the car itself at the will of the men at the tubes.

The driver threw off his power and set the brakes. Kirby, raging with impotence, shot him through the head as the car stopped. The *Ariel* settled in the soft dust of the road ahead, and Grahame appeared on deck as the whirring propellers ceased their motion and two men, with rifles trained upon the prisoner, stepped out of the hull.

"Don't move," warned one of them, "or I'll shoot."

Kirby grinned. He knew his value living far offset any possibility of his being killed. Neither was he ready to die. Defeated himself, he was still confident that the ultimate victory would lie with the Japanese. He suffered himself to be bound and led into the body of the helicopter.

"Fortune of war," he said, as he faced Grahame. "If the fog hadn't broken—" He shrugged his shoulders. "What are you going to do with me?" he demanded.

Grahame looked at him coldly.

"I am going to turn you over to General Lancaster. He will know how to deal with you while I go to end matters at Watsonville."

"General Lancaster?" repeated Kirby. "He is an old man, and should be a wise one. Perhaps," he added meaningly, "I shall be able to come to terms with the father of Miss Lancaster."

III

FATHER—AND GENERAL

General Lancaster made the ranch house at the railroad crossing close to Sargent his headquarters. The building was a modern one, and in the office library of its owner the general established his court. By the approved rules of warfare he would have been justified in taking all his prisoners who had fought without regular uniform, without flag, or apparent authorization, and lining them up before firing squads. This he was loath to do. Their losses in dead and wounded already amounted to nearly half their number under the massacre of the air-fleet bombardment. The supplies captured revealed that their rifles were modern and of uniform manufacture. Much of their ammunition had been exploded by the *Polaris* on the trip from the Pinnacles. What was left, with the guns, was welcome, but the problem of handling ten thousand prisoners was a serious one, that called for a speedy settlement. While General Lancaster debated the question with his staff, Grahame arrived with his prisoner, who was quietly defiant.

"I must leave him in your care, general," said Grahame, "while I fly to Watsonville."

"Return as soon as you can, colonel. I want your advice on this internment matter." As Grahame left the room, the general turned to Kirby with a stern face.

"You should be shot without mercy, sir," he said. "As commander of a guerrilla force you have no recognition. Whatever false ideas of patriotism may have prompted the men you led are with you, but motives bred of personal revenge in one who is neither Japanese nor American."

Kirby, standing between two soldiers, surveyed the general coolly.

"I cannot help my birth, sir," he replied. "I am a Japanese citizen, at least. As to what you say about *personal* motives"—he emphasized the word— "there is much truth. I should be glad to discuss those *personal* affairs with you in private. I have some information which you will be glad to receive, but which I care to give only to you privately."

The general flushed a little under his tan while his aids looked their contempt of the man who was apparently ready to play the role of double traitor.

The general hesitated, then asked his officers to withdraw. There were two doors in the room, one opening on the entrance hall, the other on a side porch. A bay window looked out upon a lawn.

"You may leave him here," he said to the two men who held Kirby. "Has he been searched for weapons? Good! Post a sentry at both doors."

The men saluted and left. Kirby allowed himself to smile. General Lancaster noticed it with the slightest hint of embarrassment before he spoke.

"Whatever personal matters may lie between you and me, sir," he said, "will have no bearing upon your case. My duty is paramount to my affections. If your life is spared, it will be because of information you give me concerning this war that you have precipitated. Under certain conditions I shall turn you over for imprisonment, but I can promise you no ultimate immunity for any information you may give. You have deliberately placed yourself outside the pale of military law."

Kirby, his arms still pinioned behind him, bowed with a suspicion of mockery.

"I am not without my own standards of honor and duty, general," he answered, "and neither your military nor personal viewpoint can affect them. Nor am I so much in love with life that I would, if it were in my power, rob my country of certain victory by divulging secrets. My ultimate fate will soon be decided, but not by the authorities of the United States, unless you decide to order the firing squad. And that, I think, you will hardly do."

"That we will see."

Kirby keenly scrutinized the general's face, set in resolution, the jaw rigid, the eyes determined, the torturing suspense of his daughter's fate put aside in his stern sense of prime duty.

"If I restore your daughter to you, unhurt, will you give me my life? I do not ask for freedom. I am willing to gamble that on the conviction of my country's speedy conquest. It may be that I may yet be in a position where I can extend courtesy to you, General Lancaster—"

The general rose from his seat at the desk, his eyes flashing.

"If I knew that duty to my country was the signing of my daughter's death warrant, I would still carry it out. I will parley no longer with you, sir. As for your fate, we will decide that in general court-martial, in which, as presiding officer, I shall cast no vote. The verdict, I think, will be unanimous," he added grimly.

"One moment, general." Kirby spoke clearly and rapidly. "I respect and admire your principles. Do with me what you will. If death is to be the speedy end of my ambitions, I can at least be generous. I will restore your daughter."

General Lancaster's fingers played a nervous tattoo on the flat desk top; his voice wavered a little, despite his will.

"You mean—"

"What I said. If you will allow me to write a note that is necessary. It must be in Japanese, with my ideographic signature. Otherwise any attempt to rescue her, even with the knowledge of her whereabouts, would result in disaster for her. I so arranged it before we marched."

The two men faced each other. Kirby's face was impassive, his eyes unshifting.

"Mind, I promise nothing."

"General, I ask for nothing."

The general undid the cord that bound Kirby's arms, then resumed his chair and motioned to the one on the opposite side of the desk. "There is paper and pen." He pushed them across to Kirby.

A wooden stand held two inkwells of heavy glass blocks capped with bronze covers. Kirby turned the stand toward him, and dipped the pen in one of them.

"The ink has dried. It is nothing but mud," he said, as he lifted the container. Suddenly his motion became swift as the strike of a serpent. His arm swung back, then forward, and the heavy inkwell crashed against the general's temple, a corner cutting into the skin. The blood spurted as General Lancaster, instantly unconscious, fell forward, his head rolling limply upon his arms. The inkwell dropped into his lap, then dully upon the rug beneath the desk, staining its pattern with black, while the red blood from the severed vein soaked into the desk blotter.

Kirby rose with the swift stealth of a panther. There was no alarm. The sentries had heard nothing. He continued to talk while he moved, lest the silence should seem suspicious. He was dressed in a whipcord coat and riding breeches of military cut, with puttees above his boots. His visor cap had been left in the motor. Two noiseless strides took him to a clothes rack, from which he selected a long raincoat and a cloth cap. In a moment he was transformed into a civilian who could easily pass for a resident or a visitor at the ranch. For a second he surveyed himself in the mirror above the mantel, still talking false items of information, as if giving them to the senseless figure at the desk.

On the side wall of the bay window, which held a cushioned seat, hung a pipe rack and match safe. There was tobacco on the mantel. He took a pipe, found that it drew, and rapidly but carefully filled and lit it. Then he knelt on the window seat and looked out on the lawn. It was a croquet ground sunken from the garden proper, high-hedged from the road, with a grape arbor at the farther end leading into an orchard planted on a slope, beyond which the trees were covered with brush. There was no one in sight. He lifted the sash with deft swiftness, looked out, and dropped ten feet to the lawn. Puffing at his pipe, he walked leisurely toward the arbor.

Just before he reached it, a sergeant and four men came out of the vines.

"Looking for stray Japs?" he asked the sergeant easily.

The man looked at him. He had neither knowledge nor idea that this gray-eyed man in the raincoat and cap could have any connection with the enemy, much less be their commander, of whose capture he was unaware. He saluted respectfully.

"I'd be obliged," went on Kirby, "if you could keep your men off my lawn. Unless it's necessary, of course. And, sergeant, I haven't enough to go round, but there are a few bottles of beer in the ice chest. Tell the cook I said she was to give you half a dozen."

The sergeant saluted again, while his men grinned appreciatively.

"Thank you, sir," he said. "I'll do that if I get a chance."

Kirby walked slowly through the orchard, forcing himself to an even pace until he reached the thick tangle of a manzanita thicket. Then, bent double, he tossed the pipe away, and forced his way through the undergrowth, striking a cattle trail at last and running at full speed westward across the uncultivated hills, his ears strained to catch the first sound that would force him to change his course and throw the pursuers off his trail. Within ten minutes he had caught up with the fog, retreating slowly seaward from the valleys, but still clinging to the higher ground, and was lost in the mist.

Two hours later, after the fight at Watsonville had spelled another Japanese defeat, the employees of the seashore station of the Overworld Wireless

Company, on the beach of Saugus Cove, remote from any settlement even when not wrapped in the fog that was thick along the shore line, were suddenly surprised by the advent of half a dozen Japanese armed with rifles and revolvers, evidently fugitives from the fight, headed by a white man in a long raincoat and cap. The leader usurped the sending operator's chair, and, while his men bound and gagged the staff and took up their normal duties in the engine room, transmitted syllables and sentences unintelligible to the helpless prisoners, who could only guess that they were in Japanese code.

The man in the raincoat laughed as he got up and stood over the bound men, pistol in hand. Sudden ferocity blazed in his eyes under a glaze of crimson, and he emptied the automatic, leaving the bullets in their brains.

Later yet, the Italian fishermen at Santa Cruz heard the putter of a launch, and wondered what fool among them was putting to sea in such weather. It was the next day before they discovered the absence of a skiff from the sands and a power boat from the fishing fleet anchored in the bay.

IV

THE INDIAN RAID

The fog held; but now it was hailed in friendship instead of regarded as an enemy. With the forces of the Californian Japanese subdued, the railroads set to work making repairs that would once more connect the Pacific coast with the continent at large, and permit reinforcements to enter. The civic committees labored hard to accomplish the reconstruction of their water systems, and, meanwhile, the fog held back the attack from the sea, preventing any attempts at landing. Day and night it spread its wide pall along the shore, a barrier that neither battleship nor submarine could penetrate with impunity. By day, ashore, all but the outlying ridges were swept clear by the sun, by night the mist came stealing in to claim the land. Always it kept the sea, and every hour of it meant a delay that was immensely valuable.

With the work in the interior valleys done, Grahame spared an air squadron, under one helicopter, as a special patrol for the Mexican line, fearing a possible landing on the peninsula of Lower California at Ensenada, and a march overland through the border gate at Tia Juana. And there, also, the fog was an ever-present guardian.

Half a full army corps of Japanese had been killed and captured. The prisoners were quartered for the time in San Francisco harbor, on Alcatraz, Angel, and Goat Islands, while the military authorities at Washington determined their ultimate fate. Grahame forwarded a suggestion that ten thousand men, most of them trained to agricultural work, would be a decided benefit to hand-lacking farmers, or might be used to advantage in reclamation work. Meanwhile California had to guard, as well as feed, them.

The air fleet spent another busy day following the battles of Gilroy and Watsonville. With Oriental cunning the Japanese had made friends with the Indian, claiming kinship that was not altogether outside the bounds of possibility, lamenting the fallen estate of "Poor Lo," and promising him freedom and conquest, while furtively supplying rifles that were buried on the reservations with their cartridges until the time came for revenge upon the white men.

A dozen rebellions flashed up in one morning. Agents and guards were killed, and once more the land rang with the war whoop, and settlers fought desperately for the lives of their families.

It was a well-planned diversion, that might have seriously interfered with the concentration of Grahame's air squadrons, had not the fog caused Ogden Kirby to act twenty-four hours ahead of his original schedule. The first word came from the big Klamath Indian reservation at Klamath Lake, in Oregon, not far north of the California line. This was almost instantly followed by a call from the Yuma Indians, at the southeast corner of California, and another from the Hoopa Valley reservation in Humboldt County, in the northwest.

The attacks had come at dawn. Grahame was roused out of his well-earned sleep by his personal orderly. Within ten minutes he had got in touch with his local squadron commanders, and in twenty minutes more they were assembled about the great map of the coast.

"We must assume this to be universal," said Grahame. "I've sent warning to Washington. They'll take care of the Yakima, Colville, and Quiniault reservations from Seattle and Tacoma. The Cœur d'Alenes, in Idaho, are to be watched.

"Oregon must handle the Siletz on the coast, here, and the Grande Ronde, next to them." He rapidly set his forefinger on the places as he named them: "Warm Springs, on the Des Chutes River, Umatilla, and Klamath. It's a big contract; they are three hundred miles apart, some of them, and it's nasty traveling. We've got the big end of it in California to cover.

"You, Ford, cover Hoopa Valley; you, Duke, Round Valley, in Mendocino, and you, Ryone, Tule River reservation in Tulare County." He quickly checked off his officers and their assignments. There were the reservations of Potrero, Los Coyotes, Santa Ysabel, and Capitan Grande, all in San Diego County, the Marango Cahuilla, Santa Rosa, and Torres, in Riverside, most of them in secluded spots, but all of them in touch with ranches where massacres might be in progress.

"General orders are to commence bomb firing at sight," said Grahame. "I trust superstition will prove a strong weapon. They must be disarmed, and, if possible, turned over to their agency guards, unless these have been already overpowered and killed. In that case get neighboring ranchmen to act."

Thurston, by special request, had become a member of the *Ariel's* crew, and he was among the first to report at the aërodrome for duty. His company had made strenuous efforts to rehabilitate telephone conditions throughout the state, and all repairs to the city system had been already accomplished, so that he was able to secure and bring to Grahame a reassuring report on the condition of General Lancaster.

"There was no fracture," he said, "and he is fully conscious. The only cause for alarm is his anxiety over his daughter's whereabouts and safety. He blames himself for having let Kirby get away."

"Some Japanese god of good luck seems to have established a protectorate over him," replied Grahame bitterly. "We can only trust that things are too strenuous with him to allow him to do her any harm. My hands, like the general's, are tied with duty, but there will be a reckoning some day, and I hope to be the chief accountant."

Thurston, who knew his friend's feelings for Irene Lancaster, nodded sympathetically. "Did you think of the Pinnacles?" he asked.

"Yes. I dispatched a helicopter there last night to make a thorough search and clean-up of the place to-day. All ready? Get aboard, Fred; we've a long trip ahead of us.

"I'm not much afraid of the Indians in California," he said, as the *Ariel* rose and started north at her limit speed of one hundred and twenty miles an hour, traveling at a five-thousand-foot level. "They are mostly Diggers, and easily cowed, with the exception, perhaps, of the Yuma reservation. And there are some troops there. It is the Klamath Indians I expect trouble from. They are a different type. The Klamaths and the Modocs put up the last big fight against the whites, and they had to shell them out of the lava beds from the lake. That's where we are bound for. It will take three hours."

"I know something of them," said Thurston. "I was up there when we were surveying for the new line. One of the totems of the tribe is the eagle—the sun bird—as they call it. They are likely to think us their divinity come to inspire them."

"They'll soon change their minds," answered Grahame.

The *Ariel* flew straight and fast, crossing the Sacramento River where it poured into San Pablo Bay, and swinging above Mare Island, where part of Admiral Freeman's squadron lay. Early as it was, the place was busy with loading stores onto the warships, that showed, from the smoke lifting from the funnels of cruisers and torpedo destroyers, that they were ready to steam to sea at a moment's warning. San Pablo Bay itself, with all the great harbor, was heavy with fog that halted just short of Vallejo, diverted by the barrier of the St. Helena range of coast mountains. The helicopter made a tangent northeast to Sacramento, and, high over the dome of the state capitol, darted north above the twisting river, up the fertile valley, past Chico and Redding, following the cañon of the upper Sacramento. The great dome of Mount

Shasta was now their guide, its everlasting snows dazzling in the early sunshine. They skirted it to the left, rising above the timber line and turning northeast once more along the line of the railroad from Weed to Klamath Falls, over the marshes of the lower lake, where myriads of wild birds rose far beneath them at the advent of the flying monster.

From Klamath Falls, the railroad penetrated part way into the reservation along a projected line to Eugene, Oregon, which state they were now in. The reservation, well watered and largely marshy, was practically a flat of some hundred and fifty square miles, with only the two rises of Saddle and Fuego Mountains to break the level.

The town of Klamath Falls was covered by a great cloud of smoke, through which flames broke occasionally. The heat of the conflagration reached the *Ariel* as it skirted the cloud, looking in vain for any signs of life. Another hour would see the place in ashes. Out on the lake, the steamer *Winona*, crowded with fugitives, was resisting the attack of a score of small boats and launches, close packed with yelling savages firing at the large boat from which a few rifles returned scattering shots. The paddle wheels were turning slowly. Evidently the white men had determined to make a stand rather than try for a landing in the face of the superior armament of the Indians.

As the *Ariel* swiftly dropped, a cheer came from the steamer and yells from the Indians. The savages seemed to acclaim the airship as Thurston had predicted, first with outstretched arms, then with prostrations of worship. They were quickly undeceived. The helicopter fell to two hundred feet above the lake, then swooped ruthlessly upon the Klamaths, darting here and there like a great dragon fly after water insects. Bomb after bomb dropped through the tubes with fatal precision, and, as each reached its mark, the surface was broken into a little maelstrom, amid which appeared for a moment splintered planks and dismembered bodies torn by the high explosives.

As the last boat was sunk, the Stars and Stripes broke out on her deck, while the *Ariel* circled the steamer, its crew echoing the cheers of the relieved refugees from Klamath, and sped for the buildings of Fort Klamath at Agency Landing at the head of the lake. There once more they found desolation and smoking ruins, without sign of life. To the east, along the railroad, more smoke was rising.

A dozen small stations were set along the completed portion of the railroad that lay east of the lake, and all of these had been destroyed. At the end of the line stood a work train of open cars and engine. Here the workmen of the road had evidently made a desperate stand. Several groups of bodies lay upon the ground, half of which were those of Indians. Rising for better observation, they sighted, on the banks of the Sprague River, perhaps two miles from their position, a mob of savages formed in a huge circle. The *Ariel* was over the horde in ninety seconds, five hundred feet above the ground. So intent were the Indians on their task that they failed to notice the hovering helicopter, with its muffled engines.

A fire reduced to red-hot charcoal glowed in the center of the ring. A wagon had been stripped of its wheels, and across these four men were bound. To one side was a little group of prisoners. The men stood. About their knees crouched women and one or two children hiding their faces.

Civilization had slipped back. The old lusts and cruelty of the savages were once more dominant. Six Indians lifted the first of the wheels with its living burden and bore it toward the fire as the inner circle of warriors yelled, and beyond them the squaws peered eagerly to watch the torture.

The shadow of the *Ariel* slid across the ring, and the savages looked up in awe as a bomb flashed downward, scattering the fire among them. The bearers of the wheel dropped it and joined their tribesmen in falling upon their knees, their heads bowed to the ground. In all there were about two hundred of them, now trembling at the sudden manifestation of wrath and power from the mighty bird that floated over them.

One of them, venturing to look upward, caught sight of the flag, and called to his fellows. They sprang to their feet. The situation was changed. This was not the sun bird! It was some craft of the white men who carried that flag—but had they not killed white men since dawn, and seen the flag burn at the agency? The day of the white man was over, as their brothers from across the sea had told them. They had been frightened at first by the noise and the scattering of the fire, but it was only a noise. Should they, whose hands were red with the blood of the white man, be frightened by a noise maker?

Inflamed with victory and with drink looted at the agency, they reached for their rifles. Nothing loath to avenge, the gunners of the *Ariel* trained down their rapid-firers, and the Indians fell like swathes of grass before the scythe, running in all directions through the willows, plunging into the river to escape the hail of lead that relentlessly pursued them. The *Ariel* swept in widening circles for a few minutes, then returned to the little group of whites, who had already unbound the men from the wheels, and, with rifles cast away by the Klamaths or taken from the dead savages, were ready to assist in wiping out the tribe. The *Ariel* came to earth, and Grahame offered them passage to the lake, where they could get in contact with the survivors on the steamer. The men declined.

"We've seen things to-day that there's only one way of forgetting," said the leader. "Now that we're armed, and you tell us they didn't burn the work train, we'll take care of the situation, thank you just the same. This reservation is mighty likely to need new ownership before nightfall," he added.

"I don't think many of them got away," said Grahame. "I tried to avoid the squaws as much as possible."

"The squaws are the worst. It was them suggested tying us on the wheels," said one of the men.

Grahame shrugged his shoulders. He had little time to spare.

"I am the Indian agent," said the first speaker. "I will take the responsibility of the matter. If you don't mind notifying the *Winona* that we're alive, thanks to you, the train will take us to Klamath Falls, what there is left of the town, where they can meet us later in the day, and we'll run down to the main line."

V

NEWS—AND A THREAT

It was mid-afternoon when the *Ariel* once more reached her base. At headquarters, General Lancaster was reported to be steadily improving, and there was a message for Grahame from police headquarters. Lucille l'Estrange was dying. She had attempted suicide, leaving a letter addressed to Grahame. This, if possible, she wanted to supplement by talking to him if he returned in time. Medical aid had been given, but she had been found too late, and was slowly sinking.

Grahame found her at the hospital, and the doctor in charge administered a restorative that gave the dying woman strength enough to open her eyes and whisper a few broken sentences.

"The letter will tell you," she said, "all that I did. Show it to Miss Lancaster—it will explain." She sank back on the pillows, her face as white as the linen. Grahame quickly told her of the abduction of the general's daughter and the absence of any trace of her whereabouts. So far no word had come from the Pinnacles. The news revived her, and her eyes opened once more.

"There is a submarine under his orders," she said. "He has used it once or twice. It is stationed at the—"

A tremor ran through her, and her body was shaken with a convulsion. Graham knelt beside her as the doctor forced apart her clenched teeth and a few drops of the powerful drug entered her mouth. The eyelids lifted slowly, but the eyes were vacant of expression.

"The submarine!" said Grahame. "Where?"

A light flickered in the dark orbs as he bent closer to catch the syllables she tried to form. Her head fell limply backward, the jaw relaxed.

"She's gone," said the doctor. "She must have suffered agonies to last this long. Took Lysol. Did you make out what she said?"

"Yes. The Coronado Islands. I knew they had a submarine base there. Smothered in a fog now. But while we can't reach it, they can't leave. It's a clew, and I'll make the most of it."

The letter held another, unsealed and addressed to Miss Lancaster. The note to Grahame was short:

> I have nothing left to live for. Hate does not replace love. Read the inclosed and forgive. L.L.

He looked at the second letter.

> All that I told you concerning Mr. Grahame and myself was untrue. I had never seen him before the meeting in the Palace Hotel. I did it because Ogden Kirby told me it would help him. I did not know then what I know now. But I loved him, and I pray the God whom I shall meet in judgment long before you receive this that no other woman may ever follow the example of
>
> LUCILLE L'ESTRANGE.

"That," Grahame told himself, as he refolded the last writing of Kirby's unfortunate mistress, "explains what Irene meant when she said Kirby did not furnish her with the proofs against me. She will hardly need this now, even if I can find her to deliver it. His fascination for her died with the blow she struck him in the face, I fancy. That submarine, if I am not mistaken, will be used by him as his means of escape if we win. And I'll take good care to be there with the *Ariel* when that happens. Upon which occasion Ogden Kirby will not get away before he produces Irene—nor after."

The *Polaris* arrived, bringing one passenger, the mayor of San Francisco, who had been found imprisoned in an underground cavern. The whole place had been searched, without the discovery of another person in the region of the Pinnacles. They had located large stores of provisions and ammunition, over which a guard had been left, but if any Japanese had been left at the base, they had deserted it. Grahame gave orders for the stores to be brought to San Francisco, and issued a special command to the commander of the helicopter.

"There is a submarine base at Los Coronados, off San Diego," he said. "As soon as the fog lifts, I want it and the submarine attached to it kept under surveillance. Follow any movement of the latter, and keep in touch with me. Consider that your special duty to be changed only by direct orders from me."

As the commander saluted, Grahame had little thought how soon circumstances would cause him to countermand the patrol that seemed to hold the only hope of finding Kirby, and, through him, Irene Lancaster.

Fifteen minutes later the government wireless stations on the Pacific coast, from Cape Flattery to Point Loma, including those at Vancouver, in British Columbia, thrilled with a message that came from the sea—the ultimatum of Japan:

> Unless the government of the United States shall within twenty-four hours cede to the empire of Japan the states of California, Oregon, and Washington, a state of war shall be considered as existing between the two nations, and such actions as are deemed necessary to enforce this demand will be immediately carried out.

From Congress, assembled in alarmed consultation; from the White House, where the president and his cabinet gathered in anxious conclave, no answer came as hour after hour passed by and the Pacific coast swung in the balance between imperious demand and the vacillation of a government torn by political dissension. The emergency committee, in solemn conference, resolved that the coast should not be sacrificed. Meanwhile the fog gathered its forces at nightfall, and, beyond it, none could tell how many leagues distant, lay the war vessels of Japan, waiting for the word to take possession, or invade. Scouting between them and the fog-bordered shore flew the aërial patrol in an attempt to locate the hostile fleet. Locked in San Francisco harbor by the mist were the fighting ships of Admiral Freeman, toy boats compared to the force against them, even when including the rest of the fragmentary Pacific force at Bremerton and at San Diego, similarly fogbound. The Hammond torpedoes, the mobile dynamite guns of the coast railroad, all were powerless against a fleet safe hidden behind the fog curtain, and that, cruising in clear waters, twenty miles away, could send missiles hurtling at will upon defenseless cities.

How far the wireless impulse had leaped, from which direction, could not be foretold. The Japanese fleet had three lines of battle, the first containing eight dreadnaughts and eight battle cruisers. This had engaged the Atlantic squadron in the disastrous battle off Cape Horn. Another had silenced the forts at Corregidor, in the Philippines, and accomplished the surrender of Guam. The third, perhaps, had taken Hawaii. The ultimatum might have come from Yokohoma itself. Only the airships might discover the whereabouts of the squadrons, though unassisted by guns and torpedoes, they could do little more than harass the floating forts, which doubtless carried their own complements of biplanes.

One scanty consolation remained. While the fog remained, there could be no landing. But a bombardment seemed imminent.

At midnight the first news came from the air patrols, forced to keep within the limits of their wireless. A Japanese squadron of dreadnaughts, cruisers, and destroyers, accompanied by colliers, and convoying what appeared to be transports, was two hundred miles at sea, off the coast of Lower California, proceeding slowly northward. A second squadron, approximately half that distance from shore, was off Eureka, nearly two hundred miles north of San Francisco, steaming south. Apparently San Francisco and Los Angeles were their respective destinations. From beyond the fog the fourteen-inch guns of the battleships of the *Kuso* type could toss their shells into San Francisco without fear of reprisal. Los Angeles, twelve miles inland, was in comparative safety. To get within striking distance, the dreadnaughts would be forced to enter the fog, and their range finders be rendered useless.

The night passed. Half the time for answer had gone by. No word came from Washington. The Pacific coast, prepared to secede if they were sacrificed to Japan's demands, determined to fight invasion. This they believed themselves able to accomplish, even though their coast cities were destroyed. The frontier spirit was aflame.

The air patrols reported the two squadrons seventy-five miles offshore, steaming toward the two principal cities of California at the limit speed of the transports and colliers, which still kept within the protection of the warships.

At seven o'clock in the morning, Admiral Freeman got into connection with Grahame from Mare Island.

"I have received no orders from Washington," he said. "I am going to endeavor to engage the enemy. I can creep out on the ebb and proceed toward the sea limit of the fog, which they must almost touch if they intend a successful bombardment. Unseen until the last minute, I can bring my lesser-calibered guns within range. I shall attack also with my submarines."

The total number of the gallant admiral's force, assembled in San Francisco harbor and at Mare Island, consisted of six cruisers, none of which was less than ten years old, four torpedo destroyers, and four coast-type submarines. One cruiser and a destroyer was at Bremerton, and two destroyers at San Diego. Their biggest guns were eight-inch weapons. The attempt, to Grahame, seemed worse than foolhardy, even if they could safely emerge through the Golden Gate, where the mines were fortunately arranged for shore explosion. There was the barest chance that by surprising the enemy they might, with rare luck and marksmanship, cripple him and retreat into the protection of the fog before they were blown out of the water. The submarines, antiquated as they were, might account for one or two.

Grahame confined his answer to an assumption that the admiral best knew his risks and responsibility.

"I want you to keep me in continual touch with their movements through the airships," said the admiral. "Use the special battle code. The time expires at five-thirty this afternoon. I leave on the first of the ebb, four hours from now, at eleven o'clock. I am sending launches ahead, to help us feel the way out. We'll have to creep till we strike deep water."

At nine o'clock Washington announced that, with the exception of such troops as could be sent over rebuilt lines of communication, they could guarantee no aid, and pointed out the almost certain destruction of coast cities by bombardment. To which the governors of Washington, Oregon, and California sent the joint answer:

> We can rebuild our cities if we keep our land. And we are going
> to keep it.

With this went the affirmation from General Lancaster, once more able to assume his command, that, under the Grahame plan of defense, actual invasion could be repulsed.

At ten o'clock the president sent the following:

> The nation at large is practically powerless to aid you in this crisis,
> nor can we deny you the right to protect your own frontier. May God
> and the right be with you! What shall we answer?

And the three states replied: "*Nothing*."

At ten-thirty, one Japanese squadron was a hundred miles from the Golden Gate. The second had passed Los Angeles, and was on its way to join the first, seemingly having abandoned any attack on the southern city after its air scouts had reported the width of the fog belt.

At eleven o'clock, with fifty motor boats scattered in the van, with searchlights struggling with the mist, with sounding leads cast constantly, linked by steam and wireless signals, the intrepid, forlorn hope of Admiral Freeman emerged from the Mare Island navy yard and crawled on the tide to pick up the cruisers off San Francisco naval row, and venture forth to where duty—and death—beckoned them.

VI

THE FIGHT OFF THE FARALLONS

The sun was dropping toward the western horizon, as the *Ariel*, high above the fog, flew seaward to assume command of the air patrol. In line with the flagship at intervals of a mile were three more helicopters, all that Grahame felt that he could spare for the occasion.

Somewhere beneath them, Admiral Freeman's ships groped their way toward the sea limits of the fog, the helicopters acting as their periscopes above the mist. Grahame anxiously watched the fall of his marine barometer, presaging a change in the weather that was corroborated by the masses of clouds in the northwest, from which a wind that steadily strengthened already

blew. The fog shifted uneasily. From the deck of the *Ariel* it looked like a
fabric of canvas upbillowed by the wind beneath it. The outer edge was
frayed, masses of fleecy vapor rolled up and shredded off, flung shoreward
by the wind.

To Grahame's weather-wise eyes it seemed probable that long before
morning, unless another shift of the weather altered matters, the coast would
be cleared off. The sea was rising. Beyond the fog, the Japanese battleships,
gray on a sea of dark green flecked with white, seemed as solid as if their
hulls mounted from the bottom on fixed foundations. They were steaming
so slowly that their progress was barely perceptible, even to his aërial view.
Four dreadnaughts, the *Hondo*, *Yesso*, *Kiushu*, and *Shikoku*, of thirty-one
thousand five hundred tons, mounted with fourteen-inch guns, were flanked
by eight battle cruisers of the *Kongo* type, of twenty-seven thousand tons,
and escorted by ten torpedo destroyers. To the southward showed the main
fleet, consisting of eight dreadnaughts, twelve battle cruisers, and some of
smaller type protecting four transports and several colliers. A score of torpedo
destroyers were with the first-line fleet, that lay back in superb arrogance,
leaving its second squadron to handle the work in hand.

For the first time, Grahame, as he surveyed the full menace of the invaders,
fully realized the desperate odds of the battle that must ensue to prevent a
landing when the fog cleared. He glanced at his watch. In five minutes more
the twenty-four hours' announced ultimatum would be ended. He sent down
his final reports to the little squadron, still hidden in the mist, and, with a
signal to the three helicopters, rose with them to an elevation of a mile.

The Japanese second squadron lay within five hundred yards of the fog,
which was gradually receding. Above them, like gulls wheeling in the wind,
rose and fell the biplanes of the Japanese ships and those of Grahame's
patrol in apparent amity. The battleships were stripped for action, though it
was doubtful if they expected any attack through the fog. The forward turret
of the leading dreadnaught, the *Hondo*, swung slowly, and the muzzle of the
great steel tube was elevated to supreme range as the last seconds of grace
passed.

The helicopters hovered above the fleet. Anti-aircraft guns were tilted
toward them. Grahame could see the men as they crouched behind their gun
shields. His own crew was at stations, at the bomb tubes, checking off the
range with nice allowance for windage, and on deck, by the rapid-firers. He
felt sure that he could work havoc among the enemy's air fleet, whatever the
results of Freeman's desperate enterprise.

A bugle rang out. A burst of gas and flame belched from the great gun, a
ring of smoke floated clear for a moment, then was torn apart by the wind,
as the projectile soared on its long trajectory toward San Francisco, lying
helpless on its hills, over twenty miles away. A second shell sped from the

Skikoku. The time limit had elapsed. The bombardment was on.

Instantly skirmishes commenced between the airships as they maneuvered for position and spat viciously at each other with their rapid-firers. White balls of smoke poured upward, toward the helicopters, sending out shrapnel that burst well below them. Three darted zigzag to the assistance of the biplanes, while the shrapnel shells tried vainly to follow their eccentric moves. One lifted above a Japanese biplane, gauging accurately its speed, hovered for a moment, and let fall a bomb. It struck one wing of the great kite, which tipped, tried to right itself, and then went whirling downward. Close to the fog it burst into flames, and disappeared.

Grahame remained stationary, waiting expectantly for the emergence of Freeman's ships. At last, beneath the surface of the water, he saw one of the four small submarines of the coast defense, invisible to the enemy, rising to the surface. Its periscope bobbed up between wave crests, remained a moment, and dipped as the submarine slowly settled, still unsuspected by the enemy. From the great height, Grahame, tingling with anticipation, saw the shadowy oval sinking, then the streak of the torpedo, rushing toward the *Hondo*, five hundred yards away. It struck the dreadnaught amidships, a geyser of water tossed skyward, the massive structure seemed to shudder, then slowly began to list. Figures broke out upon its decks as the sluggish movement changed to a swift roll, and the waves invaded the stern. The destroyers, smoke pouring from their funnels, sought for the death dealer. Once more its periscope emerged, and the sea about it was churned with missiles. The tube was smashed almost instantly, but its second torpedo was discharged, and, even as the *Hondo* plunged beneath the surface, its decks lifting with an internal explosion, one of the battle cruisers staggered as the torpedo found its mark against her bows. A second submarine came up to be instantly riddled. Two of the four had gone to the bottom with their brave crews, and, with their loss, nearly sixty thousand tons of fighting metal sank with them, and scores of Japanese were struggling in the rising seas.

From the fog bank came one by one the ships of Admiral Freeman, firing their guns as they swung broadside to the enemy, their weakness of calibered strength balanced for the time by the close range. Now the battle raged in earnest, with thundering detonations and spurts of fire as the great shells sped. The setting sun reddened the sea, and the shifting fog, with a prophecy of blood. One of the helicopters was down, smashed by a chance charge of shrapnel. Wrecks of biplanes floated on the waves. The *San Diego*, Admiral Freeman's flagship, one turret smashed, its armor dented like a discarded fruit can, fought on till a fourteen-inch shell from the *Kinshu* smashed through amidships. Rent apart, the *San Diego* sank within a hundred seconds.

Never since modern ships were built was such a fight. The cover of the fog had brought about an unequaled situation. Charges designed to hurl tons of explosive shells for miles sent them across the short space with annihilating impact. For a few minutes the destruction was terrific, but the end was a foregone conclusion. Before four battle cruisers, dispatched from the main fleet at thirty-five knots an hour, could get into action the Pacific squadron, the pitiful example of a nation's unpreparedness, was battered to scrap iron, set on fire, practically blown out of the water or beneath it. The third submarine, crushed like an eggshell, shared the fate of the second. The fourth was somewhere astray in the fog. Two cruisers, their guns silenced, limped shoreward through the mist. The narrow strip of sea was strewn with wreckage and crippled men struggling for life.

The defeated Americans, overwhelmed by the odds, had taken heavy toll of their conquerors. The *Hondo* and two battle cruisers were sunk. Two more cruisers were dismantled of turrets and all superstructure. Not a hostile ship but was scarred and pierced, with masts and funnels shot away and big guns out of action. One blazed furiously in the growing dusk.

Above the mêlée the American air fleet had won their share of the battle. The *Ariel* alone had disposed of five biplanes. Not one of the enemy's airships was a-wing. Grahame counted his losses. A dozen biplanes were missing, one helicopter was a total loss, another, with her fore and aft propellers out of commission, drifted shoreward on the wind.

From the main fleet a cloud of machines had arisen headed by a triplane.

Grahame hesitated. For a moment he thought of summoning his reserves from land. The blood lust and the desire of avenging the admiral's gallant sailors was upon him, but it was growing dark. The *Ariel* had not gone unscratched. The hull had been punctured by shrapnel, that luckily had missed the engines. One pair of horizontal propellers were shot away. He had wounded men aboard, and the main issue was yet ahead of them to-morrow to prevent a landing. The wind was freshening to a gale, sweeping the fog before it. All about his flotilla shrapnel was breaking from the concentrated fire of the remaining quick-firers of the ships joined now by the four battle cruisers. Their own ammunition was practically exhausted.

He signaled his biplanes to fly shoreward, to their stations. One of them fell. A puff of cloud broke about the remaining helicopter, enveloped it, and the airship, crumpled to shapelessness, dropped like a plummet.

The *Ariel* mounted slowly, hampered by the loss of her twin propellers. Toward her, on the curve of a great spiral, the triplane sped far ahead of her consorts.

It was a direct challenge, and Grahame accepted it. The sun had dropped beneath the sea rim, and night was coming fast. The triplane was barely distinguishable against the sky. A beam of light broke from it, reaching toward the *Ariel* almost straight upward as it drove beneath the helicopter, two quick-firers spitting viciously.

The *Ariel* dropped her last bombs as she flew.

"That's the last," said Thurston, straightening from the tube. "And we've missed her."

A volley of bullets ripped through the hull as the *Ariel* darted sideways. Thurston fell, shot through the foot, as Grahame sprang for the deck, shouting an order. The helicopter lowered and sped on the same level with the triplane. Her searchlight swept the Japanese, while her rapid-firers vomited in an exchange of shots. The triplane, with planes deflected, dodged downward, but not before Grahame had sighted in her gondola, clear in the glare of the beam—Ogden Kirby.

Rage swept over him with the vehement desire to cripple the triplane, and, swooping after it like an eagle after a fishhawk, capture his man from the waves and bear him back to land, triumphant, to the rescue of Irene Lancaster and the final disposal of his arch-enemy.

A shell, fired from a cruiser at the ray of the *Ariel*, burst about their stern, shivering the driving propeller, spattering through the thin sheathing, and spreading death in the engine room. Half the horizontal propellers were out of commission. Partly supported by the remainder, dragged shoreward by the still-whirring tractor, the *Ariel* dropped rapidly—faster than the triplane, volplaning after, could follow—entered the fog bank, and fell into the waves that surged beneath the mist.

> **The invasion of the Pacific coast by the Japanese, and the destruction of the principal cities, had commenced. How the defenders met their enemy, and the results of the conflict, will be told you in the final installment of this story in next month's People's.**

The Peril of the Pacific

Part 5 The Victory

By J. Allan Dunn

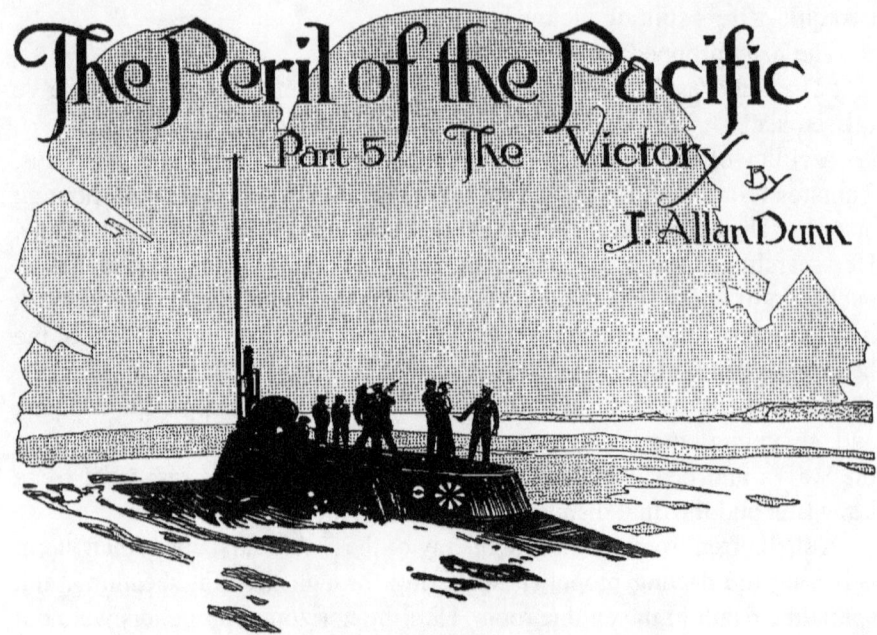

Synopsis of Preceding Installments

Bruce Grahame, an expert in aëronautics, and a believer in preparedness, especially against a suspected Japanese invasion, is in love with Irene Lancaster, daughter of General Lancaster, chief of the Pacific division of the United States army, located at the Presidio, San Francisco. To prove his assertion that the Pacific coast Japanese, most of them veterans of the war with Russia, are drilling secretly at night, Grahame takes General Lancaster, his daughter, and Ogden Kirby, whom he suspects of a connection with the Japanese government, in his triplane, the *Aërolite*, to a valley in the Coast Range. There they find a large company of Japanese drilling on the open plain, in the moonlight. The next day Grahame and his friend, Fred Thurston, trail Kirby to a Japanese club, where are gathered several distinguished Oriental statesmen, in consultation over an enlargement of an aëro photo map of San Francisco Bay. Japan delivers an ultimatum to Washington, the context of which is, "Free Entry or Forcible!" In default of immediate protection and assistance from Washington the Emergency Association of the Pacific coast meets, presided over by Bruce Grahame. Grahame outlines plans for defense. Kirby steals the plans from Grahame's safe, but is caught by Grahame after a long motor-boat chase in which Kirby escapes, but the papers are recovered. By means of a dictograph Grahame and Thurston overhear the Japanese plans at the Chrysanthemum Club. Suddenly the Panama Canal is blocked by an explosion, leaving the Atlantic fleet on the wrong side of the continent. The factory where Grahame's helicopters are being built is blown up in a night aëroplane raid. The Japanese withdraw from the big cities and gather at the ranches held by their countrymen. Suddenly the Pacific coast is segregated from the rest of the United States by the destruction of bridges, tunnels, railroads, telegraph, telephone, light and water supply. The Atlantic fleet, on its way to the Pacific coast, is destroyed near the Straits of Magellan by an overpowering Japanese fleet. The Mayor of San Francisco and Irene Lancaster are kidnapped. The small army of Americans, with the aid of Grahame's air fleet, defeats an army of the enemy at Gilroy. Kirby is captured and taken before General Lancaster. He offers to return Irene Lancaster in exchange for his life and is refused. By a ruse he escapes. The Indians, spurred on by the Japanese, rise in rebellion, thus complicating the situation. An American and Japanese fleet meet in battle off the Farallons and the Americans are defeated, but not without inflicting heavy damage on the enemy. Grahame's aëroplane, the *Ariel*, is defeated.

I

THE LOST LEADER

DRIVEN BY THE WIND, and dissipated by the change of temperature, the fog reluctantly departed, clinging here and there persistently in patches in Mendocino and Monterey Counties, but leaving the rest of the coast line clean and no longer protected when the sun rose the morning after the battle which was to go down to history as the Fight of the Farallons, the group of desolate, barren mountain peaks that form the bird-haunted islands of that name outside the harbor of San Francisco.

The sun shone on a ruined city. Once more San Francisco was devastated by a catastrophe almost as swift and disastrous as the earthquake and fire of 1906. The first great shells that had been fired before the Japanese ships had been engaged by those of Admiral Freeman had sped with unerring aim. As if prophetic of calamity, one had fallen in Union Square, at the base of the statue erected in commemoration of the victory of Admiral Dewey at Manila. The trim lawns, with their flower beds, palms, and shrubberies were displaced by a deep pit, that yawned like an enormous grave. The façade of the Hotel St. Francis was shattered, and all the buildings surrounding the park scarred and shaken by the frightful explosion.

It was the hour when shoppers and clerks mingled in the homeward journey. The occupants of two Powell Street cable cars were killed. On the sidewalks of Powell, Geary, and Post Streets, and Grant Avenue the dead and wounded lay by scores. The unfortunates seated on the park benches or crossing the square were instantly annihilated.

The terror of the affair held many of the living paralyzed, while others ran shrieking from the scene in search of safety or peered with pallid faces through the broken windows upon the place of death. Before the full horror of it all could be fully sensed, the second shell struck the Call Building midway in its height, and sent its upper stones hurtling, with their occupants, into Market Street as a child might strike a toy tower of wooden blocks. The third shell dropped on the apex of the California Street hill fairly between the Fairmount Hotel and the great apartment house opposite. One wing of the hotel fell like a house of cards, one side of the apartment house was blown inward. The fourth shell plunged into the waters of the bay.

The Fairmount burst into flames that burned in the fog like a sullen beacon. A conflagration started on Market Street, fought desperately by the firemen, handicapped by lack of water. The submarine pipes from the Sunol reservoirs had been repaired, but the city was on an allowance of half its usual supply.

The civic committees, aided by the police and their volunteer forces, tried to restore some measure of calm, and, the bombardment ceasing as the sea fight commenced, the citizens began to act according to the plans laid down for such an emergency. Stores and offices were hastily closed, and households gathered together in preparation for flight, striving to gain reassurance from the cessation of the shells, hoping against hope that the four shots would be considered a sufficient demonstration against a helpless population.

Thirty minutes later their hopes vanished. The Japanese, furious at the loss of the *Hondo* and the battle cruiser, commenced again to shell the doomed city. The great missiles came from beyond the fog, their source invisible to the gunners of the harbor-defense artillery, who, a stationary target themselves, were powerless to do more than guess the position of the shifting enemy, whose range they could not determine.

For an hour a tornado of shells raged. Buildings tottered and fell or dissolved in shapeless masses of debris amid the frightful detonations. At the end not a building of importance in the business district was unscathed. The taller erections were nearly all destroyed. The Crocker and Flood Buildings, Whittell and Humboldt, the Merchant's Exchange, the *Chronicle* and *Examiner* edifices were reduced to twisted girders of steel to which clung crumbling walls of brick and stone and cement. Great gaps on Nob Hill and the prime residence district marked the unerring aim of the Japanese behind the fourteen-inch guns of the dreadnaughts. Adding to the devastation, the flames began to sweep through the ruins and devour the surrounding buildings. The fire threatened a repetition of the conflagration of fourteen years previous. It leaped exultantly in a dozen places, roaring as it found fresh fuel, mocking any efforts to curb its appetite. The final shell, landing in the Civic Center, wrecked the City Hall.

The citizens fled. All through the night the sound of shuffling feet, the dragging of trunks, the clatter of horses' hoofs, the whir of motor cars, proclaimed the frenzied exodus. There was no zone of safety for them, as once before, in Golden Gate Park or in the Presidio reservation. The entire head of the peninsula on which the city was built was in peril of another outburst from the deadly shells.

They fled southward in a great mob, by motor car, in wagons, on foot, and in the special trains swiftly organized by the railroad, not knowing where to go, traveling until exhausted; tortured, as the fog showed signs of departure, by fears of a landing; conscious of the fierce resentment held by the enemy against all Californians who had barred their gates to a peaceful invasion, and now trembled at thought of the terrors of a forceful entry. As the night passed and the stars showed through the thinning veils of mist, those heavenly orbs seemed to be looking down, like the eyes of pitiless gods, upon a people already doomed to the reprisals of an Oriental horde, only thinly veneered by civilization, relentless, savage, bent upon wreaking vengeance for the slight of past restrictions.

Torture, slavery, degradation worse than death were the fearful topics whispered by the groups of fugitives. A hundred reports increased their terrors. The destruction of Admiral Freeman's fleet, and the inadequacy of the military force was common talk, and, while some strong hearts affected confidence in Grahame's plans, of which the general public knew little, that last hope died with the steady rumor of the loss of the leader of the defense.

Upon General Lancaster, still weak from the blow inflicted by Kirby, burdened with all the responsibility of the situation, Grahame's failure to return fell heavily. He had the plans and could, in a measure, carry them out, but the brain that had conceived them, that held them plain in every detail without reference, the master mind and genius of the defense was absent. The man of the hour was missing, shot down in the fog that was now withdrawing its protection.

Lancaster made his preparations according to the predetermined arrangements. One section of the air fleet guarded the Mexican line from being crossed by soldiers that were suspected to be close to the border. At San Diego and San Pedro, units consisting of Hammond torpedoes, dynamite guns on railroad trucks, and range-finding airships awaited possible attack. The main unit was stationed at Monterey Bay. San Francisco harbor, it was trusted, could resist a landing with its big guns and the channel mines. Oregon and Washington, General Lancaster did not believe would be included in the main attack. Each state had its quota of defense units, but it was in California that the blow was expected and the chief resistance was concentrated.

At dawn the Japanese fleet was far below the horizon. Scouting air patrols reported it still divided into two squadrons, one of which convoyed the transports. A low-lying streamer of fog was outside the Golden Gate. Monterey Bay was filled with a mist that would probably disperse with the sun, but in the meantime promised a temporary respite from any immediate attempt at landing.

With the daylight came fresh news of trouble, flashing fast by wireless down the coast. Simultaneous submarine attacks had been made upon Seattle, Tacoma, and Portland. At the first lifting of the fog, submarines already assembled in northern waters had made perilous night trips under the narrow waters of the sound and the Columbia River to deliver their object lesson in connection with the bombardment of the greatly hated San Francisco. At Portland, the railroad bridge across the Willamette had been destroyed. At Seattle and Tacoma, docks had been badly damaged and shipping sunk. But the news was not entirely one-sided. The attacks had been offset by instant retaliation. At both Tacoma and Seattle, as the submarines, their temporary purposes accomplished, were retreating to the Juan de Fuca Strait and the open sea, aëroplanes followed their course up the sound as kingfishers follow minnows in the shallows. From their rendezvous in the Hood Canal, a flotilla of speedy motor boats of the naval auxiliary issued in answer to the wireless call of the biplanes, and joined the pursuit, waiting for the first appearance of a periscope. Against their speed and quick-firers, escape was impossible. Four intruders were accounted for in Admiral Inlet, where two, blinded, blundered ashore, one surrendered, and the last, literally peppered with bullets, sank. In like fashion, two were put out of commission at the junction of the Willamette and Columbia Rivers.

But such minor victories counted nothing against the major menace of the fleet, and the tale of disaster already done was supplemented by the news that came from the southland. At San Diego, two battle cruisers had appeared almost at the same moment the submarines commenced their work of destruction in the north. There were fifteen minutes of heavy firing, and the cruisers steamed for Los Angeles, leaving the Coronado Hotel, on the beach, and the U.S. Grant Hotel, in San Diego, in smoking ruins, and the city on fire. The American destroyers, as they raced to reach torpedo range, had been sunk as easily as floating walnut shells beneath a handful of well-aimed gravel.

Los Angeles, twelve miles inland, had been spattered with explosives. The business section was wrecked and ablaze, the message said, the old mission church of Our Lady of the Angels included in the havoc, while one far-flying shell reached the Mission of San Gabriel Archangel, seven miles outside the southern metropolis. From north to south the Pacific coast had been marked by the lash of Oriental power and displeasure.

Both Grahame and General Lancaster had agreed that the probable first move on the part of the enemy would be an attempt to destroy the great guns of San Francisco harbor, a task made easier by possession of the aërial map made by the Japanese aviator. This might be accompanied by a joint effort to effect a landing at Monterey. The separation of the warships into two squadrons gave color to this anticipation, but, for the time, the lingering fog in the Bay of Monterey prevented the carrying out of the latter maneuver.

The biggest guns of the Japanese fleet were of fourteen inches caliber. Those of the coast artillery at the San Francisco Presidio, on Angel Island and the cliffs of the Marin shore, included some sixteen-inch cannon, giving an advantage of from five to seven thousand yards in range. This benefit the general determined to make the most of, and he decided to assume the offensive in the hope of crippling the Japanese dreadnaughts before their own guns could be brought within striking distance. Against this plan were the facts that the artillerymen had been allowed but scant practice, owing to a parsimonious government and the great cost of every charge; and that hitherto their records had registered only twenty per cent of hits at a range of twenty thousand yards, less than half the distance at which they must now fire. One hit in five, if enough shells were fired, should cause havoc, but, greatest handicap of all, the supply of shells, from the lack of appropriations, was limited to less than thirty minutes' supply of steady firing.

At the general's order, the various batteries sprang to action. Five helicopters rose high above them, to secure the range, hovering steadily over the emplacements of the big guns. As General Lancaster watched them, waiting for the records of their Barr and Stroud range finders, a message came from the government wireless station on the island of the Middle Farallon that brought a sudden light into his eyes and new vigor to his frame. The next moment the word was being relayed to the helicopters. One of them darted seaward at full speed. The general turned to his staff. "The luck's beginning to turn at last," he said. "Tell the batteries to commence firing at the extreme limit of their range."

II

The Bird Islands

As the *Ariel* fell into the fog, with one engine and half her propellers out of commission, Grahame acted promptly. The riddled hull would, he knew, let in water like a sieve. For a while, perhaps, his available propellers might hold them off the water if he lightened ship, and he set every sound man to getting rid of ballast and movable equipment, first ordering them to strap their life belts about them. He had Thurston brought on deck and laid down beside one of the pontoon rafts which were set free from their lashings.

The *Ariel's* fall was checked as the weight was tossed overboard, but the airship still dropped, slowly but inexorably. The carburetors began to choke in the fog. It was only a matter of a few seconds before they reached the water. The wind that drove at the fog did not penetrate the mass of it, and Grahame hoped that the waves beneath the mist would lack much of the fury of the sea outside the bank. Their only hope lay in the pontoon rafts, on which they would be absolutely at the mercy of the currents. It was impossible, in the clammy darkness that enveloped them, to tell when they were about to reach the water, though they listened instinctively and apprehensively for the swash of the sea above the drone of the propellers.

"Stand by to get clear the second we touch, boys!" said Grahame. "Look out for the horizontals!"

Sections of the bulwarks, planned for such emergencies, had been removed entire, and the crew hauled the rafts to the edge of deck, gripping the links of life line, ready to thrust clear the second they touched the water.

It seemed as if the time was interminable while the propellers fought against the gravity pull. Then the keel of the *Ariel* thwacked against a wave, and unseen spray slapped at her sides. The men flung themselves into the cold sea, striking out desperately with their legs to get free of the wreck. Thurston, helpless on the deck of his raft, called out to Grahame:

"Look, Bruce, she's going."

For a second or so the *Ariel* seemed to maintain her buoyancy. Her electric lights still gleamed dully through the mist, and gave a faint suggestion of outline. Then the water found the engines, the lights were suddenly extinguished, the whir of the propellers died in a last flutter, and the helicopter sank to the ooze, a hundred fathoms deep.

Grahame had snatched an electric lantern from its holder, and, by its ray, he dressed Thurston's wounded foot with a first-aid bandage he had shoved into his pocket.

"Well, old chap," he said, "we're still afloat."

Thurston gave a wry smile. "Out of the frying pan into the fire, or out of the saucepan into the sink, whichever you prefer. Did you see Kirby in the triplane?"

"I did. His luck is too good to last. As for ours, we're a long way from dead, yet."

"And a long way from shore. Any idea where we are?"

"Somewhere near the Farallons. I hope the drift will set us ashore. Not much of a landing, but we'll make it if we get a chance."

"Then what? Nothing there but sea birds, is there?"

"For a man connected with the public service, Fred, you are sadly lacking in information. There's a lighthouse on the Southeast Farallon, a government wireless station on the middle one, and a lightship halfway between them and shore."

"A devil of a lot of good a lightship is in this fog," said Thurston, "but here's hoping!"

The trend of the current was northerly. Grahame trusted that they would strike one of the scattered islets. He held a fairly strong conviction that they had fallen south of them. If they missed them, the prospects were not cheerful. When the tide turned, the waves would send them shoreward to an iron coast. They had no provisions, and it was cold as well as dispiriting in the fog. He ordered the men to rig the oars and rowlocks that were attached to the rafts.

"It will bring us quicker to wherever we are going to fetch up in this fog," he said. "And it'll warm you all. Row with the current."

They pulled clumsily at the crude contrivances. Grahame took a steering oar to keep their efforts to an even progress, calling through the mist to the second pontoon. There was no answer. The two rafts had drifted apart in the thick mist.

Presently the waves began to slap more viciously, and the fog seemed less thick. Despite current and ebb tide, they made little progress.

"We're bucking the force of the wind," said Grahame. "We can't feel it yet, but it's piling the sea up, just the same. We must be getting close to the edge of the fog bank. Better rest for a spell. We'll ride our luck."

The men stopped rowing, and the raft drifted aimlessly. Then it struck a current, and followed it until another helped to buffet it first in one direction, then another.

"Cross currents and tide rips," announced Grahame. "There's land of some sort hereabouts."

The sound of surf came faintly to their ears, increasing to a steady pounding.

"It's going to be a nasty job, landing," said Grahame. "All rock, and no sand beaches hereabouts. But we can't miss the chance. It may be our last. Stand by, ready to back water at the word."

It was an eerie situation, drifting on to a wave-beaten shore, blind in the fog, unable to see what best to do until they were in the swirl of the surf itself. Grahame cut loose a life line, and put it about Thurston's chest in a loop.

"You can't swim much with that leg, old chap," he said. "Take a chance with me. If I make it, in you come. Now, men, each for yourselves. Sink in your nails and teeth if you have to, but hold on. Look out for the back wash. We can't save the raft."

The next instant the raft struck. It tilted, struck again, and a wave that swept hissing out of the fog behind them smashed the frail platform against a ledge of sharp-crested volcanic rock. In a moment, each man was struggling amid a turmoil of seething waters that sucked and tore at them as they grabbed for holds. The wave receded, and left them scrambling on the reef, their sense of direction gone.

Grahame's voice boomed through the mist:

"This way, boys. Straight to me. It's only waist-deep. Hurry before the next wave gets you!"

They tumbled pell-mell in the direction of the sound, falling and getting up again, bruised against the rocks, slipping on seaweed, then hands torn by clustering mussels and abalones, fighting their separate ways through the fog to where Grahame shouted and the ray of his electric lamp glowed faintly. They found him in a little cove, paved with rough pebbles, Thurston at his feet, unconscious from a blow on the head and loss of blood.

There was a rush and roar in the air above their heads, and they looked up nervously, though conscious that sight was unavailing.

"It's the birds," said Grahame. "We've scared them off. Grope around and see if we can make higher ground. The tide will cover this when it turns."

Blundering and tripping, but thankful they were alive, the crew investigated, while Grahame worked over the senseless Thurston, who presently groaned and sat up.

"Some headache," he said. "Knocked out at both ends, Bruce. And I've swallowed a gallon of salt water. Where are we?"

"Somewhere in the county of San Francisco," answered Grahame, relieved to hear his friend's voice once more. "That's a fact, Fred. The Farallons are part of the county, but a long swim from City Hall. We're on one of them, but we'll have to wait till daylight to find which one. Thank Heaven the fog's started to lift, or we might be here for a week."

The men reported that they were in a cove, at the upper end of which they could clamber above tidewater. Two of them assisted Thurston, and they made their way to higher ground, where they grouped themselves disconsolately.

"Suffering snakes," said Thurston. "This smell would choke an oyster. Guano and rotten eggs. I'm sitting in a raw omelet, and there's a goony pecking at the small of my back. Ouch!"

The imaginary bird turned out to be the sharp point of a rock, but Thurston's indomitable spirits cheered the little crowd, doubly marooned by sea and fog. Remembering his wound, they forbore to grumble at their own bruises and sprains.

Grahame consulted his water-tight watch by the lantern.

"Seven o'clock," he said. "We're close to the edge of the fog. It'll be clear inside of an hour, and we can get some idea of where we are."

Gradually they began to feel the force of the wind and its chill, while the mist shredded gradually away, displaying star-set patches of sky. Now and then there was the swish of wings as the most venturesome or sleepy birds returned. About them rose a dozen or more islets, mere craggy clusters of crags, fit only for the breeding places of birds. Some of the hungry men searched for eggs and sucked at them eagerly but suspiciously, not always with happy results. The main fog bank, rolled up by the wind, slowly receded. To the south loomed the bulk of the Middle Farallon.

"There's a wireless outfit there," said one of the men. "With beds and hot grub, if we could get to them."

A light flashed out beyond the island, vanished, then reappeared.

"That's the lighthouse on the Southeast Farallon," said Grahame. "The keeper's doing what he thinks his duty, I suppose, but he's helping the enemy more than any one."

"It's company, anyway," said Thurston.

It was a long, cold watch to sunup when they stretched and chafed their stiff limbs to the audience of a myriad curious birds. On the western horizon distant stains of smoke showed where the Japanese fleet kept watch.

"Hot breakfast there, mate," said an airman.

"Rice!" answered the other contemptuously. "I'd like to make it a durned sight hotter for them. What's the skipper about?"

Grahame was unscrewing the glass of the electric lantern. It was of the bull's-eye variety, used for inspecting the engines, and the lens was fully eight inches in diameter.

"Going to poach eggs for breakfast?" asked Thurston. His teeth chattered, and his eyes were sunk deep in purple hollows, but they still held a twinkle.

"I'm going to get in touch with land," said Grahame. "We've got to get out of this before our friends out there get too busy."

He set the glass in the clutch of one hand, and, descending to where a cliff sheltered him from the west and the sight of the fleet, caught the rays of the rising sun and flashed them in the call of the Aërial Auxiliary. "T.K.R." repeated over and over again with his improvised heliograph.

They were too distant from the Middle Farallon to distinguish more than the spidery masts of the aërials, with the buildings at the base of one of them, but Grahame persevered, trusting that the operators would be up betimes after the cannonading of the previous evening in anticipation of coming events.

At last there came a quick wink of light, then another. Grahame answered, and flashed his message.

"They are sending ashore for a helicopter," he said quietly. "We'll be out of this in fifteen minutes."

The men cheered, and the frightened sea birds wheeled about them. It was less than ten minutes before the helicopter *Jupiter*, making sixty feet to the second, rushed toward them from the land, flying low to avoid the lookouts on the distant fleet, hovered and settled down on a tiny level plateau, rose once more with the rescued men, and sped for the shore.

As they neared it, a flash showed against the Marin Hills, something rushed overhead, toward the Japanese ships, with the sound of an express train, and the hollow detonation breaking through the wind told that the sixteen-inch guns of the coast defense were in action.

III
WITH SHOT AND SHELL

The great guns that, with sufficient ammunition and a liberal expenditure for battle practice, should have rendered the Pacific coast immune from actual invasion, rose, roared, and recoiled, belching out their defiance and trained with every effort at precision. The fog, both enemy and friend, had practically departed, leaving an open field between the hostile forces. The heavier caliber, theoretically, should win. But the Japanese guns, while inferior in range and weight of missile, handicapped by a mile or more of water, which gantlet they must pass before their artillery could answer, held the great advantage of experienced gunners. They knew the exact trajectories of their fourteen-inchers. For every million dollars spent upon ammunition for offense, one-quarter that amount had been set aside for the practice that makes perfect.

The California coast artillery had the scanty records of their own peace targetry and that of the Atlantic coast. Scarcely any gun had been fired more than thrice with its actual war charge. The life of the gun, limited to so many discharges, the cost of the projectile, in the sight of appropriation committees limited by a palisade of pork barrels, served effectually to offset what they chose to consider remote possibilities of national danger.

At top speed, it would take the Japanese dreadnaughts upward of three minutes to cross the twenty-five hundred yards of danger zone before they could effectively reply to the fortifications. Then it would be a matter of known propulsion and trajectory against established and stationary targets versus theoretical formulæ and a shifting objective.

The hovering helicopters, two miles in the air, announced the range, the officers took the figures, consulted the gauges for windage, and set the elevation for the pointers. The mammoth rifles mechanically elevated themselves on their carriages to the extreme pitch, the shells were set, the fuses timed, and the crucibled deviltries started upon their mission.

For two hundred seconds a hail of projectiles fell about the Japanese dreadnaughts, speeding to where they could successfully reply. Both squadrons were aimed at by the American gunners. Eighty per cent of the missiles, each representing a moderate man's idea of comparative wealth, plunged harmlessly into the sea. Of the apparent hits, a third struck glancing blows, that wounded, but did not pierce the armor of the battleships. One dreadnaught, the *Chosen*, received two shells, that fell at the end of their great arcs plumb upon her decks, one plunging through the bows, the other crashing into the after turret, and sank instantly. The *Kongo*, its control mast torn and blasted into twisted wire, received a wound just above the water line that practically put her out of the fight, barely able to retreat at half speed to a zone of safety. The cruiser *Matsushima* suffered a raking blow that disemboweled her of motive power, and disappeared beneath the waves in a cloud of steam.

Then, the line of advantage crossed, the real duel commenced. On both sides the gunners became unconscious of exploding shells that merely seemed to time their heartbeats. They loaded, adjusted angles, and fired automatically, unmindful of scorching heat, the gray scum of smoke and choking gas, of smearing blood and rending steel. The skies were split by man-made thunder as they aimed on order at their invisible targets, in ignorance of hit or miss, all individuality lost in the lust of war.

Incessant mandates, calling the range, crying the elevation, a swift inspection, then the cry of "Fire!" urged them to work like demons of the pit with sinewy brown arms bared to the elbows, bodies wet with sweat, soiled with the grime of battle. On the horizon, black smoke streaked from the destroyers as they strove to veil the range from the helicopters, hovering two miles above sea level. Airships from the sea and the shore wheeled and volplaned, soaring in spirals and loops in single combat, as venturous knights might have dashed out from the massed ranks in medieval times.

Swiftly the shells of the shore batteries began to diminish, while a never-ceasing rain of missiles poured unerringly from the sea as the hostile ships closed persistently in, battered, staggering under blows, in a confusion of gray smoke, foaming sea, and crashing explosions. The sea tossed up columns of seething spray, the soil was flung up in earthy geysers, trees were razed, cries of dismembered men sounded faintly in the uproar, and slowly, reluctantly, the cannon of the coast defense ceased firing.

Grahame, making the *Jupiter* his flagship in place of the sunken *Ariel*, took barely time for a hasty meal and a change of personal equipment. Thurston, against his protest, was put under medical care. The chart room of the helicopter was provided with maps from Grahame's headquarters. The principal of these, mounted on rollers, was a panorama of the California coast, enlarged from another, that was pinned on the chart table. Both showed the position of every detail of the mobile railroad artillery and the torpedo stations set within the ruled-off range squares. On a blank sheet, level with the eyes, a periscopic arrangement of mirrors threw a vision of the land or seascape over which the airship passed. Through glass partitions, arranged for soundproofing, the speed telltales, the barometers, and chronometer were visible. An indicator connected with the engine room and automatically coupled or locked propellers at the will of the commander. The wireless instruments and operator were close at hand, the messages delivered over a tape that coiled into a basket in one corner of the tiny cabin.

Grahame and General Lancaster took their stand.

"It seems a strange place for a commander," said the general, as the helicopter began to rise.

"Could there be a better one?" asked Grahame. "Surely it will be the observation post of the future. Unlimited view, immunity from danger, for we can stay above shrapnel range; a fixed point one moment, able to move at two miles a minute the next, to rise or descend; in constant communication with all your forces!"

He spoke enthusiastically. General Lancaster sighed lightly as he answered:

"I dare say you're right, Grahame. Anyway, you are actually the commander. My artillery is silenced for sheer lack of ammunition; my soldiers are only a handful; poor Freeman and his little squadron are gone. The national defenses are practically nil. It's up to you and your emergency plans. And it's a tough problem."

"We can handle it," Grahame replied confidently. "They knew our weakness, general. *They don't know our strength.* They had the exact location of every one of your batteries. They don't know anything about our dynamite guns or torpedoes. We can keep their airships too busy to give them any information, and they'll have a hard time finding the range of guns moving in all directions at any given speed up to twenty miles an hour. Now, then!"

The aneroids gave the level at five thousand feet as Grahame and the general stepped to open portholes in the side of the hull and focused their powerful field glasses on the enemy. They had risen from the parade ground of the San Francisco Presidio, and the fleet was in plain view. The inshore squadron had wheeled and was steaming fifteen miles off shore, parading in front of the shore batteries its guns had so effectually silenced in alliance with the parsimony of Congress. The first-line fleet was slowly progressing southward with the transports.

Grahame had clamped to his head a telephone apparatus communicating with the wireless operator.

"Call the *Mars*, at Monterey," he ordered, as his eyes roved over the situation. "Ask the fog conditions.

"They are very evidently not going to try a landing in San Francisco harbor," he said to the general. "Afraid of the mines. They don't want to take too many chances. They'll bombard your guns at the Monterey Presidio, and imagine the coast clear. We'll give them all the leeway they want, and then, sir, we'll teach them a lesson that will last for all time, that the white man is master. It won't be my fault if one bottom of their fleet—warships, transports, or colliers—ever gets back to Japan— Yes! Hello!"

He listened to the report from Monterey for a few seconds.

"Fog still masks the bay," he announced to the general. "It's a nasty coast to make a slip on, and they'll be careful. I don't want to show our hand until we have to."

"I'm not overconfident about those dynamite guns of yours," said the general. "Those dynamite shells have no penetrating quality, and it will take a lot of explosions to wreck those dreadnaughts. They would work havoc on trenches or advancing troops, of course—"

"Or a landing party. It's the torpedoes I'm relying on, general. That's why I want to coax them within striking distance. There are a dozen dynamite guns now on the line between San Francisco and San Jose. I could bring them up and engage that second squadron, but I want them to think that they have effectually silenced us. There is nothing much more for them to wantonly destroy, and, from their standpoint, the fight is over. I doubt very much whether Kirby, for all his foxiness, got much of an inkling of what we were really doing outside of the helicopters. Sproule managed things famously in the transportation line in covering up shipments and the work in the railroad shops."

The glasses shook in the general's hands. "Where is that treacherous devil?" he said. "I'd give the last few years of my life to come to handgrips with him. I'd choke the truth out of his throat. Duty comes first, Bruce, but—"

"We'll get him, sir; and Irene, too," answered Grahame reassuringly. "He got the best of me last night by a fluke, when I thought I had him. He's commanding a triplane, and I've made a special detail to attend to his case. Ah! They are playing into our hands."

The second squadron was advancing at full speed to join the first fleet. Grahame's conjecture about the mines that guarded the entrance to San Francisco harbor was a true one. In the absence of precise information, Admiral Kato was carrying out his invasion along the lines of least resistance. The mines could be removed by the land forces after they had invested the harbor.

With the principal coast cities destroyed the Japanese plans for a New Nippon did not include their rebuilding. San Francisco was to become once more a sand desert, used only for fortification purposes, and the capital of the New Kingdom was to be established on the mainland, on the site of Oakland and Berkeley. At Monterey, the natural sea gate to the rich San Joaquin Valley, hitherto undeveloped under the long-haul policy of the railroad, a great seaport would be built.

At present, these general plans were unknown to Grahame, but he had shrewdly surmised them as the logical action of a conquering nation, putting himself in the place of their chief councilors. The main issue that now counted was the evident intention of the enemy to land in the bay of Monterey and establish a headquarters somewhere along its shores.

The bay of Monterey, a deeply bitten crescent some sixty miles south of San Francisco, is the only practical open harbor and roadstead of the Pacific coast outside of San Diego. Between Santa Cruz Point and the Point of Pines, the mouth of the bay is twenty miles in width. Close by the headlands are the towns of Santa Cruz and Monterey, each the railroad point for a popular pleasure resort. At Monterey once called the Spanish galleons towing from the Philippines. Later the whaling fleet centered there. It is a port of call for Pacific coast steamships, but, despite rumors and opportunity, and its central position in the state, it has never been developed for shipping.

Between Monterey and Santa Cruz, fed in the center from the main lines at Watsonville Junction, the tracks of the railroad branches run in an arc between sand dunes and marshes, leaving a segment of lonely shore, where Grahame had established depots for the torpedoes and electric storage stations for their control, the latter so skillfully buried in the sand that detection, even at the closest range, was practically impossible. From Santa Cruz, along the cliffs ran the tracks of the Ocean Shore Railroad to San Francisco.

The regular lines of track had been augmented by spurs, Y's sidetracks, and runarounds for the quick handling of the truck-mounted dynamite guns. Immediately after the defeat of the reservists, hospital supplies, provisions, and ammunitions had been stored at Santa Cruz, Watsonville, and Monterey.

Now everything was in readiness. Gun crews, largely chosen from ex-navy and army gunners and artillerymen, with members of the naval reserve, were on the qui vive, as were the Red Cross doctors and nurses, equipped with Ainsworth hospital cars; and the handler of the commissariat, recruited from the railroad, under Pollok.

The aëroplanes of the enemy commenced a swift retreat beyond the fleet, and flew southward with the ships, protected by the vessels' lighter batteries. Grahame issued a recall to his own flotilla, and they accompanied the *Jupiter* in a parallel course with the enemy, following the tracks of the Ocean Shore Railroad. Their mission was to prevent the enemy from discovering the nature of the shore batteries once they opened fire.

IV

THE DEFENSE OF MONTEREY BAY

The Japanese ships, the biplanes wheeling about them like great sea gulls as they regulated their speed to that of the slowest unit of the fleet—the transports—steamed in two rows, keeping their distances as if on parade.

The destroyers were inshore, ready to pour out a screen of smoke should any necessity arise. On board, the officers laughingly watched Grahame's air fleet winging its way above the cliffs. They had only to destroy a few guns at the Monterey Presidio, of which they possessed the exact locations, and annihilate the few companies of soldiers. There they would land, fortify the railroad passes, and establish New Nippon.

Ogden Kirby, in the big war plane, with its three tiers of ailerons, was not in as pleasant a humor. The defeat of the reservist forces still rankled, and his tactics had been made the subject of sharp reprimand, followed by general comment that subsided into a situation where he was either ignored or the subject of pity. His command of the triplane had been given him with a sarcastic hint that he might perhaps redeem himself.

"Like must fight like," Admiral Kato had sternly said to him. "You should not have attempted your coup with your knowledge of their air fleet, which can only be coped with successfully by our own, backed by the fleet aircraft batteries. You have done much for Japan, and it is not for me to weigh your accomplishments against your failure. I will give you a triplane. Perhaps you can turn the tables on your late conquerors."

Kirby's dream of a glorious career had faded. The governorship of the New Nippon was not to be his. The ambition that had led him to attempt the march of the reservists to the sea, where he could have entrenched them against any assault from sky or land, had ended in disaster that might easily spell disgrace with a government that would not easily forgive the useless sacrifice of thousands.

The carefully reared edifice, planned through long years that promised success, had crumbled, and he lived now for the personal triumph of his hate against Grahame and his love for Irene Lancaster.

Grahame he believed at the bottom of the sea. He had watched the *Ariel* drop, like a desperately wounded sea fowl, into the fog, with a feeling that went far to soothe his injured pride. Irene he vowed to make his own if he had to break her spirit in the conquest. On the night of her abduction, he had conveyed her to the coast of the nearest point to the rancheria, Esteros Bay. There a launch had taken her to where she now lay, helpless, in a sea cave of one of the Santa Barbara Islands.

The sting of her hand on his cheek reasserted itself, as it always did when he thought of her, and he promised himself an ample vengeance for the blows and the scorn in her eyes. The control of the submarine that waited his orders at the Coronado Islands had not been taken from him. The undersea vessels were not a factor in the present situation. It was of the latest type, eighteen hundred tons, with a surface speed equal to that of a battle cruiser, and a radius of six thousand miles. On it was the bulk of his personal wealth, converted into gold from American securities, in which, by foreknowledge of the Japanese invasion, he had made a fortune.

Whatever the outcome of the fight, and he held no doubt of Japanese victory, he determined never to return to Dai Nippon under the stigma of a failure. With the triplane and his submarine he summoned up vague visions of establishing some island kingdom of his own in the south Pacific, with Irene Lancaster, acknowledging him as lord, as his consort. Riches were his, and power could yet be gained. Even yet he might compel the admiration of Japan. If not—

His reverie was broken by a call to the triplane's wireless. The fleet was fifteen miles offshore, passing the triple capes of Pigeon Point, Middle Point, and Point Ano Nuevo. Santa Cruz was less than an hour away at their present rate of travel. Two dreadnaughts and four battle cruisers left the main fleet at full speed to subdue the guns of the Monterey Presidio. The imperial flag was hoisted to the mainmast of the flagship, and bugles sounded as the men rushed to their quarters. The destroyers made no attempt to form a smoke screen. The American air fleet still kept to the cliffs. There was nothing to fight. The whole affair was a dress rehearsal. Kirby took up his station above his ship, as did the rest of the biplanes, awaiting further orders. From his elevation he could see that the fog had disappeared. As far as the range of his glasses, the distant headlands stood out distinctly.

The tactics of the Japanese admiral were comparatively simple. Within twenty-four hours he expected to land his troops, withdraw his main fleet across the Pacific, and report his victory in person. The submarine flotilla at Tierra del Fuego, which had so effectively wiped the American Atlantic fleet out of existence near Cape Horn, still remained at their base. Six of the thirty ships composing the Atlantic battle line had perforce remained in home waters for lack of complement, and, fully alive to the fact that by this time patriotism would see them fully manned from the naval reserve corps, he thus held them in Atlantic waters, guarding, at the same time, against possible interference of purchased warships from other nations. The gold of the United States, which would be freely subscribed and spent for such purposes in the indignation of the ravished nation—now the wealthiest in the world—constituted, he was well aware, the chief menace to the complete occupation of California.

A landing at Monterey, release of the reservist prisoners, fortification of the railroads, the establishment of a coast artillery with guns provided for that end and now aboard his ships, and the recall of the submarines, would leave him free to announce his task accomplished. A Japanese squadron, sufficiently strong to hold the new possession against attack from any scratch navy that America might gather, would be left in charge.

The immediate work in hand was the destruction of the coast artillery at Monterey, to be followed by a sortie from his air fleet, both for a recognizance of any opposition that might be planned against the landing and in an endeavor to destroy as many of the American airships as possible.

He was not greatly concerned about Grahame's air armada. They were a nuisance to be suppressed as quickly as possible, but not a serious opposition to landing. His vessels were equipped with the latest anti-aircraft guns which could toss steel to a height of two miles. If need be, he could sweep the sky with a constant stream of shrapnel, under the cover of which his troops could land in safety. It was all very simple.

At twenty miles, far outside the range of the Monterey artillery, the advance ships opened fire with murderous precision, the great shells falling on the gun positions with the same deadly accuracy as at San Francisco harbor earlier in the day.

There was no reply from the fortifications. At that distance it would have been futile. General Lancaster, at the suggestion of Grahame, had withdrawn the artillerymen.

"They can either think we've abandoned the guns or are helpless against their heavier metal," said Grahame. "The main thing is to keep their aëroplanes from discovering the dynamite guns on the railroad until we've got the fleet inside the bay, transports and all."

Ammunition charges, purposely left exposed at the Presidio emplacements, blew up one after the other as the shells showered down. The ruse worked to perfection. After the first furious bombardment, the Japanese ships fired at longer intervals shells that were evidently considered superfluous, and at last their battery ceased and the main fleet drew up to the van and assumed formation.

Five dreadnaughts made up the left wing, five more the right. Inside of them were ranged the battle cruisers, then the auxiliaries. In the center steamed the transports, their decks black with men, eager to step upon the soil of their long-hoped-for new country. About them swarmed the destroyers, ready to act as a shore convoy. They came on slowly at half speed, prepared to fight, yet not expecting resistance, entering between the horns of the crescent bay, closer and closer, while the confident officers completed preparations for the embarkation of the troops and the landing of the big howitzers they had brought to keep the coast guard of New Nippon.

They were only five miles away. Still the American helicopters hovered high and the biplanes swung to and fro. Down on the beach, part marsh, part sand, men in concealed pits patted torpedoes and batteries and listened for the tick-tack of their receiving apparatus, to tell them when to launch the deadly engines while they gazed from their hiding places at their targets. Tucked away like duck hunters in blinds were many of them, in huts built among the rushes, covered with reeds above the shrapnel-proof roofs. Others were crouched in sand burrows. All were by the sides of sloughs or lagoons that opened to the sea with channels deepened to let out the torpedoes to blue water, where the electric control would guide them, unsuspected and unseen, until their war heads exploded against the armored keels.

The last wisp of fog departed, and the day was crystal clear. Flags suddenly broke out upon the admiral's ship, and were answered from the rest of the fleet with bunting that flipped gaily in the breeze.

Grahame turned to General Lancaster with a gleam in his eyes. "They are anchoring, sir," he said. "By the Eternal, we've got them now!"

The great cables of the floating fortresses rattled out. Secure in their impregnability, sure that all defense had been destroyed, the enemy proceeded with the leisurely precision of a review to set, ship by ship, link by link, a chain of steel across the bay. Only the transports did not anchor, but came in to close moorings while the biplanes sprang shoreward, above them, like blue rocks released from the traps.

The American biplanes soared to meet them, both air fleets maneuvering for altitude. Only the six helicopters remained stationary at ten thousand feet, their horizontal propellers humming as they gripped the air. They were too valuable as range finders and observers to risk battle unless directly attacked. Back from the beach, the gunners, in the armored cars, adjusted the dynamite guns to the proper trajectory, and waited. Grahame was not yet ready. He wanted to see the transports anchored and the troops in the barges before he let loose the hell he had prepared. His brain held no thought of mercy. He remembered the Atlantic fleet, sunk at midnight, Admiral Freeman's predoomed men, the ruined cities, and their dead citizens. It was white man against brown, as it had been through all the ages. The lesson must be thorough, absolute, convincing.

The air was full of sharp detonations. Patches of smoke trailed between the planes. The whirring of the propellers, the roar of the heavily cylindered engines, created a din that reechoed dully from the sea. Here, there, machines began to fall, whirling down like dead leaves over and over in helpless gyrations, or slid off sideways, with figures tugging desperately as stubborn levers. Some dropped headlong, blazing, many of them, to smash into the shore surf or the stagnant marsh pools. The defenders were superior in numbers, but their machines, owned and manned by volunteers, were of mixed models and varying speeds. The Japanese biplanes, powerfully engined, of identical type, attached with precision in divisions of six, those from the dreadnaughts led by a triplane that carried a crew of eight and two machine guns. As a whole, they climbed better, and, working in concert, systematically singled out the isolated craft of the Americans and concentrated their fire. Machine guns sputtered at close range, and here and there hand bombs were thrown in desperate rallies that sometimes ended in collisions that sent the combatants side by side down to death.

The invaders, try as they might, could not break through the shore cordon, and soon reinforcements of the Americans, summoned from the shore patrols, began to appear in overwhelming numbers, winging from north and south to join the fight. The Japanese admiral signaled a recall, and the hostile divisions wheeled and drove to sea, with Grahame's fleet in swift pursuit, reluctantly returning to land as they received their own orders.

Grahame feared a trap, and his wisdom was proven when, the Japanese machines safe behind the fleet, white puffs of smoke spotted the sky. Soon a hail of shrapnel broke above the shore in an impenetrable curtain of bullet-bursting bombs, before which the defense retreated. The helicopters lifted to eleven thousand feet and hovered above the zone of fire. Gradually the anti-aircraft guns lowered their trajectory, driving all but the helicopters a mile inland.

Barges and launches dropped from the davits of transports and cruisers. Gunwale deep, the boats were taken in tow, stringing out behind the launches, the red-rayed sun of Japan flying at their sterns.

From the *Jupiter* the order was sparked, "Commence firing!"

Then the promised hell broke loose. From the dynamite guns the explosive shells soared upward, arched, and fell roaring among and upon the open boats and transports in a tornado of turbulent destruction, while the armored cars glided back and forth upon the tracks and seemed to multiply fifty cannon to five times that number as they shifted position after every discharge. Bewildered by the unexpected avalanche of steel, the big guns of the fleet attempted to answer their unseen foe. The shrapnel ceased abruptly, and once more the hostile air fleet rushed desperately inland to locate the batteries. Once more the American biplanes rose to meet them. On sea and land and sky pandemonium reigned. The waves were lashed into a maelstrom, the sand was tossed high as the searching shells tried blindly to find the source of the blasting fire. Two triplanes broke through the cordon, and two helicopters darted after them at the call of the *Jupiter*. The batteries were no longer masked. The fourteen-inch guns of the dreadnaughts found their range.

From the *Jupiter*, high swung in the sky, the battle looked like a panoramic exhibition. The great ships seemed tiny models, the bay a pond, the scattered boats and launches water bugs. Suddenly a dreadnaught rocked, lifted its bows, and disappeared. Another was tossed in fragments from the water in a glare of flame. Another and another sank as the merciless torpedoes, guided at will by the electric controls, hurled themselves against the hulls. All the transports had sunk from the frightful impact of the dynamite, the embarkation flotilla was only splinters strewn over the sea, to which clung a few despairing men. Anchors were torn from their beds, and, still sullenly firing, the fleet put out to sea, the remnant of the airships flying far ahead, in a disordered rout. They were unpursued. Grahame's triumphant airmen sank to earth behind the railroad. The dynamite guns vomited their missiles at the fleet, that melted as the torpedoes found their mark. The ships, a tortured fragment of the proud vessels that had so complacently entered the bay and anchored, passed with increasing speed beyond the torpedo range, but still the shells rained upon them, powerless to penetrate, but able to change thick-armored turrets into shapeless masses of scrap, to uproot masts and level superstructures.

With their funnels shot away, half of them afire, of all the pomp and power of the Japanese navy, only two battered dreadnaughts and four cruisers limped at last beyond the fury of the shells and disappeared behind the gray haze of acrid gas that masked their pitiful retreat.

A sudden silence seemed to fall upon the bay. The roar of the conflict ended with the carnage that showed so few actual signs of occurrence. The waves rolled into the beach above the sunken vessels and their crews as if the frenzy of the combat was a dream.

The American forces had not escaped entirely unscathed. Some of the Japanese shells had found their mark along the railroad tracks. The scattering fire had unearthed a few of the torpedo stations, and the gallant airmen mourned the loss of at least a third of their comrades. But there was no comparison of destruction. As an aggressive force, the Japanese power of invasion was wiped out.

V

BY SKY AND SEA

In the *Jupiter's* chart room, General Lancaster gripped Grahame by the hand. He said nothing, but his eyes, still flashing with battle lust, spoke for him his admiration and acclaim.

Grahame reached for his indicator, and the *Jupiter* darted seaward. As the general looked at him inquiringly, he nodded, then spoke:

"Time now for our own affairs, sir. Kirby's out there in a triplane. He's got a few minutes' start, but we'll overhaul him."

"Do you know which machine is his?"

"It will be flying south, I fancy. Toward the Coronados."

The *Jupiter* rushed out to sea above the dismantled warships, flying two miles to the minute, seeking for Ogden Kirby, and, through him, Irene Lancaster.

In the distance they could see the defeated airships in a cloud that swung to the west and south.

"They'll wait for the ships presently, and go with them to Hawaii, I imagine," said Grahame. "I don't envy them their reception. We must pay a visit to the islands presently, and there are one or two other matters to clear up yet—the submarines, for instance—but I think we've earned a few hours for ourselves, general."

"Airship to the south'ard, sir," announced the forward lookout.

Far off, a mere speck against the blue to the unassisted eye, they saw their quarry, and darted in pursuit. Slowly the speck increased in size, a triplane driving down the coast.

And while Kirby and his men nursed their engines, watching the wingless craft that stubbornly gained mile after windy mile, Admiral Kato lay dead upon the floor of his cabin on the shattered dreadnaught, the suicidal blade of his ancestors by the side of his disemboweled corpse.

For an hour the two machines flew with little change in their respective positions. The *Jupiter* was not as fast as the *Ariel* had been, and the advantage she gained at the beginning of the pursuit was gradually lost as Kirby's crew worked desperately over the engines of the triplane. The *Jupiter's* speed gauge moved up to one hundred and five miles, and stayed there, nor could an extra revolution be coaxed out of her.

"Some of the horizontals were hit in the fight early this mornin'," said the chief mechanician, in reply to Grahame's appeal. "I'm fearin' there's a blade or two off pitch that's hinderin'. We've had sma' time for repairs. I dinnna ken the fu' extent of the damage."

"Well, do the best you can, McPherson," said Grahame. "I'd like to get close enough to wing him, but if we can hang on, we'll get him later, when he comes down. He'll need more spare time than he's likely to get to make his landing."

Ahead, Kirby watched the helicopter fall back with but little satisfaction, realizing that his gain was insufficient for his purpose. The island on which he had imprisoned Irene Lancaster was over two hundred miles south of Monterey Bay. It would take him fully half an hour to descend, take the girl and the guards he had left with her aboard, and get under full headway again. He could abandon the guards, and decided to do so if he could save time thereby. But he had less than a third of the necessary time now in hand, and half of the distance was already covered. He might, he figured, gain another ten minutes in the rest of the flight, but the pursuit would be upon him before he could get clear again, and the triplane was no match for a helicopter with the latter's extra armament and superior maneuvering ability. And, after Santa Barbara Channel, there was another flight of close to two hundred miles before he could reach final safety in the submarine.

He decided to call the base on the Coronados. There were men stationed there aside from the crew of the undersea vessel. The base was well stocked with provisions, gasoline, oil, and extra torpedoes as a port of call for the submarines now at Cape Horn, which were to replenish supplies there before returning to Japanese waters. To it had been attached the six submarines that made the raid on the northern ports. Its equipment included a radio station, and Kirby commenced calling at the extreme limit of his sending capacity.

He had no thought that the helicopter held any but enemies who believed him cut off from the rest of the Japanese air squadron, and were determined upon his destruction from a purely impersonal standpoint. Grahame he had every reason to believe at the bottom of the sea, and he considered it more than likely that General Lancaster had been killed by the blow from the inkwell. He had flung it with all his force, he remembered.

If he could have shaken off the helicopter, he was inclined to look upon things very complacently. The admiral who had rebuked him, the officers who had held aloof from a man who was under the stigma of a failure, were now either dead, or, if living, under a ban even greater than his own.

As Orientals, there was but one end for the chiefs of the ill-fated invading expedition—the fate of "death with honor," which Admiral Kato had already achieved. But the mixed blood in Kirby's veins caused him to look upon life as a more precious thing, not to be surrendered until the last hope of enjoyment was gone. He was in no mood to return to Japan, and in America he would undoubtedly be shot if captured. He was an outlaw from both the nations that had combined to give him birth.

And an outlaw he determined to be. There were twenty millions in specie and convertible securities aboard his submarine. The woman he wanted, though there was more revenge than passion in his present longing, was in his hands. He would possess her, tame her to his will, or, if he could not, there were others to be won or bought. A vision of a little island kingdom where he would reign supreme, of palm-fringed lagoons, of pearls, of fragrant blossoms, rose before him. If he tired of the American woman, he could turn to one of the other side of his breeding. His Japanese ancestors had come from the Pacific; there were beauties there, with skins of gold and bronze, who would adore him with their ardent natures and worship him as a king. A king he would be, with a court of luxurious magnificence, a satrap of the south seas, gathering about him pomp and power—

A member of the crew disturbed his reverie with the unwelcome announcement that the helicopter seemed to be once more gaining.

Kirby went to the stern of the gondola and looked through his glasses with a frown. The pursuer was distinctly larger.

"It's the head wind, sir," his engineer reported. "We might escape it by rising, but we'd be losing as we mounted."

"How much gasoline have you got?" asked Kirby. If his supply was sufficient, he could give up his present purpose and hold his lead sufficiently to fly across the Mexican line.

The answer was discouraging. There was barely enough fuel to reach the submarine base. One of the tanks that should have been full was empty.

"A stray bullet," suggested one of the men.

Kirby cursed fluently. "Have you got the Coronados station?" he demanded.

"Not yet, sir."

"Keep at it till you do."

Slowly but stubbornly the helicopter grew larger. Kirby set down his glasses and gave an order to ascend in an endeavor to find a calmer level, where he could once more begin to pick up a lead. The great ailerons were tilted, and the triplane climbed steadily in the face of the gale. Suddenly the wireless operator caught the answer from the Coronados. They had flown within operating distance.

Kirby came to a swift determination to abandon any present attempt to pick up Irene Lancaster. He could come back for her later in the submarine. He sent a message to the base, ordering the subsea boat to proceed at full, unsubmerged speed to meet the triplane. The submarine was capable of making thirty-five knots on the surface, and every moment gained gave him more time for the transfer of himself and crew.

Back in the *Jupiter*, Grahame watched the overhauling of his enemy with grim satisfaction. Once up with the triplane, he felt confident that, with the absolute control of the helicopter, he could cripple Kirby's machine sufficiently to make her fall, without endangering the lives of her crew, though Kirby's was the only one he really cared about saving. By hook or crook, by torture, if it became necessary, he resolved to wrest from the half-breed the secret of Irene Lancaster's whereabouts.

"Then I shall turn him over to you, general," he said.

"He'll receive scant mercy at my hands. His life was long ago— What's that?"

The bow of the *Jupiter* dipped suddenly; the airship pitched, staggered, then righted herself.

"Damaged propeller given way, sir," McPherson reported. "One blade gone and put another horizontal out of commission as it went. The two forward starboard shafts. Makes it hard to trim her. I could fix it if we had time. There's spare propellers aboard."

"There's no time for repairs, chief," answered Grahame. "All I'm worrying about is the speed."

"We'd have to shut off two port horizontals aft to hold her level, sir. That 'u'd be a quarter of our lift, and more than we could stand, I'm thinking. And I'll no guarantee ye full speed flying wi' a list to starboard. The engine bed's none too strong as it is."

"Get all out of her you can," answered Grahame. "He has the devil's luck still with him."

Her decks aslant, the *Jupiter* drove on behind the swiftly revolving tractor, her speed reduced to nine-tenths of full. From the triplane Kirby saw her pitch, and then, side tilted, fall behind. In an hour he gained almost ten minutes. Soon the *Jupiter* was an indistinguishable mote in the blue, doggedly hanging on.

The triplane was above the islands of the Santa Barbara Channel. The coast of the largest of them, the island of Santa Cruz, was wave-chiseled into a line of deep indentations, of arched rocks, worn away from the land, and caverns that ran far back into the cliffs. These rocky chambers had long been used by smugglers of men and opium, both Japanese and Chinese, and many of them had secret hiding places, almost impossible to find by the uninitiated.

The triplane volplaned swiftly to the surface of a cove and skimmed lightly over the placid water to a sandy beach where a little stream trickled down a wooded glen. To one side were the low arches of a cavern known to the smugglers as Tres Bocas—The Three Mouths. Kirby sprang to the shore, entered the cave, and whistled. The interior was comparatively shallow, well lighted from the three entrances. The worn walls showed no opening. But, as Kirby impatiently repeated his signal, a Japanese, straightening from a stooping posture, came out of what seemed the solid rock. Kirby snapped an order at him, and he swiftly retreated, holding aside a mass of seaweed that masked a low cavity at the base of the wall.

Into this he disappeared. The apparently solid rock formed only a curtain for an interior chamber, roughly circular and about twenty feet in diameter. Two lanterns dimly lit the place, which was rudely furnished with benches, a table and a low bedstead, on which was lying the figure of a woman, motionless.

The Japanese roughly shook her shoulder.

"You come," he said.

Irene Lancaster sat up. The terror of her own situation, the suspense at what had happened in her absence, had rendered her face pallid and haggard, though her spirit still gleamed in her eyes.

"Go where?" she asked.

"I don' know. You come. Quick!"

Anything was better than the dreary cavern, watched almost constantly by her sullen warders, and she followed the man outside. She was not altogether unprepared to see Kirby, and her head went up proudly. Her captor wasted no words upon her.

"Take her aboard!" he commanded two of his crew, then swung upon the man who had played jailer.

"Where's Amaki?" he asked.

"He's gone fishing."

"Well, we can't wait for him. In you go."

"You're not going to leave Amaki here?" protested the man. "We've got no boat. I won't go without him."

"Then you can both stay here till you rot," said Kirby. He entered the gondola, the triplane was backed gently from the beach, the great propeller spun, whirred to a roar, and the machine raced for the open waters of the channel, then lifted, and wheeled to the south. Five miles away the *Jupiter*, still canted to one side, glided in pursuit.

The helicopter was not to be shaken off so easily this time. McPherson consented to speed up his engines another notch, keeping his bearings literally afloat in oil.

"That's the most I can gi' ye," he declared. "Any faster an' they'll rock themselves to junk."

And with that Grahame was forced to be content, though the triplane steadily forged ahead, furlong by furlong.

Kirby anxiously kept track of his gasoline gauge, and figured out his course of action on his chart. From Santa Cruz Island to the Coronado the distance by air line was approximately one hundred and eighty-five miles. The submarine was nearing him at thirty-five knots to his mileage of one hundred and ten. An hour more should see the two meet somewhere in the neighborhood of Catalina Island. At the rate the fuel was being consumed, he realized that he would, in all probability, have to abandon the triplane and perhaps some of its crew.

To the latter prospect he was callous as long as he could get Irene and himself safely below the conning tower of the submarine, with twenty fathoms of water between them and the surface as a shield for any bombs the helicopter might let fall. Had he dreamed that the father and lover of the girl were in the flying machine, he would have been more reckless, calculating on their fear of endangering her life. Even then his nature might have prompted him to choose the more dramatic course of sinking out of sight and reach.

The islands of Santa Catalina and San Clemente showed like purple shadows on the sea, then resolved themselves into craggy peak and rocky shore as quarry and hunter ate up the fast-flying miles. Across the channel, beyond San Pedro, a blue mist marked where Los Angeles was burning. Grahame had not confined the hours of the pursuit entirely to the purpose in hand. As they flew, he was in constant touch with the mainland, and already movements were started that sent two helicopters to hover above the submarine base in the Gulf of California on the island of Tiburon, ready to destroy any submarines that, leaving there, should pass the neutral limit. The threatened attack across the Mexican border had not materialized, and General Lancaster's troops were dispatched to the line against any such emergency.

"Then," he said to General Lancaster, "we'll send a helicopter squadron down the South American coast to find that submarine flotilla, and chase them, if needs be, across the Pacific, with seventy-five-pound bombs falling at the first peep of a periscope. We'll volunteer for an Hawaiian expedition after that. The remaining fraction of the Atlantic fleet, with the dreadnaughts bought from Brazil and Argentina, should crack that nut, but, if they need our help, they are welcome to it. Then I fancy we shall have done our share."

"More than that, Grahame," protested General Lancaster. "Your plan and the preparedness of the Pacific-coast citizens have saved the country. There's no honor within the gift of the nation you are not entitled to. It would not have been long before the Japanese would have ceased to be content with the territory west of the Sierra."

"You'd have a hard time making the Middle West believe that, I imagine," said Grahame. "Confound those propellers of ours, that chap's got the speed of us. Look at him scud."

Off Santa Catalina the triplane was fifteen miles ahead, a gap of ten minutes. Below the two airships the waters of the famous fishing district were crystal clear, emerald in the shallows, sapphire and purple in the depths, with shadowy patches where submerged peaks and plateaus lifted from the ocean bed. A strip of dark brown marked the great kelp bed that stretches down the Pacific coast, a great curtain of weed, a veritable sea forest, where sea bass, twice the weight of a man, browse amid the trunk-like stems and the jungle of floating branches and fronds.

The triplane began to descend in long swoops toward the surface. The submarine, its decks awash, its two guns manned, a group of Japanese on the deck anxiously gazing at the flight, was tearing toward them. Kirby gave an order, the triplane's sending apparatus crackled, a hatch opened in the after deck of the submarine, and a small boat automatically appeared on davits that swung outward. Two sailors took up their stations in it, ready to make a swift dash for the plane the moment it came to a rest on the water.

With ailerons banked, the big machine plowed through the wave crests, scattering foam, until, as the propeller ceased its whirl, it slid to a standstill, rocking to the motion of the sea. The side door of the gondola opened as the boat came alongside. An airman stepped into it, followed by Irene Lancaster and then Ogden Kirby. The rowers swung to their oars, and the tiny craft, laden to its limit, hastened back to the submarine. The girl gazed about her, her eyes widening as they saw the helicopter rushing swiftly toward them, Grahame recklessly speeding the engines to their limit in the endeavor to prevent the transshipment.

"It's Bruce!" the girl cried intuitively. "It's Bruce—come to rescue me."

"Not unless he swims—*upward*," said Kirby. "Bear a hand there. They'll be within range in a second."

The girl was dragged aboard. In the minds of Kirby and the crew of the submarine there was no time to lose. The helicopter would be directly above them in five minutes, and it took almost that time to submerge. The little boat was left to drift, the last figure disappeared below, the automatic hatch closed, the cover of the conning tower followed, and, amid a swirl of water, the submarine slowly sank as its tanks were filled with water ballast.

It was twenty feet below the surface when the helicopter arrived above the spot where it had disappeared. They could see it sinking slowly down, like a great fish, in the translucent sea.

The general turned to Grahame, with anguish in his eyes.

"Too late, my boy," he said. "It's not your fault, but she's lost to us now."

"We can follow his course," said Grahame. "But I can't attack."

"I'd rather you dropped a bomb and blew them all to atoms, than leave my daughter in the power of that hybrid devil."

VI

IN THE KELP

A rattling volley came from the triplane. Abandoned, practically out of fuel, its crew had determined to fight rather than surrender. It had lifted, and was mounting in a great spiral, both machine guns and the rifles of the marksmen striving to cripple the *Jupiter* in a surprise attack at close range.

It was over inside of five minutes. Handicapped though it was by broken horizontals, the helicopter rose far more swiftly than its antagonist. Once above the triplane, the *Jupiter* shuttled for position, hovered, and dropped a seventy-five-pound bomb directly in the center of the great kite. With the explosion it seemed to disintegrate, lost in a blinding smother of flame and smoke, that swayed the helicopter as it sprang upward from the force of the explosion.

Keeping the higher level, it darted in search of the submarine, hopeless though the pursuit seemed to be, ranging like a sea bird after herring, a dozen pairs of eyes scanning the transparent waters as easily as tourists in a glass-bottom boat watch the fishes in the sea gardens of Catalina.

Kirby, thirty fathoms down, laughed as he thought of the ending of the chase in his favor by the margin of minutes. He laughed again as the captain of the craft asked him if he should return to the base.

"No," answered Kirby exultantly. "You are full supplied? Then steer southwest. We've a long trip before us."

The man looked askance at his superior, with a curious glance at Irene Lancaster. The airman who had come aboard with Kirby and the girl had already spread the news of disaster to the Japanese fleet, and he could not reconcile the situation with Kirby's mood.

"Special orders?" he asked, at a venture.

Kirby's smile turned to a scowl. "*My* orders," he said, with an oath.

The Japanese looked at him stolidly for a moment, then saluted with a swift precision that was overpunctilious.

"There's a barrier reef lifts parallel with the shore," he said. "We'll have to rise to twenty fathoms to clear it."

"That's your business," Kirby curtly answered. "I've given you your course."

The fin keels were set, and the submarine's nose rose until the twenty-fathom level was reached. The course was set, and it steered for the open sea, under the drive of its engines, at a fifteen-knot clip.

Kirby had not yet determined upon his exact destination, but there was plenty of time for that, he decided. He had yet to win the crew over to his plans for freedom. That, too, could wait. The main thing was to keep below the surface as long as possible. After the helicopter's gasoline supply began to run short, they would perforce give up the chase, perhaps they had already abandoned it. Steering southwest, the nearest land was Hawaii, two thousand miles away, with nothing in between—

Slowly, insidiously, the progress of the submarine slackened. It seemed to be thrusting aside something that resisted elastically. The propeller shaft turned with gradually diminishing speed, then it stopped all revolution. The lights burned on, the newly charged batteries held their strength, nothing had gone wrong with the machinery, but the craft was held powerless to proceed, suspended twenty fathoms under the surface. The tanks were emptied of water and charged with air. The submarine lifted a trifle, her bows pointed upward, and stayed in that position as the boat swayed slightly to and fro, gripped by some unseen force outside.

High above, Grahame had located it as it changed its course, and had foreseen its peril. It had attempted a passage through the kelp curtain, and the supple cables of the weed held it as securely as the tentacles of a mammoth octopus might clutch. The propeller was inextricably locked in a tight-wound tangle of living rope rooted to the sea bed, moving with the current a little, holding the submarine as securely trapped as the chain nets of the English Channel and the Scottish locks ever gripped a German U boat.

"We've got them, after all," he said to General Lancaster. "I knew his luck must break some time."

"How are you going to get them out of that before they smother?"

"That's not such an impossible problem if we can get hold of a couple of tugs at San Pedro. The submarine's hard and fast. They could live easily enough for days, but we'll have them out before sunset."

As the *Jupiter* crossed San Pedro Channel to the mainland, he outlined his plan. A government tug was secured, and another commandeered for war purposes. Within thirty minutes both were steaming for the kelp, the helicopter ahead of them, to relocate the submarine. The tugs stopped their engines inside the belt of weed, lying a quarter of a mile apart, two bases of a triangle of which the *Jupiter*, skidding slowly seaward over the surface and settling well beyond the kelp curtain, formed the apex.

The airship towed a pontoon that the government tug had brought as a deckload. On it was a length of heavy iron cable, its ends fastened to six-inch hawsers, that, in turn, were attached to the stern bitts of the tugs. The *Jupiter* rose, leaving two men on the pontoon with the cable. The submarine, a hundred odd feet down in the kelp, was now in the triangle, nearer the base. The heavy cable was tossed over from the raft and sank through the kelp, forcing down the stems that slid aside in the line of their least resistance.

At last Grahame gave the signal. The tugs steamed forward, dragging the hawser and the iron cable in a great V, in the clutch of which they hoped to grip and break the mass of stems that held the submarine.

Suddenly the lines tautened, and the screws churned the water as the powerful vessels fought the resistance. For a minute the sturdy kelp stems held, then, with a jerk, they were torn from their roots as the propeller of the submarine was torn from its shaft and the imprisoned craft shot to the surface.

The helicopter dropped to meet her emergence, her deck guns trained on the conning tower. The lid lifted, and the form of the Japanese commander of the submarine appeared, megaphone in hand.

"We surrender," he called, in good English.

"Where is Kirby?" asked Grahame.

"Below; he surrenders, also." There was a grim smile about the lips of the Japanese that made Grahame think the surrender of Kirby had not been entirely voluntary.

"Bring your men on deck!" he commanded. "We'll tow you in. Send up the lady first. We'll send a boat for her."

He signaled the tugs, and a boat put out and rowed across the kelp to the airship, embarking Grahame and General Lancaster, with four of their men bearing side arms. The quick-firers of the *Jupiter* still dominated any attempt at treachery.

As they stepped aboard the submarine, Irene appeared, wonder growing in her eyes as she saw her father, and rushed into his arms. The impassive Oriental crew followed, and then came Kirby, the Japanese commander close behind him. He caught sight first of Grahame, then of General Lancaster. His face distorted with astonishment, then with rage. Snatching a pistol from his belt, he fired at Grahame. The Japanese commander struck up his arm, and the bullet went wide.

Irene sprang from her father's side to that of Grahame, and Kirby, before his weapon could be wrested from him, turned it upon himself. With a bullet through his temple, he held his balance for a pulse beat, glaring at the reunited lovers with implacable hatred in his fast-glazing eyes. Then he pitched to the narrow deck and rolled down the sloping side of the submarine into the sea, slowly sinking amid the waving fronds that parted to receive him, finding a grave in the surge of the Kiroshiwo, the black current of Japan.

The End

Index

OFF-TRAIL PUBLICATIONS
Specializing in the era of American pulp fiction

THE WEIRD DETECTIVE ADVENTURES OF WADE HAMMOND
By Paul Chadwick
Volume 1: 10 stories, 180 pages, $18
Volume 2: 10 stories, 172 pages, $18
Volume 3: 10 stories, 202 pages, $18
Volume 4: 9 stories, 232 pages, $18

The Wade Hammond stories complete in four volumes. In these chilling adventures, all from the classic 1930's pulps, Detective-Dragnet *and* Ten Detective Aces, *freelance investigator Wade Hammond battles a series of weird enemies. Some of the best of '30s pulp fiction.*

DOCTOR COFFIN: The Living Dead Man
By Perley Poore Sheehan • Introduction by John Wooley
8 novelettes, 178 pages, $16

Weird stories from Thrilling Detective, *1932-33. A former character actor who faked his own death, Doctor Coffin runs a string of mortuaries by night and fights crime at night. One of the strangest detective series.*

SUPER-DETECTIVE FLIP BOOK: Two Complete Novels
From the pulp *Super-Detective*:
"Legion of Robots" (November 1940) by Victor Rousseau • Introduction by John McMahan •• "Murder's Migrants" (March 1943) by Robert Leslie Bellem and W.T. Ballard • Introduction by John Wooley
2 short novels, 174 pages, $18

Super-Detective started as a Doc Savage-like adventure pulp, then changed format to hardboiled detective. The Flip Book *features a novel from each of the two phases with intros exploring the historical background. Exciting!*

PULPWOOD DAYS: Volume 1: Editors You Want To Know

Edited by John Locke • 180 pages, $16

*Numerous articles from the writers' magazines by and about pulp editors, with ample biographical profiles. Editors include: Frank E. Blackwell (*Detective Story, Western Story*), Ray Palmer (*Amazing Stories, Fantastic Adventures*), Edwin Baird (*Weird Tales, Detective Tales*), and many more.*

GANG PULP

Edited by John Locke • 19 stories, 294 pages, $24

Hardboiled stories of the criminal underworld from the first year (1929-30) of the gang pulps: Gangster Stories, Racketeer Stories, *etc. These violent tales came under immediate censorship pressure; the history is explored in an in-depth essay. "A remarkable work of popular-culture scholarship"—*MYSTERY SCENE, *Fall 2008.*

THE GANGLAND SAGAS OF BIG NOSE SERRANO

Volume 1: Dames, Dice and the Devil
Volume 2: Horses, Hoboes and Heroes
Volume 3: Hell's Gangster

By Anatole Feldman • Introductions by Will Murray

Each: 4 novels • **Volumes 1-2**: 266 pages, $20 • **Volume 3**: 224 pages, $18

The complete Big Nose Serrano novels from Gangster Stories, Greater Gangster Stories, *and* The Gang Magazine, *1930-35. Feldman was the best of the gang pulp authors, and Big Nose was his most inspired creation, the berserking king of Chicago gangsters.*

CITY OF NUMBERED MEN: The Best of Prison Stories
Introduction by John Locke
12 stories, 278 pages, $20

> *During Prohibition, famed publisher Harold Hersey turned America's disintegrating prison system into the hardboiled* Prison Stories *(1930-31). Included are stories from all six issues of this ultra-rare pulp, the startling history of* Prison Stories, *complete cover gallery, and "Harold Hersey: Tales of an Ink-Stained Wretch," the first comprehensive biography of pulp publishing's most colorful character.*

THE MAGICIAN DETECTIVE: And Other Weird Mysteries
By Fulton Oursler
Introduction by John Locke
7 stories, 210 pages, $18

> *Fulton Oursler was one of the great editors of his time, ruling over the Macfadden publishing empire for two decades. But stage magic was his first love, and, in his heart, he remained a conjurer in a black cape and top hat. In this collection of early fiction, Oursler's bewitching imagination takes flight in tales of magic, murder and mesmerizing mystery. Also featured is an in-depth exploration of the astonishing career of Fulton Oursler.*

GHOST STORIES: The Magazine and Its Makers
Edited by John Locke
Vol 1: 19 stories, 256 pages, $24 • **Vol 2**: 15 stories, 272 pages, $24

> *Macfadden's* Ghost Stories *(1926-31) presented haunted tales in every exciting arena: the Western Front, gangland, aviation, the Klondike, the circus, etc. The personnel behind* Ghost Stories *were a fascinating group: poets and scholars, war heroes and war correspondents, adventurers and Bohemians; a few became prolific pulpsters; a few became bestselling authors. And a few led haunted lives. Vol 1 includes the history of* Ghost Stories, *bios of every editor, and every Vol 1 author. Vol 2 includes bios of every Vol 2 author, every cover artist, and a gallery of all 64* Ghost Stories *covers.*

www.ingramcontent.com/pod-product-compliance
Lightning Source LLC
Chambersburg PA
CBHW021016180626
46814CB00003B/1312